Filtered

Through

Time

S. R. Lee, Editor

Editorial Committee
Claire Henry
Joyce A. O.Lee
Louise Strang

PUBLISHED BY WESTVIEW, INC., KINGSTON SPRINGS, TN

PUBLISHED BY WESTVIEW, INC.
P.O. Box 605
Kingston Springs, TN 37082
www.publishedbywestview.com

ISBN 978-1-937763-63-3

First edition, August 2012

The author gratefully acknowledges permission from Sony, Inc. to reprint the
lyrics to *Pony Rider* by Alan Rhody.

Good faith efforts have been made to trace copyrights on materials included in
this publication. If any copyrighted material has been included without
permission and due acknowledgment, proper credit will be inserted in future
printings after notice has been received.

Printed in the United States of America on acid free paper.

To all those over time
who have worked
toward peace.

S.R. Lee

Appreciation

The people whose help was essential to this book are far to numerous to name. I will point out Claire Henry, Joyce Lee, and Louise Strang whose editorial suggestions and patience with my stubborn opinions have been a support for many months. I thank the publisher, Mary Catharine Nelson, whose skill and common sense made the book possible. I thank Rick Warwick for his important support, consistent encouragement, and quick offers of help when I really needed it. I thank Emily Nance, the young photographer whom I asked to take many specific pictures, and Peg Fredi whose skills in rehabilitating pale old photographs are most remarkable. I thank Sandy Zeigler for her creative work on the cover. Then I thank all the authors, those who are friends in local critique groups and those who live far away in other states, all of them for trusting us with their creative work and their insights and points of view on a cataclysmic moment in the history of our nation and the long term effects it has had on our society.

TABLE OF CONTENTS

Table of Contents

Introduction

I wrote a story which was out of sync with what is published nowadays. Because the story covered the years 1849 to 1865 and was placed in Tennessee, something in connection with the Civil War Sesquicentennial seemed a possibility. Details of the idea fell into place. I would create a home for the story in an anthology of fiction and poetry, not a history. It would be more about the effect of the war over the intervening one hundred and fifty years than about the war itself. The name, *Filtered Through Time*, fit the theme. Rick Warwick, historian for the Heritage Foundation, suggested giving people plenty of time to write; we set the deadline a year and a half out from our initial conversation in January, 2011. I made and distributed fliers.

The result has become a book which lives up to the flier's statement that we "welcome a variety of points of view." Local authors describe in both fiction and poetry the terrible battle in Franklin, Tennessee. Authors from North Carolina, Colorado, and Illinois sent work. There are student submissions and octogenarian submissions.

In one poem, the young woman threatened by Union soldiers

> screamed in rage,
> "You blue bellied devils you,"

while in another a Union man mourns the pain of war:

> They toil over malevolent matters
> Whose sovereignty is a pillar of strength
> The American flag is in tatters
> And thus humbles our noble selves by length

Many of the stories and ideas come from more modern times. One poem tells of a cannon ball found in a school playground in the 1930's. A "fictional essay" tells how a 21st century teen imagines her ancestors' lives contrasted with her modern, technological life.

I thank all the authors from near and far. All were willing to send fine quality writing to an unknown editor for a local anthology. Through these months of submissions, the book has grown in dignity and variety of style, perspective, and content. Together, we offer to the world good reading.

S.R. Lee

1. AT BATTLE

Photograph by Emily Nance
Monument for the Battle of Nashville

At Battle

A Prayer for Stillness
[Williamson County, Tennessee, 1864]

Thelma Battle

If you could read my thoughts,
you can read this heah...silent prayer.

The sounds of rumbling cannon
move across the distance.

Soldier boys... soldier men
noisily tromp along these roads and fields.

Pray for Stillness!

Soon bullets will fly and musket balls race
to make arrival time aboard their destinations
of brave hearts, flesh, and bones.

Pray for Stillness!

The beat of drums make sounds of roaring thunder.
The coming gunfire will seem like blazing lightning
striking trees.

Pray for Stillness!

I sense the moments coming of agonizing cries
of the mortally wounded.

Pray for Stillness!

3

When the death angels visit this heah place,
may they hurry to those who needs 'em most.

Pray for Stillness!

All through the day I wait and weep as young
children jerk and tremble. Soon the night will come.

Pray for Stillness!

The men folk is gone away to fight.
The ladies, they's heah struggling on.

Pray for Stillness!

Here we await the war beneath this house
crowded full with my Missus, her family,
mine and me.

Pray for Stillness!

Missus, she prays for victory. Me, I pray for freedom.
Hush...the war's done come to this heah place.

Just be Still and Pray!

Battle Morning

Alan Rhody

The day arrives, my mind it reels
Like a wagon flying down a hill
Full of burning smoking hay
With no one at the reins.

The horses charge without restraint
Bounding toward a speeding train
With pumping locomotive veins
This calm but frightful day

I sit so still, stare at the haze
Sit so still and watch blood stains
The lonesome sky is turning black
This calm and frightful day

No one's at the reins

Battle

Susie Margaret Ross

As he aimed his gun,
I shot him straight through the breast.
He fell to the ground.

I said a prayer,
Asking forgiveness of God,
For his soul and mine.

The Searcher

George Spain

On December 15 and 16, 1864, the Confederate Army of Tennessee is destroyed four miles south of Nashville. Over five thousand Federal and Confederate soldiers are casualties. Two of every five men in the 13th United States Colored Troops Regiment are killed or wounded attacking Peach Orchard Hill at the Battle of Nashville.

It is nearing late afternoon of the second day after the Confederates have retreated southward. The shell-torn hills and fields are covered with debris. Bodies, and parts of bodies, are still being found and buried. It stinks with a moldy odor: the Confederate dead in their shallow graves, buried where they have fallen; parts of men and horses scattered in the mud and litter; the blood of the wounded; the dead and the sick filling the hospitals, churches, homes, and schools; the stench of the unwashed bodies of thousands of prisoners packed into abandoned buildings and warehouses; the burning of dead horses and the wreckage of battle; the piles of rubbish, the piss, the shit and decay of all the living and the dead. It is the odor of war rising from a city of 30,000, now filled with 70,000 Yankee soldiers and thousands of Rebel prisoners and hordes of refugees, freed slaves, laborers, teamsters, gamblers, drummers, prostitutes, and herds of cattle and horses and mules. Wood smoke rises from campfires in and around the city; coal smoke pours from the chimneys of factories and homes, trains and riverboats. Wagons, trains, gunboats, and steamboats come and go continuously, some bringing fresh troops, ammunition, and supplies, others heading North filled with the wounded and prisoners.

It is bitter cold. At times snow and sleet mingle with rain. Fires burn night and day as the smoke drifts high above the city, spreading a dark smudge across the sky, a cloud that can be seen and smelled from miles away. Where the battle has raged, trees are torn apart, limbs strewn upon the ground, stone walls crumbled. The muddy earth is plowed by cannonballs, grapeshot, and canister, and rutted by wheels and galloping horses and the boot prints of running men who had done everything they could to kill one another. Within the city, the air is filled with the crunching of wagon wheels and the clopping of horse and mule hooves on the unpaved streets, the high-pitched whistles of steamboats and gunboats on the Cumberland, the chugging and clanging of trains, the ringing of church bells, the sounds of music from the theaters and of soldiers singing and officers shouting orders, of teamsters and drovers cursing animals, and of campfires hissing as the freezing rain continues to fall steadily all across the fields and hills of middle Tennessee.

A tall woman, thin almost to gauntness, stands ankle-deep in the muddy remnants of a cornfield that lies below a high gray hill. Her head and shoulders are slumped from exhaustion. She is so tired she can barely lift her feet, but her mind does not stop thinking. From a distance, she seems small. Her long red hair cannot be seen for the green woolen shawl that covers her head and shoulders. She was beautiful once, but now her face is so sunken and withered she appears old and without life. She wears three long dresses, a ragged blue Army coat, high-top button boots, and gloves that have no fingers. In the cold air her breath makes little white clouds. She is searching for the body of the father of her baby; his name is Joseph Vann. He is a Negro soldier. She looks up the hill. *Ay, here it tis, whair they said ta come ta, whair he wus, tha place he did nay come back from. Right here whair I stand. Ye fought haire, in this vairy*

*field an up thair on that hill.   O, Joseph, me precious.
Whair are ye? Ye said nay to worry, ye'd be back. But ye
did nay.*

She was born Katherine Lynch in County Donegal at the
northern tip of Ireland, the daughter of a healer granny-
woman and an alcoholic poacher father.   When she was
eleven, her father was hung on a snowy day just before
Christmas for killing a deer on the land of an absentee
English landlord.   Three weeks later the landlord's farm
manager and six constables drove her and her family from
the land.   The next spring, she with her mother, three sisters,
and two brothers emigrated to Boston.   There, three years
later, she married an Irishman named John O'Conner.
Even though she didn't love him, he was a kind man and a
devout Catholic with dreams of a better life.   He had come
to America to take possession of 160 acres that he had
bought in Dublin from an American Catholic land dealer
who John trusted because of his frequent references to Holy
Mother Mary's blessings.

After traveling for two weeks in a farm wagon over rain-
washed and rutted roads, they finally came to the land that
the salesman had said was all "milk and honey bottom-land
in a cove in the Tennessee mountains."   What they found
was 141 acres of steep, bouldered mountainside and 19
acres that could be farmed only after he removed two
hundred trees.   His dreams kept him there.   Two years later,
while trying to save his best mule from drowning during a
flood, John slipped on the muddy bank, fell into Crow
Creek, and so was drowned himself.

Katherine did not leave.   She loved the mountains and
the people.   Like her mother, she made her living as a
healer granny-woman.

Joseph was born a slave on a plantation in northern
Georgia.   His owner was an old Episcopalian who rarely gave

God or Jesus much thought but used the Bible to support slavery and whatever else he felt strongly about. He considered Joseph to be his best field hand as well as the best carver of wood in the area. He and his wife both thought Joseph loved them, which led to a moment of brief surprise when Joseph cut his throat with a sickle on the evening of the day he sold Joseph's wife and daughter, Sara, to a slave dealer. As the old man lay on the ground with his eyes stretched wide, Joseph knelt, tore his shirt open and ripped from his scraggly neck a leather strap from which hung a small carved figure of Christ on the cross, standing on a coiled snake. He put the cross and strap in his pocket. *Now you got nuthin o mine. I swear by my lil Sara I'll kill all of you debils an get her free.* He plunged his fingers into the gaping wound until they were covered in blood, then lifted them to his lips and licked them clean. He stood up, turned, and began to run north. He ran without stopping until he was well into the mountains; he knew if he kept going north he would eventually find the Union Army and join it.

Just as he crossed the border into Tennessee, he was bitten on his right ankle by a timber rattler. He quickly took his shirt off and tied it around his leg above the bite and cut the fang marks with a piece of flint. He let it bleed for a moment, then pressed moss into the cut and hurried on, following a game trail beside a creek. An hour after he was bitten, his leg had swollen to twice its size. He began to stumble and fall, and his vision started to blur. He went on a hundred yards. The trail steepened. He could hear roaring ahead and for a brief instant thought he saw something huge and black. Then he could not feel himself. He swayed, went to his knees, and fell forward into a thick patch of ferns.

He would have died there if Katherine had not been digging ginseng nearby. A storm was coming, and she had worked her way toward a large cave to go inside until the lightning and rain passed. She would have missed him if not for the trunk of a fallen chestnut tree which she stepped up on. From there she saw him.

She looked around. Seeing no one else, she jumped down and went to see if he was alive. Lying in the midst of the crushed ferns lay a powerfully built black man. His back was crisscrossed with old scars from what had been long and hard lashings. She saw the swollen leg, the tourniquet, and the cuts above the wide fang marks, and she thought, *Ah, me Lord Jasus, some wuns beat hell inta yair back. An haire ye be a runin all this way just ta be bit by a serpent.*

At that moment the storm struck. A strong wind began to blow and the rain fell in torrents. *I've got ta git thee in the cave.* Though she was strong, he was so heavy and lifeless that she could barely pull him up the mossy slope. She fell three times and each time stopped to rest but finally dragged him to a level spot. From there she pulled him inside the mouth of the cave, far enough that the blowing rain could not reach him. Then she went out into the storm. A short distance down the gorge, she entered a large grove of trees where black snakeroot grew. She dug up seven plants, then ran back to the cave, placed the roots on a flat rock. With a round stone she crushed them into powder and pressed it into the cuts.

When the storm was gone, she went to her cabin and returned to the cave with a lantern, two blankets, a bundle of herbs and plants, and some food. Then she removed his filthy clothes, washed him all over, and covered him with a blanket. During the first nights, she lay against him to give him more warmth; but as the days passed and she sensed that his strength was slowly returning, she found herself staring at his naked body in the lantern light as she washed him. When she saw him watching her and his responses as she washed him, she began to want him. And she saw in his eyes that he wanted her.

In the weeks they were in the cave, Katherine cleansed the poison from him; and once he was strong enough, she began to make love to him. When he was able to walk without her help, she took him to her small cabin in a beech grove at the north end of the cove. She dressed him in John's clothes, and began to take care of him as if she were his wife. And he began to cut her wood, to plant and hoe her garden, and to make her furniture and carve for her beautiful spoons and forks and plates of walnut and chestnut. The more they talked of their dreams and of their love, the more Joseph forgot his vow to join the Union army to free his daughter from slavery.

Nine months later she had his son. When he held the dark-skinned, curly-haired boy and looked into his black eyes, Joseph suddenly saw Sara cuddled there. He felt a sudden pain in his chest for his vow came back to him. In that instant he knew that no matter how much he loved Katherine, he had to go north and find the Union Army to fight for his daughter and son.

Katherine saw it in his face and knew.

Two weeks later she was strong enough; they left the cove. They walked a hundred miles in six days to reach Nashville. On the second day there, two old free blacks, a husband and wife, rented them a one-room shack in Black Bottom,

They realized that Black Bottom was the only place in the city where they could stay together; no where else in Nashville would this be allowed. Whites, even northern whites, would not tolerate it; and some would want to lynch Joseph and drive Katherine out of the city. Even in Black Bottom, most of the Negroes thought that a white woman living with a black man was going against nature and God's will and so shunned them, Few would look at Katherine when she went outside. Only the old couple treated her with kindness. She wondered if they did it just because they felt sorry for the baby, since their granddaughter had a child the same age.

The day after he moved his family into the shack, Joseph joined the Army.

Katherine has walked four miles from Nashville between the stone walls that run along both sides of Franklin Pike. Mud is caked on her boots and the hems of her skirts. Her hair and face and body are splattered with it from the passing horses and wagons. She is cold and wet from the rain that has come with the ending of the snow and sleet. She turns slowly and looks up at the hill and then across the field. Except for the pike, which runs nearly in a straight line between parallel stone walls, there is no order or familiarity. In every direction she sees trees seared of bark and trunks and limbs scattered over the ground, wrecked wagons and caissons, dead horses and mules in their harnesses, pieces of muskets and rifles, canteens, jackets, caps, tin cups, haversacks, and the earth gouged and torn by shells and wagons and horses and boots.

Great flocks of crows and buzzards have fed here all day long. Now as evening comes they are leaving, rising all around her, black flecks against the gray sky heading to their roosts for the night, only to return at the first light of tomorrow. She has almost reached the hill where, two days before, Joseph had fought with the Colored Troops who charged again and again up the hill through the sharpened wooden stakes and abates put down by the Confederates and against the breastworks and cannon at the top. Hundreds were killed and wounded here; their bits and pieces feed the birds in the day and the animals that come in the night. *He is haire. O, dear God help me find im.* Then out loud, "Please take me ta im."

All across the cornfield and the slope of the hill dark shapes of people are standing or moving slowly through the mist like specters. Most are men, but now and then there is a woman or a horseman urging his animal through the mud. Some are spread out in lines, soldiers searching for the wounded and dead. Others are in clusters: the black gravediggers and cleaners of battlefields who are filling Army wagons with whatever they can find that is still useful for killing. What cannot be used is thrown on the dead horses and mules and burned, the flames flicker far across the fields and hills. Smoke rising from the burning pyres hangs near the ground; handkerchiefs and torn strips of shirts cover the faces of those working near the fires.

Katherine sees families and friends looking for loved ones, soldiers looking for comrades, and many who have walked or ridden in carriages all the way from town just to gape and ponder the destruction caused by the two days of battle. What they see is more horrible than what they have heard or imagined for two days from the tops of their houses and the hills of the city. Mixed among these seekers of horror are thieves who have come to steal from the dead. Like crows and buzzards, they wait for when no one is looking to take their turns at feeding on the corpses, peering from the corners of their eyes for that quick instant to slip a ring from a finger or a watch or billfold from a pocket.

For four days Katherine has eaten only hard bread and cheese. She fears that her milk is drying up. Hunger and fear and lack of sleep are causing her thoughts to break apart. For long moments she has to concentrate to remember what she is doing here. She has to stop and shake her head for her thoughts to clear. *Ay, ay know now, ay'm lookin for me Joseph.* Three times she reaches into her coat pocket and pulls out a dirty, wrinkled paper and reads out loud, "Private Joseph Vann of the 13th Colored Regiment, Company B." Each time, she shakes her head trying to fix it in her mind. But on the third time, just as she begins to walk on across the field toward the high gray hill, she hears a voice whisper in her head, *But he's dead, don't ye remember...Joseph's dead. This be the place whair he died. He's haire...He's haire.* She shakes her head *Nay, Nay, Nay, Nay,* and answers the voice out loud, "But what if ye be wrong? What if all this be a dream? What aye saw yesterday could niver be real, nothin that 'orrible could be real...nothin."

The day after the battle, a rumor had run through Black Bottom that every Negro solider was either dead or wounded. The next morning, long before light, Katherine had taken her baby to a wet nurse. As she kissed him goodbye, she had prayed, *Holy Mother uv Jasus lead me ta Joseph today so aye can feed me baby afore night comes.* As she prayed, she pulled from between her breasts Joseph's small wooden cross and touched it to her baby's forehead. Then she handed the baby to the woman, walked out the door, and rushed to the hospital for Negro soldiers, an abandoned, three-story brick building near the river. When she entered the front door she almost fainted. *Sweet Jasus! This is what a slaughterhouse smells an looks like, this is whair they cut the throats uv beasts.*

Blood was everywhere: on the floors, the steps, the handrails, and had made handprints and smears on the walls. The air reeked with the odor of chloroform, turpentine, alcohol, blood, and overflowing honey buckets. Nurses, their fronts covered with bloody aprons, moved among the beds, stepping over those lying on the floor, carrying buckets of water, for drinking and for washing away the blood and filth. Most of the wounded still wore their bloody battle clothes and lay in their own waste. There were not enough nurses to clean them or to change the wet and dirty field dressings that covered their wounds. Stretcher bearers passed her, bringing in more wounded; one was groaning loudly in the surgical room. Most were quiet, though some were moaning, and, now and then, someone would scream. A few asked her for water, but she didn't stop or answer them – she went on.

The surgery was in an old office at the back of the building, next to the door that opened into the alley. Here, chloroform was given, the flesh cut, the bones sawed apart, the flesh stitched back together, and then turpentine was poured over the wounds. In this room were the buckets and boxes used to put the feet and hands and legs and arms. When they were full, they were carried outside and dumped onto the bodies that lay in the carts in the alley. From here the dead and the parts of those still living were taken to the Dead House.

Katherine had hurried from floor to floor, going into every room, looking at every face, calling his name out, over and over, asking if anyone had seen him, if anyone knew him. No one had. She had gone to every man in bed and to every man on the floor. Men were everywhere: some were lying on the floor on blankets black with blood and shit; others sat with their backs against the walls, talking quietly, smoking, playing cards, while many were sleeping. Four men sitting in a corner of the second floor hallway were singing a hymn, while one beat the rhythm on his hand with a spoon, to the words of a song of longing –

"Hear dat mournful thunder
Roll from door to door,
Callin' home God's chil'en
Get home bimeby.
Little chil'en, I do believe
We're a long time waggin' o'er de crossin'
Little chil'en, I do believe
We'll get home to heb'em bimeby.

See dat forked lightin'
Flash from tree to tree.
Callin' home God's chil'en
Get home bimeby.
True believer, I do believe
We're a long time waggin' o'er de crossin'.
O, brudders, I do believe,
We'll get home to heb'en bimeby."

As she passed them she thought *Will any wun a ye leave this slaughterhouse alive? Will any a ye get to heaven by an by?*

When she had reached the top floor, she had come onto three men whose faces were completely covered with bandages. She looked closely at each: one was too tall, another almost white, the third man she wasn't sure about so she put her hand on his shoulder and asked, "Joseph, is it ye?" and the man shook his head, No. On the floor, next to him, was a boy with the side of his head above the left ear partly gone; his eyes were wide open, they did not blink; they stared straight at the ceiling as though there was something that they must stare at forever and never forget. Beside him was a man with no jaw or tongue making gurgling sounds with every breath he took. *This be hell! This be what it looks like, an smells like. O, dear Father, forgive us all.*

She had hurried from the room and gone as fast as she could down the crowded stairway. Just as she had reached the first floor, two men came out of the surgery carrying one of the large boxes filled with pieces of bodies; they pushed past her and went out the back door. She stood for a moment watching them. Then she looked down and saw that the bottom of her skirt was black with blood. *Do I smell like death?* She walked out of the building, down the steps and onto the street. There she turned and looked up at the building and spoke out loud in her mother's language, "Dean oram triaire, Thrionoid! And then again, "Blessed Trinity, have pity!"

Late that night, she had found his company headquarters. A Negro guard took her into a room where three white officers and two black sergeants were smoking cigars and drinking whiskey. Immediately one of the officers stood up and offered her a chair and then sat down behind a table filled with papers. "How can I help you Ma'am?" She was so tired her voice was almost a whisper, "Ay'm tryin ta faind Joseph Vann. He's a private in yair Regiment and tis supposed to be in Company B. Is e hayr? Nay one seems ta know whair he be. Please, Sirs, help me faind him." The room became dead silent. The men's faces showed no emotion as they stared at her. Finally, the officer behind the desk looked down at a stack of papers in front of him and began slowly thumbing through it, one page at a time, until he stopped and put his forefinger down on a page and looked up at her and said "There he is, but his name's got a check by it." He looked up at her, "I'm sorry, Ma'am, but that means he didn't make it back with his men, so's most likely he's out there in the ground, near that big hill where a lot of my men got slaughtered by them goddamn rebels." He paused, "Now, may I ask why are you lookin for this man? Did he work for you or your folks?" She looked at him with no expression on her face and shook her head. He didn't speak for a long moment; his mouth hung open as he stared at her, then he shook his head, "Well, Goddamm it! If that don't take all...I'll be a...." He looked at the faces of the other men. They showed no emotion. They just stared at her. Finally, the officer said coldly, "Well, come over here an take a look at this map." She stepped nearer the table and looked down. "See where I'm pointing? This here line is Franklin Pike. You stay on it for bout four miles an there'll be a big hill on the left, an likely they'll be a gang of gravediggers there an they'll tell you where they've put im." As she left the room, she had heard him say in a low voice, "Well, I'll be goddamn! If that don't take the goddamn cake."

Night has almost come. The air grows colder. The crows are cawing to one another as they depart for their roosts. The gawkers and scavengers are departing with the crows. From the pike, a mule brays; a man shouts, "Git up!" and a wagon rattles as it begins its way back to town.

As the light fades, she can hardly lift her feet for the mud and exhaustion. She is standing on the lower slope of the hill where Joseph and the 13th fought. Soldiers are there searching for wounded and the gravediggers are there burying the dead. She hears someone shout, "Here's one alive!" Then, a moment later, "Stretcher, stretcher!"

She stops near three men digging a grave. Two are leaning on their shovels while the third man, whose face is dappled with white blotches, stands almost knee deep in the ground, swinging a pick with a smooth steady motion. Beside the grave lies a small barefooted body dressed in a tattered butternut jacket and pants. With the face of a boy, his mouth is slightly open as though he is grinning. His eyes are closed. A jagged hole is in his forehead. His hands and feet are crossed. The men leaning on their shovels look at her as the pick swinger continues to dig.

"Can ye tell me whair the men of the 13th Regiment be buried?"

The man in the grave stops digging and wipes his brow with his sleeve. He looks up at her and points beyond the boy's head, "Missus, you sees where I's pointing, it's over der. We buried sum of em yes'erday and de res dis morning. They wuz layin all over de side of dis hill, all de ways up to de top. We put em in four big ole long ditches over der. An when we finish we put up a board an got one of da soldiers dat could make words to write on it, U.S. COLORED TROOPS. Les me get out uv dis hole an I'll lead you to it."

He climbs out of the grave and tells the two men, "Ya'll have dis boy in de groun an get im covered over real good by de time I be back." Then he tells her, "Now you follow close behin me, Missus." He leads her a little ways across the slope to four long muddy mounds of earth and waves his hand, palm down, as though giving a blessing. "Here dey be." His voice is almost a whisper. He stands there, watching her, as she walks slowly past him and along each of the long graves, pausing now and then, looking down, her lips moving without a sound as she moves on. At the far end of the third mound, she bends down and pulls out a half-buried dark blue cap. She wipes the mud off, holds it up near her face, and turns it slowly as she examines it. She shakes her head and walks on, carrying the cap in her left hand at her side.

The board with the inscription is stuck into the ground above the fourth grave. She stops there and reaches out with her right hand and touches the board. Then with her forefinger she traces each of the letters. After the last S, she turns to the man and says, "Thank ye," and walks away toward the pike.

The mist is spreading over the field and up the slope of the hill like a white pall slowly covering the dead and those who continue to put them in the ground. Behind her, from the top of the hill just beyond the breastworks, she hears men talking and laughing, "Dat po ole Cracker won't use dat little ole pecker of his anymo." Another voice asks, "Did ya'll get ever thing out his pockets?" And a third one says, "Jus thro sum dirt on him and les get on back, cause damn it's getting colder, an I'm hongry. There is the dull sound of dirt falling onto the body of another man dressed in butternut who had died on the hill two days before.

As she walks through the cold dark, she thinks *O, me precious Joseph, tis an awful place fer ye to die and be buried! My heart's breakin for ye...I luv ye so much.* For a brief instant she feels such a sadness that she almost begins to cry. But she doesn't. Instead she shakes her head and walks faster and lets the cap slip from her hand to the ground.

When she reaches the pike, she falls in behind a wagon, close enough to hold onto the back to help support her on the long walk back to town. In the bare bit of light that remains, she sees a white soldier lying in the wagon's bed. His eyes are closed. He doesn't moan or wake when he is jostled hard by the wagon's wheels dropping into the deep ruts. The stillness on his face never changes.

When the wagon comes to the outskirts of the city, Katherine turns away and goes on alone to Black Bottom and to her baby.

Blood Red

Susie Margaret Ross

Red against skin.
Violence is a sin.

The Fifth Tennessee

Arch Boyd Brown

In the beauty of a setting sun
Alone and silent as day is done,
I think of those who've gone before
Serving with honor in peace and war.
In my own family they stand tall
Who bravely answered freedom's call.
They never wavered in the hour
When lesser men would flee or cower.
From the fields of Birchwood, Tennessee,
Came John B. Brown and such as he
Left their families and their farms,
To preserve the Union took up arms.
Amid bugle blare and cannon roar
At Franklin, Resaca, and many more
They stood their ground through blood and tears
By the grace of God and in spite of fears.
'Mid stones discolored through the years
Is etched the history of volunteers.
With names like Gamble, McCallie and Brown
They sought no fortune or renown.
I stand here now a soldier's son
Who was a soldier just as well,
And I am thankful for the One
Who protected me from shot and shell!

Author's Note: The 5th Tennessee Volunteer Infantry was organized in Barbourville, Ky. in 1862 and saw action at Cumberland Gap, the East Tennessee Campaign, the Atlanta Campaign, Franklin, Nashville, and Wilmington, N.C. The regiment suffered severe casualties during the Battle of Resaca, Georgia, and was engaged in the battle near the Carter House cotton gin during the Battle of Franklin, Tennessee. Many of the soldiers in the 5th Tennessee regiment were from Roane Co., Monroe Co., Blount Co., Meigs Co., and Hamilton Co. in East Tennessee.

Photograph courtesy of Arch Boyd Brown
Private John Boyd Brown (1835-1872) of the 5th. Tennessee
Volunteer Infantry, U.S. He is the great-grandfather of author,
Arch Boyd Brown. His widow, Louise Adelaide McCallie Brown
was left with six children, the oldest of which (my grandfather,
Archibald Boyd Brown 1856-1917), was only 16 when his father
was struck by lightning in 1872.

Marching Orders

Veera Rajaratnam

A soldier I am...marching on!
To capture that hill,
To put up our flag, to
Remove all resistance—
Red and vivid—Blood
Shed for the land. I
Shed no tears for the hearts
That stopped beating—for
That will be me in a beat, if I
Stopped to think with my heart.
A soldier I am...marching on...
[Dead beat!]

The Courage to Quit

Charlene Jones

When the Southern states seceded from the Union, Herbert Ledbetter, a young farmer in southern Middle Tennessee, wrote to his cousin Daniel in Georgia to come on up and join him in a Confederate regiment. They would be together in this adventure. Now as dusk fell on a cold evening two years later, Herbert and Daniel were pinned down in a dense Maury County cedar thicket near Stones River. Daniel raised his head to peep around the syrup-bucket sized knot on the cedar log. A shot of acknowledgement connected to the brim of his Confederate cap and sent it sailing into the woods behind them.

"Damn Yankees!" Daniel cussed in a hot whisper.

"Amen to that. Damn sons-a-bitches in Tennessee, ain't good news no way you look at it," Herbert said softly and spit a stream of tobacco. "I been telling you to keep your head down. Maybe them Yankee boys shooting your hat off has got you alerted enough you will now. Be a shame to mess up that copper hair you got." Herbert gave a bitter chuckle and spat again.

Daniel still whispered, "Georgia boy stuck here in Tennessee ain't the best news I ever heard, neither."

"What you talking about?"

"Talking about I'm sick hugging black earth in black woods over black slaves."

"For that matter, Daniel, who ain't?"

"Why don't we get the hell out of the black Yankee infested God forsaken mess and take ourselves home?"

"Whatcha mean black?"

"Just that! Black! The woods down in Georgia got some light. Pine trees let a little sun and moon in, ground's red.

All up here is cedar, maple. black gum, and black ground. Woods is shady and black as Satan's own hell.'

"Well, I shore did think you had sense enough to recognize good farming land when you're a-laying on it."

"Tell me what in the cat hair we are doing on black ground in black woods fighting about black slaves? All I ever knowed about slaving, was being pore myself. But I am used to a warm place when it's cold, a shade tree or creek when it's hot, and a roof over my head when it's raining. I ain't a bit used to a growling belly. I doubt a man that knows how to plow would ever get used to it. God knows what I'd give for a mess of turnip greens and cornbread."

"Dream up enough of that for both of us.'

"Another thing, I'm sick of this rich man's war. It don't make sense for folks like you and me. We don't have slaves."

"I don't reckon we had no say in it one way or the other."

"So now it's time we made our say."

"How so?"

"When it comes dark, let's git home to Georgia."

"Daniel, I am home, but I ain't got no place to go. Yankees on my own home ground is why I'm a-fighting. It ain't got a damn thing to do with no rich man's war or slaves neither."

"That's just perzacly what I'm talking about, Herbert. It ain't like the British was coming. We ain't got nothing to do with this war but fighting and dying in it. You don't see them rich slave owners or Yankee bleeding hearts that got this damnation started laying here starving behind this log like us. Only time them rich boys ever even spoke to us was when they wanted something."

"What something, Daniel?"

"Our votes, Herbert. We don't know nothing about their way of living. We won't after this war's over neither. Just saying there is an 'after it's over' for us. I'm beginning to feel mighty like there ain't gonna be no 'over' for me, like it gonna last longer than me, if I don't get started toward making it over."

"What you talking about? You know everybody wants this war over, and you're old enough to know wanting ain't getting."

"I'm talking about making it over for me and mine. You do as you like. I'm the last one to try and run another man's business. I'm plumb wore out with other folk's running mine."

"How you aim to do that, Daniel Ledbetter?"

"I finally figured out one good thing about these black woods that don't let you see your hand before your face ."

"What's that?"

"After dark, when ain't nobody paying attention, I'm excusing my homesick self just quiet as I know how. If you want, we'll slip out of here together. Slip on down to the south side of Winchester and collect your folks, then down across the Georgia line and get mine. We'll take us all on down to north Florida. We got kin there."

"Hell, Daniel, who?"

"Uncle Malcolm Ledbetter, that's who. He tried to get me to come down couple of years ago. Wrote me this war was coming and I better git while the gitting was good. Said there's farming round for the taking and a growing season for something all year round."

"Why didn't you go?"

"Didn't believe him about the war. Had to slide up to my ass in one before I could believe anybody would go to war over somebody else's slave."

"You don't think that's important, Daniel?"

"Not to me it ain't. Herbert, slaves been around since dirt. You don't believe me read yore Bible and that's just the official ones. They don't even keep count on poor white trash like you and me. Don't keep count on the bastards behind us that come from all over Europe too poor to be slaves. Folks do desperate things to keep from starving. They was just like us. Work all your life and then get killed or all mangled up fighting for somebody else's goods. Who's gonna feed our families if we get ourselves shot, Herbert?"

"What kind of feeding will you be doing if they shoot you for deserting?"

"With as much hell as they got going on here, they ain't got time to come looking for two scraggly corporals."

"They might. Everybody hates a deserter."

"Herbert, this whole mess is on the down hill skids and our side ain't on top. Ain't no Yankee outfit gonna give a damn about two rebel deserters"

"We really could get shot."

"Guess you ain't noticed somebody's been trying to shoot us most ever day and night for years now. I don't reckon as we'll be any deader whoever fires the bullet.'

"Daniel, I believe you done gone plumb crazy."

"Could be. Then maybe I been gone crazy and now I'm coming sane. Our kin folk down in north Florida ain't fighting. Ain't fought a day and ain't going to."

"Maybe we got us a bunch of cowards for kinfolk."

"Naw, they ain't cowards. They'll fight on a hummingbird minute over their women and young'uns and land. But they won't even consider fighting no war about slaves or secession either one. Hell, they done seceded. They seceded from the whole she-bang when the war was just talk. They got so far back, they just about got their own country."

"How they done that?"

"Well it seems they raised a litter of triplet sons Uncle Malcolm and Aunt Sue were plum foolish about till boys ended up spoiled rotten. They got fond of robbing banks. County sheriff gave Uncle Malcolm a warning he better move his family out of state. Don't nobody but kin know where they are. Game and land is ready for the taking. That sounds miles better than looking down a gun barrel for God knows how much longer. So come dark you can mark this old boy gone."

"Deserting's, deserting."

"Do what you want to. Lots of folks gave my uncle hell for running off with his bank robbing boys. But right or wrong his boys are healthy and alive. They ain't buried from dangling on a rope. That would have killed their Mama. Uncle Malcolm said he's moved them from temptation like the Book says. Banks are unknown in the parts where he took his family. Says he ain't missed banks a day."

"He's still harboring fugitives."

"You got your choice. Go or stay. Once it's dark tonight, this old boy is gone sure as sundown."

Write A Letter Home

Robert McCurley

Night's black shadows of uncertainty will engulf us soon.
Mercifully, we'll be forced to adjourn this foul and endless
    march.
In another dreary and desolate encampment,
Once again, I'll find a cut of earth to plant my ragged tent.

It's been awhile, I should write a letter home.

My body aches from obeying commands of abusive
    authority
Delivered by men intoxicated with the power of war.
I need a respite, just a moment to close my eyes and reclaim
    a shred of the sanity
Stolen from me in the midst of this continual conflict and
    hardship.

Then I'll sit and write a letter home.

Suddenly jarred awake from my unintended slumber and
    exhaustion
By the sounds of ravenous men, famished like wild animal
    in need of a kill
To soothe the gnawing in their empty bellies,
I realize my own discomfort and rise to take my fill of beans
    and bread.

When I'm done, I'll write a letter home.

Few are the pleasures allowed to quench a soldier's carnal
    nature,
Only those garnered from the earth along the way

Or secured at trading posts too few and far between.
I think I'll pause, light my pipe and relish the flavored ritual
    of an evening smoke.

And then I'll write a letter home.

Haughty laughter breaks the cold night air and I wander
    toward its source.
There in the soft light of a campfire I find Ben and William
Testing fate with Kings, Queens and Jokers as shadows
    dance across their countenance.
I reckon I'll linger and digress in their foolishness, but only
    for a spell.

For I must write a letter home.

Settled in my tent, pen in hand, I listen to the restless
    shuffling of my weary companions
As they try to find sleep amid the demons who roam dark
    battlefields,
Reminding us that the sins of war will forever live in our
    dreams.
My mind struggles to harness control of my being.

God help me, I need to write a letter home.

Blank paper rests by my side as I awaken to the terror, chaos
    and shock of an ambush
Deftly executed by wild-eyed enemy rogues thirsting for
    destruction.
My pen, lodged loosely in hand throughout the night, drops
    silently to the ground.
As I frantically scramble to mount a defense, a perplexing
    memory flashes in my mind.

I have to write a letter home.

Photograph by Robert McCurley

I feel the power of the weapon as it bucks in my hand and
  spews a screaming ball true to its mark.
A lump forms in my throat and I wonder whose wife I just
  widowed, whose child I just orphaned.
The Commander's screams rock me back to my senses and
  I realize that something evil is taking control,
Something of which I must never speak.

When I write a letter home.

Death is a mystery throughout our lives, its true essence
  known only by the Creator.
As the hot lead separates my flesh and rips through my
  chest, I know that death's secrets will soon be revealed,
The meaning of life finally made known.
Dying in the dust from which I was formed, I have but one
  desire unfulfilled.

I wish I could write a letter home.

For Want of a Match

Charles W. Rush

June 1863, Southeast Tennessee
Confederate Cavalry Encampment

The Yankees attacked the last week of June. Union infantry and cavalry rolled out of Nashville, Murfreesboro, and other camps in Central Tennessee. They intended to chase General Bragg out of his headquarters and across the Tennessee River. It reminded me of the push when the Bluecoats streamed out of Louisville, and I was wounded at the Salt River. I shook off a bad feeling.

My name is Sergeant Austin Robinson. In September 1861, I had joined Terry's Texas Rangers to look out for my young cousin, Billy Jones. He had been schooled at a Texas military college so they made him an officer. I had ridden with a Ranger force against the Comanches in Texas and had more fighting experience than most. They made me a Sergeant, although controlling these wild Texas boys took more than stripes on my sleeve. My brawling experience helped. Several of our friends had joined up with Billy and myself, and we had fought side-by-side at Shiloh, Nashville, and in Forrest's Raid on Murfreesboro.

Rangers streamed by us while Billy and I gathered our gear. I grabbed my gun-cleaning paraphernalia and jammed it into my saddlebag.

Billy held the halter of the pack mule while I cinched down our goods.

Unlike me, he had a slight frame and was trying to grow a wispy goatee to make himself look older than his nineteen years.

"Captain wants to see ya, Lieutenant," Corporal Folk shouted. "He's coming over with scouting orders."

Captain Pearre walked toward us while issuing orders to several other cavalrymen. He halted in front of Billy. "Lieutenant, we need to make sure the Yankees don't flank us from the north while we're trying to cross the Elk River. Take ten men and ride upriver to Pelham. Check out the town. I want that bridge burned so the enemy can't bring wagons and artillery across."

"Yes, Sir." Billy handed the mule's lead rope to a trooper and swung into his saddle, shotgun slung across his shoulder, one pistol in his belt, another in a scabbard hung from his saddle horn.

"If you run into a strong force," Pearre said, "try to delay them. Burn that bridge whatever you do."

Billy pointed at me. "Pick eight men. Check their loads."

Not much need in that, I thought. We'd taken to practically sleeping with our weapons primed. Hard lessons learned in over a year of battles and skirmishes.

Several hours later, Billy led us by the bridge and continued another half-mile to Pelham. We walked our horses toward the small village. The dirt road ran straight through. A general store dominated the center of town. A blacksmith shop farther along had no blacksmith or horses in sight. A dozen homes were scattered behind the main street, the people gone or hiding.

"Ride out to the north a ways," Billy ordered Folk. "Hightail it back if you see Yankees."

"Want me to check out the town?" I asked.

"No, send the rest of the men," Billy replied. "You and Charlie stay with me." Charlie and Billy had grown up best friends. Like Billy, he was young and slim, but he was fast with a pistol and had saved my life a few weeks before.

I nodded to the other men, and they began to spread out to cover the village.

"Charlie, find some fuel oil to burn the bridge," Billy said.

"We got company," I pointed to a gentleman in a dark suit and bow tie walking toward us with the use of an ivory-headed walking stick. His white mustache drooped, giving his face a stern expression. Blue eyes sparked in anger.

"What can I do for you, Sir?" Billy asked.

"I'm the mayor," the old man said. "What you boys want in my town?"

"Don't mean you any harm, Sir. But the Yankees are attacking the Southern Army all along the Elk River. We want to make sure they can't get across that bridge back there."

The oldster shook his cane at us and raised his voice. "Don't want no fighting here. You can't burn our bridge. Y'all git outta my town!"

I kneed my horse, leaned and stuck my face next to the mayor's. "Go tell your town folks to stay inside their houses. If we see anybody that even looks like a Yankee, we'll shoot to kill. Now you git, or I'll think you're a sympathizer."

He returned my stare. "Goddamn soldiers. Goddamn war, killing women and children. Anybody come into my house, I'll let 'em have it with my bird gun." He hobbled off.

I spit on the ground in his wake. "Goddamned civilians."

Charlie came back to us grinning. He had two galvanized cans roped to the back of his horse. "Got enough kerosene to burn our bridge."

Billy nodded. "Good."

The pounding of hooves got my attention. Corporal Folk galloped around a street corner. "Yankees. At least two companies of cavalry. A couple hundred troops comin' at a fast trot."

Billy jabbed my shoulder. "You and Charlie get going and burn that bridge!"

We rode off in a clatter of hooves on the hard street. We had almost made it to the bridge when shotgun and pistol fire roared behind. "Hurry, Charlie." I led him across the bridge, swinging out of my saddle.

Grabbing a can of kerosene, I ran down the river bank, splashing through shallow water to a supporting post. I poured fuel oil over the post and waded to the next one.

More gunfire rang out in the distance. I tossed my empty can aside and patted my pockets. Damnit! I had used my last match this morning. Cursing, I crawled up the bank where Charlie poured kerosene around the base of the bridge. We were head-high to the road bed.

"I don't have any matches. We need to light the posts," I yelled.

Charlie fumbled for matches and handed me two. "Them and my two is the last we got." He showed me his typical grin, then slid down the bank. Splashing to a post, he struck a Lucifer and yellow flames chased black smoke upward. He moved to the next post.

"Com'on, Billy, I need to light this fire," I murmured. I held my matches ready, listening to the gunfire get closer.

The Rangers came in a hurry. Their horses pounded across wooden planks. My match flared and died. I tried the other. The kerosene whooshed.

Shots rang out from both sides of the river.

"Get out of there," Billy shouted.

A bullet ricocheted off a steel rail beside me. "Com'on, Charlie." Seeing him light the last support girder, I stepped on the bridge and untied my horse's reins. The animal pulled to get away from the flames and smoke.

Fifty yards behind me, Billy aimed his pistol and fired at the column of Yankees a hundred yards from the bridge. Blue flies circling for a feast.

I glanced at the creek bed. "Charlie! Get up here." I kept low behind a bridge railing, firing my pistol. The frightened horse tugged at the reins in my left hand.

The Yankee cavalrymen milled in a circle. They returned my fire, splinters flying from the bridge planking.

Charlie climbed the river bank ten yards away. He had almost made it clear when he clutched his leg and fell in a roll to the water's edge.

Fear spiked through me. I slapped my horse's rump, and it bolted for the patrol's horses. "I'm coming, Charlie." When bullets kicked up dust around me, I ducked back behind the railing.

"Get back here," Billy yelled.

The flames flared higher and a large mass of black smoke erupted, covering the bridge. *I'm not leaving Charlie.*

I crawled to the bank's edge. Charlie had wriggled to the center of the stream and hid behind a girder in knee-deep water. Flames burned over his head. "How bad is it?" I shouted.

Charlie squinted up at me. "Ain't too bad. But I can't make it back. Y'all get outta here."

Billy crawled up behind me and placed his hand on my shoulder. "Can we make it down to Charlie?"

"No. Can you circle around behind them and attack? Maybe I can get him out of there if you do that."

Billy studied the Bluecoats. "Austin, I don't want to lose more men. And that's what will happen if I try that. They outnumber us twenty to one."

I didn't want to run away and abandon Charlie. But I thought if he surrendered he would at least be alive. "When we leave, hold out your white handkerchief and give up. They'll treat you okay. We'll see you again soon."

Charlie waved to us, a smile plastered on his face.

My guts churned as we used the covering haze to crawl back to the Confederate position. Black smoke billowed up from the bridge. Parts of planking fell into the river near Charlie. Billy ordered our men to mount up.

As we rode through the thick woods, a half-dozen rifle shots snapped behind. I reined in, causing Billy's mount to run into my horse. "I'm going back."

Billy put his hand on my arm. "I can't let you do that. I need you alive."

"Let go, damnit!" I snatched my arm free.

"Listen to me. Charlie's either dead or a prisoner. Nothing you could have done. Nothing you can do now." Billy's eyes glistened.

I jerked my horse's head around, spurring away from the damned Yankees.

If I'd just had a match . . .

Author's Notes:

The Texas Rangers arrived in Nashville in late 1861. Their first major battle was at Shiloh in April 1862, and they fought almost continuously in battles and skirmishes in Tennessee and Kentucky until mid-1864. The true-life characters in the short story, "For Want Of A Match," were: Austin Robinson, wounded and captured at the Salt River, Kentucky, October, 1862, and later exchanged at Vicksburg in the Spring of 1863, and fought with the Rangers until the Surrender in 1865; Charles Allday, wounded and captured in Tennessee in July 1863, then exchanged in January/February 1864; and William H. (Billy) Jones, critically wounded at Mossy Creek (now Jefferson City), Tennessee, in January 1864. He recuperated at his Grandparents home in Evergreen, Alabama. According to oral family history, many years later he scratched at a scab on his back and a rifle ball from his Civil War wound fell on the floor.

Photograph courtesy of Charles Rush
William H. (Billy) Jones, Lieutenant, Terry's Texas Rangers,
8th Texas Cavalry (CSA)

Mustered Out

Jeff Richards

Isaac Greer stared through the campfire smoke at his wife stirring a cast iron pot of dried vegetables and beef that came off the Cracker Line. Jenny's skirt, bunched tightly around her legs, revealed her petticoat and army issue brogans. She rolled up her sleeves, exposing her muscular arms covered in freckles. Her hair was tied back; but it kept coming loose, hiding her pretty gray cat eyes. She brushed the hair away. Smiled at Isaac.

"Are you hungry?"

"I expect," said Isaac.

"How about you boys?"

She was talking to Harold Naylor and Walker Thomas, Isaac's shadows.

"We're ready, ma'am," said Harold spitting tobacco juice on the fire. He banged his fork on his tin plate like he was ringing the dinner bell.

"Yes ma'am," said Walker. These two fellows had followed Isaac all the way from Stones River where he had ripped the 18th Alabama flag from the hands of the dying flag bearer, bullets flying all around as thick as fleas. They believed his life was charmed. Maybe they were right in a peculiar way, considering that what Isaac believed was that he wanted to die. Not by his own hand because he was a God-fearing man but by some other: a bullet slapping into his gut, a saber slicing across his throat.

They sat around the fire partaking of the stew that Jenny had sprinkled with herbs and the bread she had baked that morning and the coffee she begged off the loyal farmer, a veritable feast. Isaac hardly believed she was the same retiring spinster lady that he married seven years ago.

"Ain't this the tastiest vittles I ever swallowed," yelled Harold to Jenny as she ladled out the stew to the rest of the company, all forty-seven of them, calling each by his Christian name. They were her boys and Harold was one of her favorites though no boy. He was old enough to be her father.

"I try, Harold. I try," said Jenny, brushing the hair out of her face.

Harold turned to Isaac. "What time we line up tomorrow, Sarge?"

"Around six or so," said Isaac, sopping up the gravy with his bread.

The soldiers had been pouring over Brown's Ferry since morning. Now they covered the valley below Lookout Mountain.

"But you know how it is. We been marching and countermarching just to keep ourselves busy."

"But Grant's here and he's no lay-about," said Walker in a squeaky voice. Isaac favored the young man because he reminded him of his son Asa who had disappeared the day Isaac asked for Jenny's hand. "I know exactly where we're headed."

The men scowled at Lookout Mountain, a steep edifice guarded by thousands of Secech backed up by cannon. They saw the muzzles glinting in the sun on the ridge top. They knew like Walker and were afraid, all except for Isaac who felt in his bones that maybe tomorrow he'd be mustered out.

He leaned back in his camp chair and lit his pipe while Harold railed on about how he was once in love with a woman who reminded him an awful lot of Jenny Greer.

"She was like one of the boys. A sure shot, for one thing. She bagged an old buck, hung it up, slit it down the middle, sliced off some of the meat. We had us a feast. Then we carried it home. She smoked the meat and we had us more feasts. She was a damn good cook," he said, biting off a plug of tobacco. "Once a fellow grabbed her from behind. She flipped him over and crowned him with the butt of his own pistol."

"She must've been a burly woman," said Walker who knew the story from many retellings.

"No, she was a tiny thing like Miss Jenny," Harold growled at Walker. "A real beauty."

Isaac laughed along with the other soldiers around the fire. Walker and Harold were at each other's throat, but they were also like father and son. Once Harold said that Walker was like the son he never had. Walker said he already had a father; but when he saw how that hurt Harold's feelings, he raised two fingers and said, "Now I got two fathers."

Harold spat a thin stream of tobacco juice in the fire. "I swear to God I should have married that gal. Only I'm a fool and let some other fellow snatch her up. Not the Sarge, there. He's one lucky fellow."

"Why thank you, Harold," said Isaac, banging the spent tobacco out of his pipe. He stood up, stretched, sauntered to the tent, and opened the flap. His wife was asleep, her tiny hands curled under her chin, exhausted from all her work. Harold was right, and it made Isaac feel bad considering what was on his mind. He closed the tent flap and sat down against the trunk of a pine tree. He looked up at the sky crowded with stars and thought maybe tomorrow night he would be somewhere up there behind the crowded sky, looking down from heaven.

When he took that 18th Alabama flag, he had looked down at the eyes of the dying flag bearer and saw a sorrow too deep to imagine. It was the kind of sorrow he felt now thinking about Marion laid out in a pine-box in the parlor, a frown on her lips. She was a schoolteacher when he married her, the happiest of women. Maybe if he had left her with her students. Then Jacob, two years after his mother died, broke his neck when he was thrown from a horse. Maybe if he didn't let him ride or found a horse that didn't spook so easy. Asa was the only family left, and he couldn't care for him proper and work his wheelwright business at the same time. When he told the boy that he was going to marry the spinster lady, Asa had said, "Ma wouldn't like that." Maybe if he had not gone over the next morning and asked for her hand, Asa wouldn't have run away and he wouldn't feel this emptiness in his gut that wouldn't leave even though it'd been so many years.

Jenny Greer threw her arms around her husband's neck and kissed him on the mouth. "I love you with all my heart," she whispered in his ear. He could feel her warm breath. Made his ear tingle. "You swear to me you come back."

"I swear," he said, raising his hand as if he was taking an oath that he didn't really mean.

The men lined up and marched towards Lookout Mountain.

"Bet you there's gray backs behind every tree," said Harold, shaking his head. "We're going to get all mixed up in those woods. It'll be like a turkey shoot."

"You always say that before we march off to a battle," said Walker, "and usually you're wrong."

"I wasn't wrong about Stones River," Harold pulled a plug of tobacco out of his haversack, stared at it for a second, and stuffed it back in. "I ain't going to chew tobacco, least I swallow it when I'm shot."

"Nobody's going to shoot you."

"How do you know? How do you know it ain't like Chickamauga when the woods was on fire. Maybe the woods'll catch fire here and I'll be wounded in the legs crawling away, the flames licking my boots."

"Shut the hell up," growled Greer. "It's bad luck talking like that."

"Sorry, Sergeant."

They marched up to a creek and waited forever until everyone else in the army marched up in line. Then they waited more while the officers consulted. Isaac looked down the ranks seemed to stretch for miles in front and behind him, the flags unfurled, flapping in the wind, the bayonets glinting in the sun. Across Lookout Creek a field covered in dew sparkled like diamonds and, beyond that, the woods, birds on the wing from tree to tree, chirping, the squirrels chattering, and two hawks soaring in the thermals above it all. Isaac could hardly believe there was a Rebel behind every tree.

They commenced to march parallel to the creek and came to a bridge downstream from a ruined dam, the water spilling over. They crossed the bridge and tunneled into the woods bunched together, an easy target for anyone who wanted to take a pot shot at them. But there wasn't much of anyone. A few errant rounds zinged over their heads and plowed up the dirt at their feet. One fellow got shot in the foot, fell out of line screaming like a stuck pig until another fellow dug the minie ball out with his bayonet and covered the wound with a bandana. He helped the fellow hobble off to the rear.

"Lucky soldier," said Harold. "That's the kind of wound I want."

"He'll be back in line in a week," said Walker. "You need a better wound than that."

"Like one that'll carry off my legs?"

"Yeah, that'll do," said Walker, laughing.

Out of the corner of his eyes, Isaac Greer spied a bright reflection like the sun glinting off of metal. He turned his head and saw a Reb lying flat to the ground near a tree taking a bead on Harold's chest. He pushed the old geezer aside and ran towards the soldier who was no more than a couple of hundred feet off on the other side of a little, lopsided meadow. The soldier dropped his gun, scrambled to his feet, and skedaddled into the darkness of the woods; but Isaac caught up, knocked him to the ground, and was about to ram a bayonet down his throat when the gray back raised his hands in surrender.

"Why didn't you shoot me?" screamed Isaac, the tendons standing out on his neck.

The Reb lowered his hands and looked at the Sergeant, a puzzled expression on his face. "What are you some kind of nut?"

"I asked you a question."

"Okay," said the Johnny, getting to his feet slowly, brushing himself off. "If I shot you, your buddies over there – they must be ten thousand at least, they'd fill me so full of holes I'd be like Swiss cheese. Now the only thing that can kill me is prison food."

The Johnny smirked. Isaac shook his head sadly. Everybody's a comedian, he thought.

He handed the prisoner over to the provost and made his way up the long, snaky, blue line until he was with his company once again.

"Why, Sarge," said Harold, squeezing his shoulder gently. "I'll be damned if you didn't save my skinny little rear."

"Ah, come on," Isaac growled, pushing Naylor away.

It was a bright day, a chill in the air, the leaves mostly gone from the trees. The men could see deep in the darkness of the woods until a fog descended on their lines. Through the fog, they saw tiny flashes of light like the glow of fireflies, first one place than another, the videttes retreating to their lines, and worse, a brighter glow followed by an explosion and the sound of artillery shells and canister whining over their heads. The fog lifted long enough for them to see the ridge and the cannon barking on top of it.

"How the hell we going to get up there?" asked Harold, the thought on every soldiers' mind because below the ridge was a two hundred foot vertical cliff, shining in the sun from the moisture dripping off it and below that a rock strewn field. "We ain't mountain goats."

The fog descended again and before long the soldiers had their answer. They turned north. They were going around the ridge and approach it from another side that was not as steep, they hoped. Nayler putting words to their thought, said, "It's nice to see our officers have more than sawdust for brains."

"Would you stop your bellyaching," said Walker.

"I'm not bellyaching," said Naylor, taking this opportunity to bellyache some more. "I'm just a footsore, old man. I got calluses on top of calluses on top of calluses. If I had more calluses my foot would look like this mountain, full of rocks and boulders. All I want is to sit down."

"We'll do that soon enough," said the Sergeant who heard the rattle of gunfire to his front. The fog lifted as they climbed up to a plateau and bunched behind a stone fence. On the other side of the fence about two hundred yards east, the gray backs were packing up, beating a hasty retreat after the stand they had made around a white house.

"We're too late for the fight," said the Sergeant, disappointed.

"Ain't that too sad," said Harold. He was in the process of untying his brogans to get at his feet when the colonel rushed up, his sword drawn and pointing to the east.

"Come on boys, there's more fighting to be done."

They followed the colonel past the white house to the north side of Lookout Mountain where they bunched up so tightly they didn't move for another hour. They heard gunfire to their front.

"Looks like we're missing another fight," said Walker.

"Could be," answered Greer, who was transfixed by the view of the valley below him. Far off, to the east beyond a bend in the Tennessee River, he saw the smoke rising from the chimneys of houses in Chattanooga and the tiny wagons on the Cracker Line waiting for the ferry so they could cross the river and feed all the soldiers. To the southeast, two lines of blue trickled down the roads towards another mountain where, God forbid, the Rebs were fixing to make another stand. He turned to the left to the valley they came from, but he didn't see his camp. He imagined Jenny down there busying herself for their return, trying to keep darker thoughts from crowding her mind. It occurred to him that maybe he was lucky to have such a woman as this whom the boys in the company admired, who kept his wheelwright business thriving while he was gone - he'd seen the books-- and who loved him, at the same time, with all her heart. This thought stayed with him until the fog descended once again and he couldn't see the valley.

They started marching towards the sounds of battle that dissipated somewhat, then rose up like thunder claps bouncing off of one mountain and another. They heard the Rebel Yell.

"They must be making a charge," said Walker. "We have hell to pay."

Harold laughed, "Now it's you doing the bellyaching."

By the time they reached the front, it was all over except for the screaming and jabbering of the wounded that they heard but could not see because of the fog. It was spooky, thought Isaac, sitting down on a flat boulder. Harold sat next to him. He pulled off his shoes and socks. Rubbed his feet.

"Oh, God Almighty, I been waiting this pleasure forever," he sighed deeply, rubbing harder.

Walker took a sip from his canteen. Tightened the cap, he sat down on the other side of his buddy. Sniffed the air. "Boy," he said, "if I didn't know better, I think I sat down in a field of skunk cabbage."

Harold threw his head back in silent laughter and seemed about to deliver a retort when a minie ball flew out of the fog and ran smack in his chest, the force of it so violent that it pushed him backwards over into a ravine.

Walker jumped up screaming as if he'd been stung by a hornet, ran down the ravine, and disappeared in the fog. The Sergeant ran after him. Found him on his hands and knees, rocking back and forth. Reaching out to Harold's body but not touching, afraid of the huge, red ragged hole where the minie ball had exited his back.

Isaac grabbed Walker's shoulder, trying to lift him up, but the younger man was as heavy as one of the boulders. He looked up at the Sergeant, tears running down his cheek. "I can't leave him. He was my best friend."

"You have to," the Sergeant said, softly. "This is war and he's a casualty, son; and if you don't leave him behind, you won't be able to go on yourself."

He had said this very same trite litany to other men in different situations; but, for some reason, this time as he helped Walker Thomas to his feet, it didn't sound like something he said in a perfunctory way to calm the nerves of the soldiers in his charge. It sounded like something he said to himself.

He dragged Walker up the ravine to the boulder.

"I'm not sitting there," said Thomas in a shaky voice.

So they leaned up against a tree surrounded by the rest of the boys in the company. They were all silent, though a few coughed and squirmed like they were sitting in pews at a church before the preacher commenced the sermon. They waited for the fog to lift; and when it did, they saw all the wounded and dead littering the field. What caught their eyes most of all were the Confederate trenches. They were empty.

Some of the boys stood up and cheered. Not Isaac Greer. He was thinking about the litany and what it meant and how glad he was not to have been sitting in the same spot as Harold Naylor, or it would have been him, not Naylor ,who was mustered out.

Author's Note: "Mustered Out" is a completely imagined story about my great-grandfather (Walker Thomas in the story) who was a veteran of the Civil War. He lived until the 1930s so both my father and uncle knew him and told me stories about what a terror he was, mainly because he chased the two boys out of his apple trees, but also because two of his five children ran away to Texas. He was a one-armed doctor in New Philadelphia, Ohio. The other arm hung limply

At Battle

at his side, the result of a wound he received in combat. His own father was also a Civil War veteran, but he didn't last for long. He contracted dysentery and was sent home after the Battle of Stones River. He was also a doctor. Hanging on the wall in my living room is a copy of a pre-war tintype of father and son that always fired my imagination. Through the years, I tried to find out information about my two ancestors. In the Pension records in the National Archives, I discovered that the wife of the father received a one-dollar widow's pension that commenced in the 1880s. I found nothing about my great-grandfather. In "Mustered Out," he is one of the soldiers who storms Lookout Mountain in "The Battle Above the Clouds." I doubt that he ever did this because it was Hooker's soldiers in the battle and I know for a fact, because my uncle told me, that my relative was in Crittenden's Corp, Wood's Division. But that's the advantage of writing fiction.

The Drum and the Fife

Kathleen Jack

1-1-2012

2. OUTSIDE THE BATTLEFIELDS

Photograph by Emily Nance

Going Home: Black and White

Thelma Battle

I'se carrying my master
On a wagon...home.

The war's not over,
but we's going still.

I promised Ole Missus
I'd stay with him

And bring him back to his four
little daughters and little son Jim.

His soul's gone on,
But his body's with me,

And I'se bound and sworn
to handle it safely.

One day they says I'll be buried
at the foot of his grave,

Me, born into bondage,
me, forever a slave.

I'se carrying my master
On a wagon, home.

The war's not over,
but we's going still.

Me and my master is finally home today.
Home we has come to. Home he will stay.

But if I gets a chance, I'se heading away,
North to freedom, North to a better day.

He's home...but I'se going still.

For William

Christy Cole

War torn and weary,
Going home...finally going home.
To see the child...a breathing legacy....
With hopes of what could be
With fears of what could be lost...
Going home.
The smell of new life
Like the smell of new green grass in the spring.,,
Breathing deeply...home...

Back to the smell of smoke and decay...
Death and cannon fire all around...
The taste of fear...shattering sounds...far from home...
The taste of death....searing pain...
Every thought of the child ....
Meadows and fields..
Again breathing deeply ....
Going home....finally going home.

Author's note: William Winsett was killed in the battle of Atlanta in 1864. Cole is his great-great granddaughter.

In My Shoes

Dorris Douglass

One million men are needing shoes
Beneath their ragged gray pant legs
To march in war against the blues
For our bare feet oppose the Feds,

Repel the northerners' advance,
Defend our precious States' Rights soil,
In blistered, bleeding, freezing stance,
Bragg's limping army, ever loyal.

Our brogans are all worn out
Beyond repair, but we still fight
While country cobblers help us out.
At Richmond, Congress sees our plight,

Allows 2,000 soldiers sent
To factories throughout the south,
Detailed to make us shoes to sprint
And dodge the minie-balls in route.

It's April 1863,
Shoes for Bragg is quite a task,
A near impossibility.
But Major Cunningham now asks

For soldiers skilled in leather-craft
Transferred to Quartermaster crews.
He asks for sixty, but gets half,
From duty, deathly grim, excused.

Atlanta bound, we lucky thirty
Arrive to join the forty there,
In making Rebel shoes so sturdy,
Which are to say, "We care, we care !"

Day in, day out, we ply our trade,
Except for Saturdays we drill
In case the Yankees should invade.
And Sundays are for prayer with zeal.

We've done our time to face a gun.
Are not ashamed to serve this way.
We've shirked no duty, have not run
In spite of what you're apt to say.

A year has gone, and it's July.
Brand new and frayless blue pant legs,
And brogans called gunboats, Oh My!
Are marching on Atlanta's edge.

Overhead, across the sky,
Sherman now shells the town like hell.
Eight days we shoemakers stand by,
Then under orders say "farewell."

Slip through the lines, Augusta, bound,
Its arsenal, our place to stay,
And space to make our shoes is found,
For Major Bridewell has his say.

Nine months have gone, and it is May.
Soldiers no longer need our shoes
Beneath defeated pant legs gray,
To march in war against the blues.

Now homeward bound we take our leave,
Embrace our families once more.
The times we hardly can conceive.
Behold! The wolf is at the door

With Union paws, extending claws,
For carpetbaggers soon arrive
In two-tone shoes to change our laws
And buy our land so we survive.

When Northern boys and girls meet ours,
A life together they so choose.
The love they find has healing powers
And Grandpa has complying shoes.

Burnin'

John Neely Davis

Papa decided we'd cross the river 'bout a mile upstream from the town.

Down river to the west, the moon was a-startin to set. Hit was not giving up easy and hung on to the night sky, a big silver disk a-feared that once hit dropped below the horizon, hit might never find the path across the darkness again.

I rode the little bay gelding off into the cold water, grabbin his tail as I slid off the back of the saddle. Soon as his feet cleared the bottom of the river, he started the strong, kickin strokes that are pretty much natural to a horse. The swift current carried us down stream; but in no more than a hiccup, we got to the south bank.

I could hear Papa fightin with the stole mare behind us. She was not used to swimmin, and I could hear the ruckus as Papa forced her off the muddy riverbank and into the deep water. I pulled myself back into the saddle as my bay climbed up the bank. "She's not gonna to win," I told the him, I've never seen Papa lose no battle with a horse.

Papa and the mare came scramblin up the bank behind us. "Damn fool," Papa said, "acts like she is too good to swim. Been petted all her life, prancin up and down them cotton rows carryin that highfalutin foreman." The wet saddle creaked as he leaned forward and rubbed the mare's neck, "Sister you've got some changes comin, let me tell you. Some changes comin. You'll never see that plantation again – not under my saddle you won't."

I slipped off the bay, shed my pants and shirt, and wrung the water out. Papa, hoppin first on one foot and then the other, took his boots off and poured the water on the ground. The long-bladed knife he carried inside his right boot tumbled out and shined right wicked in the moonlight.

He stripped off his pants and shirt. We stood there in the darkness, naked as the day we was borned. Probably looked like some ghosts outta a haint story or somethin like that.

Papa took an oilskin pouch from the back of his saddle, unrolled it, found a dry shirt and handed hit to me. After I had dried myself, I pitched hit back to Papa, and he runned hit over his stomach and back.

We found dead grass, wadded hit up, and dried the horses. Papa tousled my hair, "Good job, Geoff. Better than most men could've done. You are gonna be a good horseman. Wish my brothers back in Dubbo could have seen you go off over the back of that saddle. You went off like a cat; you was top notch."

I worked up my deepest voice. "I wasn't scared for me, but I was a-feared bout you on that mare. She ain't got a lick of sense"

Papa laughed and tousled my hair again, "I know and I love you for hit. We got better days comin; I can just feel it,"

We rode out across a cornfield; last year's corn stalks stickin up like pale, boney fingers. There was a light breeze and some of the corn leaves moved real quiet, small ghostly banners warnin intruders to be wary of things hidin in the dark.

"If they are raisin corn, there's got to be a corn crib somers close," Papa said, his voice just over a whisper. We crossed a small creek at the end of the field and, just like he said, there was a log crib standin right there in the edge of the woods.

We dismounted and Papa left me with the horses, told me to hold the mare's nose so she wouldn't answer in case a horse sumers whinnied. He shoved the pistol down in the front of his britches and worked his way through the darkness round the edge of the woods to the crib. Way up the valley, I could see the dim outline of a house and maybe another barn or two. There was no lights at the house, but I heard a dog bark and sumers on further up the valley nother dog answered. The mare was gettin restless, tryin to free her head from my grasp, when Papa just come easin up out of the shadders.

"Good place to spend the night," he whispered. "There is corn in the crib and some loose hay in a side shed. We can feed the horses and you can sleep in the hay – all of us can use some rest!"

We hung in the edge of the woods til we reached the crib. The horses fed, we sat in the open door of the crib and looked up the valley. "Be nice to have a little place like this, wouldn't it?" Papa said. "We could run a few head of cows, three or four horses, maybe grow some corn, and have a little garden. Bet I could get a job blacksmithin, and we could get you some schoolin."

I heard this talk before and knew hit wouldn't never happen. But hit made Papa feel good and that was the important thing.

Papa unrolled the oilskin again and took out some slices of hog shoulder and four biscuits. "Bet you are hungry, ain't you boy? If I member right, we didn't have no chance to eat yet, have we?"

"Apples. We had them apples this mornin."

Papa laughed, "Kinda hard to eat a apple when you're settin on the back of a lopin horse, ain't it?"

"Yes sir, but we made out, didn't we? Bet them other fellers wished they was as tough as we are. Reckon that's where we lost um, sumers round Murfreesboro. Reckon they stopped to eat and after that rain they couldn't raise our tracks no more?"

I'd finished my meat and biscuits; Papa shoved his over to me. "Wish you'd eat um," he said. "I ain't hungry. Believe I'd druther have a dip of snuff. Hit's more settlin to my stomach."

I pushed the biscuits back toward Papa. "I'm 'bout full. I'd druther you eat um."

Papa ate half a biscuit and a bite of the meat before rollin up what was left in the oilskin. He said, "We'll save the rest for tomorrow."

With the moon gone, the stars come out in the blue-black sky and we sat there in the darkness. Reckon both of us had our own thoughts. Finally, Papa said, "We need to turn in, get some rest, tomorrow might be a long un. You lay down back there in the hay; I'll sit round out here for a while. Don't spect we'll have no company, but you can't never tell."

"Will you wake me up in a while? You need some sleep and I can watch out just good as you can."

Papa said yeah but I knowed he wouldn't. I got up and he said, "Careful, there is a pitchfork there at the side of the shed. Don't want you hangin up on it, maybe tearin your new britches." We both laughed a little because my pants were so ragged, 'bout as much skin showed as cloth.

The hay was soft and smelled sweet. I blinked twice and the second time I didn't open my eyes again.

A sharp pain in the ribs sliced through my sleep. A man's gravelly voice, "I've got the thevin little wolf-eyed bastard, half rat, whatever the hell he is!"...another pain ...this time in the head...and before I could get my arms up, I saw the boot comin and this time there was stars and bright lights and kinda a roarin in my head.

From the front of the crib, a man shouted, "No trouble outta this rascal for a while, put a knot on his head the size of a goose egg. I spect he'll sleep til daylight. Be damn lucky if he ever sees nother sunup."

I stayed down on the ground without movin, my arms round my head, knowin that nother kick was comin. A yellow light come oozing around the corner of the crib, followed by a man carrying a lantern. He squatted down side me and jerked my arms open, "Hell, Luke he's jest a kid, ain't he?"

The man what kicked me said, "Little sum'bitch'll grow up to be just like his daddy!"

"No, I don't reckon he will. I'd say his growin days are about over and done."

"What you think we ought to do with um, Bill?"

"Well, we damned shore ain't gonna carry um back cross the Georgie state line, I'll tell you that right now. Ain't gonna waste no bullets on em, neither."

"Hell, Bill, they jest stole that mare and at pistol. We damn shore gonna get that reward anyhows. I figered we'd just bust um up some, take both the horses and head on back to Chick'mauga."

"Yeah, we do that and we'll be lookin over our shoulder all the way home wonderin if that big bastard is followin us. We'll just end all this right here and now. I'll go drag that sum'bitch back here, we'll use a choppin ax on his head– and that lil'un too - pour some coal oil on um, set this crib on far, and git the hell outta here. Folks what find um will just figure they us some kinda no goods that wus sleepin here. Smokin or drunk and caught the hay on far. Died fore they could wake up."

"I don't reckon I can stomach that - not the kid no how. Let's jest do the big'un, and we'll figure out somethin for the boy."

"Luke, I ain't askin, I'm tellin. Go get the big'un and drag him back here. We ain't found that pistol they stole. It ain't on the big'un. Bet the kid is hidin it. He'll tell me where it is fore you git back with his daddy." He gave me a kick in the side of the face, "Won't you, boy – you gonna tell me, ain't you?"

I wanted to be tough, wanted to be a man, but I couldn't. "I ain't got hit," a jerkin sob, "I ain't seen hit, I promise."

This time he slapped me in the mouth with the back of his hand, fingers rough and thick as corn cobs. "Don't you lie to me, you little bastard, I'll cut your damn tongue right outta your mouth." He knelt and put a knee on my chest.

His greasy hair brushed against my face, and his breath was foul. I smelled the stink on his hands as he cupped his palm under my chin and forced my mouth open with his dirty thumb and middle finger.

"Don't. Don't," I cried and struggled to turn my head to the side.

There was a thump and a groan from the front of the crib. Bill shouted, "Quit beatin on that feller and drag his ass on round here. We need to get this over with and get outta here."

Bill wrapped his hand in my hair and jerked me to my feet. He slapped me and I fell to the side, pulling him around so that his back was toward the front of the crib. "You comin, Luke, or am I gonna have to come round there and get the both of you?"

Luke shuffled around the side of the crib, his head down, hands hanging loose at his side, movements jerky like one of them marionette things at a stage show. He took another stumblin step forward, kinda staggered to the side and his head dropped back. Two tines of the pitchfork stuck outta the front of his neck. He coughed and blood spewed from his mouth, made little dark spots in the dirt.

Bill turned, saw Luke, and shoved me to the side. He took a step back and said, "What in the hell...?"

From the shadders behind me, Papa jumped a straddle of Bill, wrapped his left arm around his head and pulled hit to the side. With one lick, he shoved the knife into the right side of Bill's neck and sliced forward, severin the jugular. Bill's face crumpled, crimson blossomed on his lips and ran down on his shirt. There was a gurgle as blood was sucked down into his windpipe and, without no noise, he fell forward across Luke's jerkin body.

My knees buckled and I fell into the hay. I started screamin, and Papa held me in his arms. When I couldn't stop, he held his hand over my mouth until vomit squirted outta my nose and spewed out between his fingers.

Everything got black - goin unconscious ain't always a bad thing.

I woke up with Papa washin my face by the river. "Ht's gonna be all right son, trust me. I want you to stay here with the horses; I'll be back in five minutes. There is a couple of other things, I've got to do."

"Papa, those men..."

"Don't worry about um again. They ain't gonna bother us no more. You'll be okay here. I promise I'll be right back." Fog was risin up off the river and the light breeze caused hit to swirl through the woods borderin the cornfield. In the dim light of the dawn, Papa patted my shoulder before disappearin in the fog.

Chilled, I sat huddled under willow bushes, holdin the horses' reins. A loon sent a quiverin call down river, and hit went up my back like little scratchy fingers. I stood and leaned in against the bay's neck, trying to absorb some warmth and comfort. The big plantation mare snorted and pricked her ears forward. A warm glow forced its way through the fog, silhouettin Papa as he come outta the trees.

He put his arms around me and I smelled kerosene. He laced his fingers together. I put a foot in his hands and climbed up on the bay. He got on the mare, and we sat there watchin the orange glow gettin stronger; I could smell the smoke from the burnin crib. Lips tight against his teeth, Papa muttered, "Let the bloody bastards stew in their own grease and meanness."

I'd never smelled men burnin, and hit would be better an thirty years before I'd smell hit again.

On a bitter day in November, we come over Winstead Ridge with General Hood's boys. Franklin laid right there in front of us and Union troops behind breastworks as fur as we could see. Our band was playin the "Bonnie Blue Flag." We was spread out in a long line, everybody runnin close to the ground, our britches' legs flappin and cold steel shinin on the end of our rifles. Nobody knowed hit, but hit was the beginin of the end for most of us.

I took a minie ball in my leg, knocked me flatter than a flitter and that was hit for me.

Both my boys was blowed up in a munitions wagon. Their bodies was all tore up; I couldn't hardly tell um apart. They was all crusted over from the heat.

Next day, my wife and me took our boys back home to Leipers Fork. Uncle Fate hope us dig their graves, and we buried them in the rocky ground down below the apple orchard. Ever spring when the trees bloom out, I go down there and watch them little petals go swirlin off in the wind. Pore li'l things never got a chance to get growed - minds me of my boys.

Folks said, I'd get over hit. But I ain't. Man don't ever need to smell human flesh a burnin - specially when hit's his own true blood.

Ole Billy

Robert McCurley

Ole Billy lies in my tent, his head restin' on a soiled blanket.
He's got the Fever and it's makin' him crazy.
He don't know where he is,
And he don't know who I am anymore either.
I wipe the sweat off his brow and tell him stories,
But I know he don't hear me.
I'm just another ghost in his dreams and nightmares.
He's been like this two days and two nights,
And I don't know if either one of us can take much more.
His old glassy eyes stare up at me without seein'.
His parched lips mumble words, but I don't understand
    'em.
The old jackleg doctor says he might not make it,
But Billy's tough and I don't believe him.
Nigh on two years now we've been together; he saved my life
    once.
Shot a man clean through the heart
Just as he was gonna stab me in exactly same place,
I always thought that was kinda poetic.
Billy's from Kentucky; I'm from Tennessee.
We got put together in the same outfit right at the start.
I've always admired him, even though he's stubborn as a
    mule.
I've seen him shoot the tip off a matchstick from forty yards
    away.
And can't nobody beat him arm-wrestlin' neither.
I'd never let him hear me say it, but ole Billy's my hero.
One time, me and Billy was on what they call
    reconnaissance,
That's a fancy word for spyin' on the enemy.
Out of nowhere, three of them ole Union boys

Come up from behind and jumped us.
Billy killed one of 'em with his pistol and another with his
    knife.
Then he come over helped me finish off the last one.
Later when we's a talkin', I made out like
I didn't need his help, but I was a lyin'.
I'da probably been a dead man if it hadn't been for Billy.
I guess that makes twice he saved my skin.
I can't get him to eat nothin'
And he fights me when I try to give him a drink.
I don't want to tell him, but I'm startin' to get scared,
'Cause Billy ain't gettin' no better.
Another time when we's a marchin', a little ole puppy
Ran out of the woods and started to follow us.
One of the others was gonna shoot him for the sport of it.
Billy grabbed his gun just as he was takin' aim;
And before that old boy knew what happened,
Billy done took his rifle out of his hands and stuck it right in
    his face.
He told that stupid soldier that if he shot that dog,
He'd break all his fingers so's he wouldn't never
Be able to shoot nothin' else.
The Sergeant ran over to see what the commotion was all
    about.
Billy told him wasn't nothin' wrong, old dumb-ass Zeke
Just needed some pointers on where he should aim his rifle.
Then Billy picked the little puppy up and put him in his
    pack.
Next town we come to, Billy gave that puppy to a little ole
    boy.
You shoulda seen the smile on the little feller's face.
And the tear that run down Billy's cheek when he done it,
He wiped it away, though, 'fore anybody could see it.
I ain't never seen nobody had more courage than Billy.
He's survived many a battle, but it looks like he's losin' this
    one.

The fever's takin' over, and his breathin's slowin' down.
The breaths is comin' fewer and farther between.
I ain't never had a friend like Billy before.
It hurts me to see the life just slowly leakin' out of him,
But Lord knows I'm exhausted from tryin'
To stay up with him day and night.
As I look over at him, I can see that his chest has done gone
    still;
Billy ain't takin' no more breaths.
As the tears start to burn my tired old eyes,
I realize that ole Billy's gone,
And a big piece of me just went with him.

Etta's Law

S.R. Lee

Etta McKissack was not a cruel woman though few would call her kind. "The Lord maketh the rain to fall upon the just and the unjust" was the Bible verse most often running through her head. It wasn't her favorite. Her favorite was "Jesus wept."

Etta never wept. She had a Presbyterian sense of duty and a good head for numbers. She took care of the farm accounts. They showed average circumstances when the Tennessee weather held. If a drought came, the year would be lean.

"Fatback and beans all winter," Jeb might moan, but Etta had been raised not to complain of food.

"Lord, make us thankful for what we are about to receive," she intoned when he had neglected to say the blessing. Within a few years of marriage, she was the one to say it each meal.

Come spring, Etta would almost envy the black children grabbing dandelion leaves and the poke sallet along the back fence. The small ones were scavengers for their mammies. Etta kept an eye on what they took.

Beginning in 1849, when the oldest of these children was age three, Etta's ledger books showed them as an expense. Jeb bought them shoes once a year from Pollock, the harness maker. Etta measured out cloth to the mothers as each piece came off the kitchen loom. Knowing some cloth would come to them, the mothers were not lazy about weaving.

Women's work usually went well enough, but field labor was a worry. Jeb had borrowed to pay for four healthy slaves, two women and two men to work and breed profitably.

Within a year, one of the men fell under wagon wheels crossing the rocky creek with a full load of corn. His skull was crushed. They had lost half a day of harvest while they buried him in a corner of the side field. Etta did not hold with careless burials. She told Jeb to say a prayer over the grave once it was filled in.

They hadn't yet planned where to put a cemetery, but haste demanded decision. That corner would do, Etta supposed. The following winter, Etta gave birth to a bloody disfigured shape four months too soon. Jeb laid it in the ground beside the other body and built a fence to mark the cemetery.

Faced with spring plowing, Jeb's winter gloom deepened.

"Haven't even paid my loan off. Three mules out there and only that man David to help me."

"Rachel can hold a plow. Strongest woman I ever seen."

Jeb looked up. Etta rarely spoke, sad after her miscarriage he supposed. This was the strongest he had heard her voice for four months. In his surprise, he hardly took in the rest of her ideas.

"Chloe and I can manage the garden and milking. You use the others in the fields. Rachel's not with child."

The mules pulled, firm arms held the plow shafts, the big field was planted with cotton, the smaller one with corn. Chloe and Etta spaded the garden by hand. Etta planted peas in the cold mud of early March and followed along with everything in its season, as the Bible said.

Chloe had a healthy boy.

Once the growing season was underway, corn and cotton needed chopping. All five adults went out with hoes.

Jeb felt it was Etta's drive that got them though that year and the next. Chloe's baby grew, and the next winter she was round again. Etta put more wool on the loom.

But Etta herself never came into a family way again.

During the third autumn, Rachel showed round. The child was born near Christmas, and by spring Rachel was field worthy again. Chloe nursed the new baby along with her growing second one except when Rachel was back at mealtime.

Etta hardly looked at the babies. Until there were five of them racing for dandelion leaves in the spring rains, she pushed them to a small dark corner of her mind. None were old enough for real work yet. Three were black as the dirt in the corn bottom by the creek, but two were pale brown as the dust from the hillsides.

Etta took refuge in the farm accounts. Jeb was doing better than mere survival, but they were not prospering. Jeb had paid off his loan. She would not suggest he borrow again. The slave children were healthy. Soon, the two oldest might be set some household tasks.

Jeb never spoke of sons, but Etta knew she was not doing her duty by the farm. So the light-skinned children? Who was to blame? She was glad Jesus could weep.

More babies came, some light, some dark. As the older ones began to be useful, Etta made sure that only a dark one went to hold the team when she shopped at the general store or Jeb and David took wagons of corn to the Nashville market.

Gradually, Jeb put the slave children to work at tasks near the house, hitching the buggy, picking apples, work Etta's sons would have done, had she had sons. She watched the work and thought of the rain on the just and the unjust. Which of these children deserved the rain?

The farm needed cash. Etta thought to become a teacher. Her Presbyterian father had taught his girls along with his boys.

"Jeb, I could start a school."

He didn't seem to be listening.

"The county is paying now, two dollars per pupil per session. If I sign up enough scholars, then they'll pay."

"And if you don't?"

He was listening after all, wasn't even forbidding it.

"I'll charge subscription. Allens over there think school is too far for the young ones to walk. Cherrys have three children, Tuckers have five."

She would need a schoolhouse. Jeb offered to mend the leaky roof of the Baptist church down the road. The preacher struck a deal.

"But it has to be clean for Sunday mornings, no whittling on the seats, no mud inside."

So on Fridays Etta took Isaac, nine years old, light-skinned, and small for his age, to clean up the room and grounds. Later she took him every day. He seemed suited to the work.

Isaac knew how to be quiet. Oh, he was quick and obedient enough in the afternoons when it was time to go home and in the cold mornings when Etta needed to get the fire started in the iron stove. Though small, he could unhitch the horse from the buggy and tie it round back among the trees. She had him dip water from the creek to fill a bucket for the horse. Afternoons could get hot.

In the warm days of autumn, Isaac lay outside in the sun till she called him to sweep the floor. When the cold drizzly rain of November came, the boy came inside, to a back corner, where he stayed very still although she saw that he looked always toward her desk.

Etta used recess time to read over the coming history lesson. On cloudy days she would wash down the blackboard from chalk dust gathered during a morning of arithmetic and spelling. Gray light from a winter afternoon kept the room dim. Chalky boards only made the work harder for all to see.

On a cold, bright morning when the children had rushed out to shout and race about, the corner of her eye caught movement and she turned to a light brown hand and wet rag moving across the lower half of the board. As she took the rag to reach the top, she murmured, "Thank you, Isaac," then wondered that she had spoken to him as casually as she might if one of the white children washed the board unexpectedly. Why thank a slave? A light brown slave boy that might be her husband's child, as were his brothers and sisters? If the school children didn't comment, it was only because the scandal was so old, the common knowledge almost forgotten.

Etta needed someone to do the work in the schoolhouse. This boy was the one her husband would spare. What could she have said to object?

She was starting the second grade on their spelling when she heard the thunk. The room went quiet. Charlie Winston was standing by the back table; Isaac's head was ducked low to his knees. Charlie held some papers, wrinkling them in his fist as he started forward.

"Mrs. McKissack, that little black devil was writing. Don't he know he can't do that--against the law--and he was using up good paper too while all I have is a slate." He tossed the balled papers on her desk.

Blood was seeping between Isaac's fingers, but he wasn't making a sound.

She dipped a rag in the water bucket and walked back to the hurt boy. The gash on his head was not long but was bleeding down his clothes. She lifted his head to lie on the table and began to bathe the wound.

"That's our drinking water."

The little girl's voice was frightened.

"Tom, pour that water in another bucket and go get fresh." Etta wasn't going to get into arguments if she could foresee them.

"And Margaret, come help me."

Margaret loved to care for anything hurt. Etta showed her how to hold the rag against the seeping blood. It was already slowing.

"Isaac, stay still until I come back. Don't move at all."

The boy gave a small sigh and tightened his fingers on his knees.

At her desk, Etta confronted Charlie Winston who looked a little confused by the order of events. Why wasn't she whipping that black boy?

"Charlie, I'm glad you have respect for the law. You have just injured some of Mr. McKissack's property. I hope you understand the issues of property rights. If this boy's head heals soon, we won't be coming to your father for reparations." Etta wanted the word to sound long and official.

The next day she left Isaac at home. His head would heal soon, but he was a little boy and could use a day to stay with his mother. At school she made a chart of chores. She explained that only the older children would fetch water for the horse. As each child was assigned to stay after school to tidy up, brothers and sisters would stay to help. Mary Bright objected.

"There's six of us. Every time round, we got to stay six times, but Charlie's got only one brother so he'll only stay twice. Charlie, what'd you hit that boy for?"

"Hush, Mary. The plan is fair. Everyone has to take the same turn, and Jesus expects you to help your family. He says in the Bible "For if ye love them which love you, what reward have ye? Do not even the publicans do the same?"

Etta thought the logic of her quotation was not quite clear, but she knew Mary would not challenge it.

She left Isaac at home through the rest of the week.

Then Jeb said, "Take him on back with you, too puny for plowing yet."

On Monday they went early with a small load of sturdy sticks and a good-sized knife in the back of the buggy. Before Etta set Isaac to his usual tasks, she had him take the sticks and knife to a little table at the back of the room. She put a stool beside it. She took down the list of chores.

Even while the children were playing outside before the bell, Etta knew they had noticed Isaac and his knife. Once she finished the morning Bible reading, she announced,

"Mr. McKissack has sent Isaac back to help at school. When you see my husband at church next Sunday, you need to thank him. Isaac now has more work, learning to make handles. That knife is sharp. No one is to touch it, whether or not Isaac is using it. Should some of you older boys wish to learn handle making, you may stay in from recess to practice as long as I am in the room."

Handle making was a useful skill, but she did not expect any requests to learn with Isaac's knife. None came.

Etta put five half-sheets of paper on one side of her desk. She stayed longer at school in the afternoons to plan lessons while Isaac tidied the room. She told him not to wash the schoolwork from the blackboard until last. He finished his work and then was very quiet. She listened. Sometimes he folded a piece of paper and put it inside his shirt. He was a neat and useful boy.

Etta believed in duty. Her father had kept a quiet, scholarly household. Now things were different. Politicians were worried and fretful, shouting from their platforms that states rights must be preserved. Legislators made more laws controlling the slaves, capturing runaways. The Bible said, "Slaves, obey your masters."

Isaac always obeyed quickly. He was careful in his work, and she was careful in her speech. She made sure that sheets of paper were on the corner of her desk and pencils with them.

Isaac cleaned her school for three years. When he finally began to grow sturdy, Jeb wanted him in the fields. Etta made another schedule of chores for the school children. Chores used up some of their excitement over the political tension rising in the 1860 autumn season. The government in Washington was far away, but the Tennessee state legislature was filled with rumors that found their way even down to country churches. The children said rude things about those they thought enemies. Isaac did not need to hear that anger and scorn. As soon as school finished each afternoon, Etta took her buggy homewards. What would happen would happen.

The school had few books, and the children were hard on them. Etta set about to repair them one at a time. She was in no hurry, best to do a careful job. She left each book on the end of a kitchen shelf for she would use flour paste and small strips of paper to mend torn pages and frayed corners. If the book was missing for a few days, she didn't notice. It was there when she was ready to make her repairs.

From her kitchen window, Etta noticed that Lizzie, oldest among the slave children and now a strong girl of eighteen, was pestering Isaac. For several days, she kept after him in the mornings when he was milking and in the late afternoons when the men were back around the barn, feeding, storing tools, whatever. One evening Lizzie brought the milk pails up to the house while Isaac was turning the cows back out to pasture. When Etta saw the two of them go back into the empty barn, she had reason to worry: no need for an early pregnancy. She called as she walked across toward the barn, "Lizzie, Lizzie" but on entering heard only a quick rustle in the farthest stall. Silent with anger, she looked at footprints in the dust, all going away from her. There on a smooth space in the dusty floor, clear for any to read, was scratched the word "Lizzie." Etta smoothed it out and turned back to the house. No point in Jeb seeing that and getting worried, but no harm either in Lizzie being able to sign her name. A change was coming.

The War didn't touch them at first. The sun shone and the rains came, sometimes too much, sometimes too little, just as most years. Then two years into the conflict, 1863, Jeb found the slave cabins empty one autumn morning, every single person gone. He had known slaves were escaping into Nashville, now occupied by Union forces. Although not surprised, he was grim. Etta had given them shoes and cloth every year, but they seemed to feel no loyalty. Well, the corn was in the cribs and the tobacco hanging to dry. Maybe they were good riddance for the lean winter.

Etta taught. She had six new students so twelve more dollars. Jeb sold his tobacco and had enough corn to take the stock through winter. They made it better than they expected.

In April, Isaac came walking back into the yard. He was taller and bony, not much flesh anywhere.

"Mrs. McKissack, it ain't good in there."

Etta sat the lean boy down on the back steps and gave him a glass of buttermilk. It was gone in three gulps. She refilled the glass and brought some cornbread. She had not known how she loved him until she saw his hunger, this one child she had been able to nurture.

"Go clean out a cabin for yourself. Put fresh straw in your mattress. But split me some stove wood before dinner; and when Mr. McKissack comes up, you'll have to ask him if you can stay."

Jeb was calm enough about Isaac's appearance.

"Thought as much," was all he said.

Isaac stayed on, living alone in a cabin, working in the fields with Jeb, milking morning and evening, weeding and picking the garden well into autumn. He spent the winter evenings whittling legs and rungs for a chair.

Yankee raids for horses and mules were becoming more frequent. Jeb decided on a spot in the woods to hide his stock and told Isaac, "When we need to hide them, you stay there till I come back. Keep them calm in the night."

Jeb said to Etta, "No need for that boy to be pressed off to serve in some army. Hide him too."

In April, 1865, the war was over. By July the Freedman's Bureau was established in Washington. In early September, the Bureau's Commissioner for Tennessee, General C.B. Fisk, made a speech in Spring Hill defining the purpose of the Bureau in Middle Tennessee. His speech was reported in the *Nashville Daily Press and Times*.

When she read the article, Etta cut off the whole length of linsey-woolsey from her kitchen loom. She hemmed the raw edge and folded the piece neatly into a small packet. She wrote a note and placed it beside the cloth. She made an apple pie. She fed Jeb his noon dinner at the table and Isaac his dinner on the back steps. While Jeb was eating pie, she took the packet and note out to Isaac.

"Stand up and read this note to me."

Isaac read steadily,

"To Whom It May Concern,

The mulatto boy, Isaac McKissack, can read, write, and cipher. Try to employ him in such a way as to use his education.

Mrs. Jebediah McKissack"

"The Freedman's Bureau office is in the county courthouse," she said. "Now go."

Back in the house, she did not watch from a window as he walked away. She turned to clearing up after the meal.

Concluding Remarks

Robert McCurley

Yet another discourse lies before me
To a people spared, but scarred by the ravages of war.
Their surroundings are littered with remnants
    of blue and gray,
Their enervated minds desperately ready
    for an epistle of reverence and hope.

Judge Wills asked for my support in dedicating
    a few acres of land
Destined, he said, to be revered as hallowed ground,
Baptized by blood and purchased to house
    the flesh and bone
Of courageous soldiers, of fathers and sons, of men
    destined for long remembrance.

This is not a desirable task, for I am wearied
From the weight of grave circumstances past and present,
Yet even more from the consuming province of uniting
A nation universally unaccepting of simple equality
    and freedom.

Given short notice, "just a few closing remarks"
    was the humble request.
Even so, Wills knew, as well as I, that Everett
    would exploit the moment to display his oratory skills
And further his repute amongst peers and common folk,
Eradicating contingency for anyone to challenge
    his prowess of language or ability to mesmerize listeners.

Such vanity these empty and endless speeches,
Written to promote conceited popularity, political influence,
     and unmerited financial gain.
Sometimes I think it more than I can bear to suffer
     another fool against the pressing of my patience,
Knowing that some perceive me as delivering
     exactly the same.

This time, though, I will dare to stray from the expectation
     of another long-winded oration
Bloated with mind-numbing verbosity and foolish dramatics.
My thoughts, though scattered upon arrival, are now
     assembled, adduced in my mind and sealed in my heart,
Ready for dispatch, as valued seeds
     carefully counted for planting in tilled, fertile soil.

Reporters and politicians may scorn the brevity of my words.
Nonetheless, I will bestow my message with resolve,
Disregarding the opinion of those unwilling
     to rise above petty criticism
And embrace my renewed call for devotion
     to the unfinished work that lies ahead.

Two hours past and Everett is winded; it is almost time,
Yet, predictably, he is hesitant to relinquish the stage.
The crowd, restless and wandering, was lost some time ago
Upon discovering little substance to hold their attention,
Or nourishment for their troubled souls.

Photograph by Robert McCurley

Finally, my moment is here; my time has come.
Wills stands and announces me to an emotional crowd,
A people afflicted by hardship, uncertainty and loss of kin
Now finding themselves at a moment
    designated to bring closure
To the hellish misfortunes of war
    and dedicate a resting place
For those forever lost in being,
    but eternally present in memory.

I stand, wholly immersed in the moment,
    and survey the throng
Scattered over hills still sorely disfigured by enemy fire.
These faithful have endured to hear a President's message
    of inspiration, words they can embrace,
A charge that will fortify them to bury
    the horror of battle and of their dead,
To forge new lives, a new day, a new beginning,
    a new freedom in their land.

And so I begin...

Fourscore and seven years ago...

Author's Note:

The Gettysburg Address is, undoubtedly, one of the most famous Presidential speeches in history; it is also one of the shortest in length, maybe two minutes from beginning to end. When has a politician voluntarily limited himself to two minutes? Unheard of! Long and dramatic monologues were the norm in Lincoln's day and he was more than capable of skillfully articulating his agendas in captivating style over the course of an hour or two...or even three.

As Lincoln sat listening to Edward Everett deliver two-hour dedication speech at Cemetery Hill, knowing he would immediately follow with a very unconventional delivery of his own, what was he thinking? 'Concluding Remarks' intertwines factual history, speculation and imagination as to what could have been going through Lincoln's mind in the minutes immediately preceding the Gettysburg Address.

3. LEFT BEHIND

Photograph by Robert McCurley

Vicksburg, 1863

Micki Fuhrman

*He came to in a cotton field somewhere outside
  Vicksburg
As the last rays of sun were going down.
His Union blues were soaked with blood and he
  struggled to his feet
And started slowly walking toward the lights of a big
  white house.*

Sarah Louise Montgomery lit the lamp beside her bed
And began to brush her long and auburn hair.
Her eyes rested on the photograph of two brothers dressed
  in gray
And, for their souls now gone, she breathed a silent prayer.

She could not go to war herself, so she fought back how she
  could,
Giving horses, food, and blankets for the boys who fought
  for Lee
And when she walked the streets of town, they met her with
  respect.
She was a five and a half foot pillar of the Confederacy.

A knock came at the door, and Sarah grabbed her daddy's
  gun
And flew down the stairs still in her stockinged feet.
When the door cracked open, she found herself staring
Into the hungry young face of the enemy.

"Mother of God" she whispered and caught him as he fell,
Then dragged his body in beside the fire
She tore away the navy coat and bound the bleeding wound
And for six days while the fever burned,
She never left his side.

As the weeks flew by and he grew strong, he talked of
     Illinois...
About his Ma and Pa back on the farm.
Sarah told how Charles and Edward died at Seven Pines
While she sewed the last of his coat buttons on.

> *And he thought how much her hair looked like a Delta*
>   *sunrise*
> *And in his eyes, she thought she saw those northern*
>   *lights.*
> *Then he reached across the many miles*
> *And gently touched her face.*

Sarah received a letter postmarked Christmas Eve
From a woman up in Litchfield, Illinois.
It read, "My son worte me about you on his way to
     Chickamauga,
So please accept this token because you took care of my
     boy."

Sarah Louise Montgomery lit the lamp beside her bed
And began to brush her long and auburn hair.
Her eyes rested on two photographs of two in gray, one is
     blue
And, for their souls now gone, she breathed a silent prayer.

Photograph courtesy of Micki Fuhrman

I'll Be Here

Amy E. Hall

I'll be here
when you come home.
I've washed your favorite sheets.
I'll be here
when you come home.
I'll make your favorite meats –
legs and thighs
and ribs piled high.
Our reunion will be sweet.

I'll light a fire
and warm you up.
I'll pour the wine
and fill your cup.

As your gracious host,
with breasts to broast –
or perhaps a rump roast –
I'll make the finest toast.

But until I learn
of your safe return,
one, lone candle will I burn.

Author's note :While her husband is off to war, sleeping on the cold, dank
ground next to his old, dank comrades, eating hardtack and drinking dirty water,
she's dreaming of the day when she can warm him up - in every way...   This
piece was inspired by Robert McCurley's photograph "Left Behind."

Jenny's War

Randy Foster

My war ended the day Johnny's began,
though I did not know it at the time.
I had married him in obedience to
my father's insistence as paterfamilias,
in daughterly submission to my God-given
duty to go forth and replenish.

In trepidation, I had met Johnny in our marriage bed,
and morning's sun testified to my tears and
to my darkening bruises at his rough and callused hands.
As season passed into season, his anger grew
with every imagined wrong or inadvertent slight,
and only the remoteness of our modest farmhouse
masked his shrieks and his marks upon my flesh.

The night before he went to join his corps,
he had his final, brutal way with me
to stake, with lasting punctuation, a husband's claim
on wife and never-willing concubine.
I pondered for a while, as Johnny marched away,
upon his solemn-promised threat to return,
and hid within my heart the silent hope
that he would not.

Season passed into season, and I rose to the challenge
of getting in a crop and caring for the land.
No more did starlight and moonlight's gentle glow
presage an assault upon my womanly defenses;
no more did daybreak threaten broken bones.
Now, those threats of harm were his to
bear at the hands of a none-too-gentle enemy,
whilst I slept the sleep of the innocent.

Upon a season, a weather-stained letter came
to tell of bravery, honor, and sacrifice and
to share my regret at the loss of such a
steadfast friend and good and noble man.
As word got out, the neighbors came to share
with me their grief and ask me how I got along.
I cut and sewed my dress of widow's black
and patiently waited out my bereavement,
bearing only a ghost of a smile on my lips.

"Jenny's War" was inspired by Robert McCurley's photograph, "Left Behind"

Rumors

Randy Foster

What news of battle
comes on the wind?
What word of war
to buffet like March gusts?
It seems so long ago
you marched away,
so fair and handsome
under the regiment's
homemade banner
to the shrill tune of a fife
and the beat of an old drum
carried by a child, a boy
younger than our son.
I've heard rumor of
our army's victories
and heard rumor
of its far, far,
too many defeats;
but I have heard
no rumor of you,
not the smallest
fleeting rumor of you.

I watch for you,
scanning the horizon
for the first glimpse
of your dear, sweet face,
but all that comes is the
biting winter wind
to chap my lips and
mock my hopes
as my checked gingham
dress flaps on the breeze
like a flag of surrender.

"Rumors" was inspired by Robert McCurley's photograph, "Left Behind"

Instruments of War

Amy E. Hall

I've had just about enough
of this marchin' music.
In fact, I've had all
the death march drivel
that I can take.

Instead of the music
of devastation,
let's make music
of celebration.
Instead of the music
of destruction,
let's make music
of jubilation.
I wanna hear
some dancin' music!

So, break out your fiddle
and strike up the dance.
You can take your
bugles and snare drums
and drumsticks and fifes
and start to make some music
worthy of this life,
or stick those bloody, blasted
instruments where
the sun don't shine!

Come Home My Love

Louise Colln

"Anna...Anna...I brought Bill home. He's...at the great house."

Anna stood motionless with her linen shift drifting sensuously about her soft body in the dim firelight. Flickering shadows moved across her face, making her look now softly pleased, now grotesquely angry.

Thomas thought her face under the shadows might be empty of any feeling; he might just be dreaming his own emotions over it. He had wakened her too abruptly, mentioned Bill too soon.

"Back from Montana? Back to stay?"

"He...he'll stay, Anna." He had to give her time, let her come to the truth slowly.

He forced himself not to touch her. Not to put forth any claim on her now. When it came to a fight between words and feelings, words couldn't hold a candle...even words spoken before a preacher.

"He's left the Yankee army?"

"I brought him away."

"Not at his choosing?"

"No."

"Then he'll go back."

"No...he won't, Anna."

She stared past him at the window as though there was something important in the windy darkness outside. Her eyes didn't move when he walked to a willow rocker and let his body slump into it. Dear Lord, but he was tired.

"You're dirty...and your uniform's torn. I'll heat some water."

He might have been one of her pupils who'd fallen on the playground. She might have seen him just this morning instead of six—or was it eight?—months ago. Lord, how time ground together when it was mixed with heat and cold and the chack—chack of bayonets against solid young flesh and feet trying to hold in the slimy mud.

"We got in a battle in Franklin.'

"We heard. We won."

He shook his head. "It's hard to tell. Lots of them killed. Lots of ours killed. I found Bill there."

She busied herself dipping water from a bucket set carelessly on a mahogany table...as though caring for good wood was something done only in distant kingdoms, far away times.

She poured the water into a blue granite pan and set it into the fireplace to heat, then reached for a piece of cloth from a shelf nailed high over the table. It tore easily into washcloth size.

She went into her bedroom and came back with a blanket.

"Move over by the fire."

She waited for him to rise, then spread the blanket over the rocker and carried it to the fire.

"Or do you want to lie down?"

He shook his head. It seemed like his body wanted just to lie down and never get up, but his brain fought it. Sitting upright kept some of the mind-pictures away.

He leaned back in the chair as she knelt before him. She took the pan from the fire, barely frowning at the heat on her fingers. She floated a bar of lye soap in the water, swished her cloth in it, and ran it over his forehead and sharply curved nose. She scrubbed harder against the stiff bristles on his lean cheeks and neck.

"Why'd you move here from the great house?" It was important. Was she setting distance against him when she set distance against his family?

Photograph by Truman McKillip

"There's hardly enough food for them up there. When the slaves left, it just seemed best to move into the overseer's cabin." Her detached voice seemed to slip around the question rather than answer it.

She brought the blanket up lightly about his shoulders. She unbuttoned his gray shirt, letting her fingers linger on each button, as though she were teasing him into lovemaking, working his sleeves off his arms without asking him for help. The warm suds slipping over his aching shoulders and chest brought something soothing, almost like loving completed.

He could no longer see her. He let his eyes close.

He saw figures, squeezing under his eyelids, raising screaming guns, letting their own brains and blood shatter against him...

It was getting dark and the Yankees still wouldn't move and let the Confederates take back their own yards, their hill above the river, even their houses. If they'd just get up and get out of the land, run from the shells, stop shooting back, they could all quit and go home.

Go home. Go home. The guns were saying it, the cannon on both sides. Go home. You're going to make something even worse in this branch of hell.

Had someone heard? Somehow the guns had stopped and he was wandering over the mounds of bodies, doing what he'd done after every battle when the blue and gray bodies were so clumped together no one could know for sure which side owned the earth under them...looking at every blue clad figure. Looking for Bill. Not sure if he was looking for him for his brotherly love or for Anna. Or just to bring some kind of an end to it. To them.

This time, he found him. It had always been like looking into his own face with a few lines skewed. He wasn't sure now even that difference might show. There was blood on Bill's blue coat. His eyes were open, but there was nothing inside them.

Thomas knelt, bowed over him. He saw someone coming with a flare and quickly laid down beside him, pretending death.

When the flare passed, he picked Bill up and staggered back into the shadows of a chinaberry tree. He left him there and went back to the mass of bodies. He took a blue coat off the nearest dead Yankee and changed it for his gray one, then took a gray coat off the nearest Confederate dead and folded it into his. In this tangle of colors, he couldn't know which army he'd have to go through to take Bill home.

He felt Anna's hands tugging at his waistband and lifted his hips for his dirt-stiff pants to come off, followed by the tags of cloth he wore as underwear. There was a momentary chill on his naked body, then comfort of the blanket. The warmth of the cloth slipping back and forth over his stomach, his thighs as she lifted each leg, his private parts, brought a sort of ragged relaxation, an almost sleep.

He heard her go to the door to pour out the water and come back to pour more in. He felt the warmed water on his foot.

Anna washed his feet, putting each one into the basin and scrubbing carefully between and around each toe, digging stubbornly at the caked dirt.

She discovered that her memories had shapes, stuffs that she could touch with the fingers of her mind. The big shape of Thomas standing before her in the schoolroom door, turning his wide-brimmed hat nervously in his hands. Awkwardly, carefully, telling her that Bill had run North to the Montana territory, with the sheriff at his back, after a killing over another woman.

Then he'd stood up with her himself to keep her from being shamed.

The day she and Bill had planned to marry was as any other day. Only she had marked it. She had awakened before dawn in the bed she shared with Thomas in the great house and thought about it for awhile. Then she went down to the day's duties

The years between then and now had been dry of children, as though none could come to a marriage that had a ghost in it. Bill's letters had been few and addressed to his parents while she and Thomas lived in the great house. At last the word come that since he could never come home, he was joining the Union Army. Then nothing else.

She lifted Thomas foot from the basin and dried it carefully. Again, she took the basin to the door and stepped out with it in her hand. She barely noticed the chill air against her wet gown.

Bill was there. Up at the great house. This house was lit up in his honor.

She went back in and stood looking down at Thomas. The face so like Bill's, but not quite him. Was he sleeping? Could she say her thoughts to his sleeping face?

Sleep teased him, floating him out of control but not into rest, opening a door that let impressions rage through his mind.

He needed a horse. Sometime, hours or days before, he's used one of his bullets to put his own Thunder out of pain from a tearing abdominal wound. There were other horses all around them now, dead and dying, just as the men were. One dark-bodied animal, unsaddled, tried to graze with the bit still between his teeth. Thomas didn't remember catching the horse. Maybe it sensed his need and came. In this nether world, it could have happened.

Somewhere he had found a cart and hitched the horse to it. Or was the horse already hitched to it? He couldn't remember. He supposed it would be considered stealing, even in wartime. No matter. No one noticed. Here and there, shots still sounded, and flares lit up the lawn of the house where they were finding wounded and taking them in or covering them where they lay on the ground. They couldn't be of help to Bill.

He whipped the horse into place with soldiers crossing the river on the railroad bridge, then turned east and south into the darkness

Once into the strange silence of the empty countryside, he wrestled the blue coat off Bill and put the gray one on, shoving the unresponsive body back and forth in the cart. A memory of watching their black nurse dress this baby brother skipped through his mind.

He put his own gray coat back on and threw the blue coats away. They'd be most apt to run into Southerners if anyone dared to be out on this night. But he'd have to hide from soldiers of either side. He was a deserter now.

He had no idea how long it took, weaving in and around hills and fields on rutted back roads, never sure if he was in Confederate or Yankee held territory. He seemed to remember a morning, a night, and another day.

He must have stopped somewhere to let the horse rest from climbing up and down the hills. Or maybe not. He wasn't sure he remembered to feed the horse. When, in some night, it laid down and refused to get up, he unhitched it.

He was tempted to leave Bill there, never tell their parents, never tell Anna, that he'd found him, He stood over him, feeling the anger burning through his spirit, pushing against his skull.

"Damn you, Bill... damn you. All our lives, I've taken your side, lied to get you out of trouble, taken your leftovers, the food you didn't want, the women...Anna...Damn you, Bill, why'd you go off North and come back killing us...making us kill you...Damn you, Bill...Damn you..."

He laid down beside the cart and cried.

A dawn, red as blood, woke him. He couldn't see a house or any sign of life though the terrain was familiar enough to him to know that a neighbor's plantation existed...or had existed...not far from them. Who was in it now, soldiers or sympathizers for one army or the other?

He was too exhausted to find out or to go on or try to find another horse. He pulled the cart into a copse of trees and slept again. Near dusk, he got up and pulled the cart himself.. He was too close to home to stop now.

He was strong...exceedingly strong. When he felt his feet staggering, it seemed to be someone else's feet. It was someone else who slipped and fell. He had two missions: to leave war forever and to bring Bill home. Neither mission gave any quarter to weakness.

Close to home. Just a little further, and he could lay down his burden...down below, by the water...

He could see the great house across the creek. He left Bill and the cart and waded across. The slave quarters were strangely dark and empty, but he found Vernon. Vernon waded back across and brought Bill home, cradling him in his big arms the way he'd done when Bill was his favorite of the children. Vernon took Bill into the great house and directed Thomas to Anna.

He could feel Anna standing over him, feel her eyes, her hands, though she wasn't touching him, though his eyes were closed. Had she been serving Bill in her mind when she washed him?

He would give up and lie down on the bed. The pictures were coming anyway. If he slept, she could go to the great house. Go to Bill. but she didn't know...

"Thomas" It was a whisper. "I want to tell you...'

He opened his eyes. something inside himself demanded that he stop her before she could say Bill's name. He couldn't let her throw away their marriage for nothing.

"He's dead, Anna. I brought his body home. He won't be buried in an enemy grave."

She nodded. "We'll go up later. We'll cry for him together. Come in to bed now, Thomas. Let me hold you while you sleep. Then let me finish loving you.'

Lilacs in the Rain
(A Victorian Lament)

Lydia Esmer

Lilacs in the rain,
Through my window pane,
Reminding me he's faraway,
And calling him in vain.

In the breeze they blow,
Gently to and fro,
But they cannot wipe away
The tears that freely flow.

Memories of love long past,
Like phantoms in the night,
Seize my mind and hold it fast,
Until the morning light.

Lilacs in the rain,
Mirror of my pain,
Telling me he's gone away,
And won't return again.

In life's springtime you were there,
Your blossoms sweet and fair
Inspired my heart to you confide
Its every woe and care.

Lilacs in the rain,
Theme of my refrain,
Though my love has passed away,
With me you shall remain.

Author's Note: The poem is also a song, set to pentatonic scale

The Drinking Gourd

Susie Margaret Ross

I hear slaves in the night,
Running through the forest,
The big dipper above them.

They run from fear,
They run from bondage,
They run toward freedom.

How I wish I were one of them,
So resolute in their purpose,
Their journey so well defined.

I hear the slaves running,
I hear them in the night.
I join them in my dreams.

4. MOUNTAINS, PLATEAU, AND UPCOUNTRY

Photograph courtesy of Arch Boyd Brown from family collection.
Soldiers are Henry Monger and his son, Dwight T. Monger.
Private Henry Monger served in the 3rd. Cavalry Regiment,
Company G, U.S. according to Federal rosters.

The Silent Wall

Joyce A.O. Lee

April 15, 1940

My name is Mary Elizabeth Taylor. I was named for my mother, Elizabeth Fish, and for Mary Todd Lincoln, the wife of our heroic and slaughtered president, Abraham Lincoln. I'm proud to carry her name, for she suffered greatly with the loss of three children as well as the sudden loss of her husband. And I too have suffered.

I was born just prior to the onset of the bloody War Between the States in an area of Tennessee that was racked and torn by northern and southern sympathies. Because my family remained loyal to the Union, we were always in danger of a raid by the Nightriders of southern sympathies.

It was a terrible time of families against friends, fathers against sons, and brothers against brothers. Neighbors and life-long friends were all divided by that brutal and silent wall of loyalty.

Before my birth, my grandfather, Dred Fish, was a member of a gang of Bushwhackers, riding reckless and wild, terrorizing southern sympathizers. He would lead this burly gang to isolated homes to frighten and burn and drive away the livestock of any family suspected of southern loyalties.

By the last year of the war, however, he had joined the Union Army, making himself respectable and eligible to collect pensions and other privileges allowed by that action. When the war was over and hostilities had ceased, my grandfather was appointed Deputy Sheriff of the County.

During those days of riding, raiding, and misadventure, Dred Fish had made an enemy of Walk Hayes by insulting his mother. One afternoon, Walk Hayes, now grown, with a bloody act of revenge, gunned down Dred Fish on the steps of the Courthouse.

My father, Wilson Taylor, had been barely fifteen years old when he ran off to join the Union Army's Fifth Cavalry Regiment. His poor mother cried and begged him not to go, trying to keep her youngest son from harm. Already, her two older boys had quarreled and split, with one going North and the other South. She struggled mightily to keep young Wilson with her, but he was determined. His loyalties for the Union were strong.

Following Lee's surrender at Appomattox, he returned home unscathed. Soon he met and married Elizabeth Fish, the daughter of Dred Fish. By that time, the Bushwhacker had become an outstanding legitimate member of the community.

With their three children, the Taylor family settled on a farm near Indian Creek where an ancient stone wall trailed across the fields till it ran out of sight. This same stone wall, so close to our cabin, divided neighbors and kin of stanch loyalties and split opinions.

My father was a straightforward man and did not hesitate to speak his mind. I'm certain with little encouragement he continued to spread his strong Union sentiments about the community, keeping alive the enmity and angry silence that his Confederate neighbors had felt during the war.

When my grandfather was murdered by that waylaying boy, I'm confident some of his and my father's enemies decided it was a good time to dispose of Wilson Taylor as well. We'd barely placed the old man's body in his grave when they came, the Nightriders with their flaming torches and terror and fear.

There was little light to see by when they came riding high and hollering loud and screaming like hoots in the night. Looking for my Pa, they stomped through our little cabin, overturning furniture, breaking crockery, setting fire to curtains and quilts.

We suspected they had plans to do away with our father, but he was smarter and knew they'd soon come after him. An hour earlier, he saddled our old horse, packed a few things, and made a run of it, figuring if he was gone, they would do no harm to a mother and her children.

With a gripping terror, like Beelzebub himself was after us, in our nightshirts, we all ran toward the stone wall. In the shadows of the dark night, we huddled close against the far side of that cold stone wall, down small with the spiders and newts. We watched through crack and crevice with a hideous curiosity while those strangers in long coats and broad hats with kerchiefs across their faces laid waste to our beloved home.

From out of the dark, one spectral man directed his horse our way toward the wall. He stopped on the opposite side near me and removed the bandanna from his face. I held my breath in fear he would hear the pounding of my heart. Figures of fire reflected along the top of that silent wall as dancing apparitions like great orange grasshoppers in a hot iron skillet.

From an inside pocket, he removed a drawstring bag with his tobacco and fine papers. We watched breathlessly while he carefully creased and rolled a practiced cigarette. The loose-pinched stub dangled from the corner of his mouth when he struck fire and lit it, throwing the match over the wall beside me. It expired in the wet grass as he turned with a laugh and rode back to the house. Not long after, to our great relief, they galloped away through the wooded path leading to town.

We four waited and then moved to follow our mother's lead. She directed us cautiously to the home of our Granny Fish. At every sound, we took cover, hiding, not knowing if those Nightriders would return to look for our Pa. They didn't know he was gone—gone to Illinois.

Some time later we received a letter form Pa's sister, Sarah Winfree. She confirmed that Brother Wilson had arrived safely and she encouraged mother to bring us children to join him there. My mother did as he (or she?) instructed.

In a wagon pulled by a horse and a blind mule, my mother, Elizabeth Fish Taylor, joined a group with six other families on their way North. Full of fear, not one of us ever returned to Tennessee. My father, Wilson Taylor, remained a strong outspoken Union man his whole life long until his passing in the year of 1922.

I give this information as testimony to the trials and tribulations of my family and our migration to the northern state of Illinois. I understand that to this day there is some squabble and disagreement among my northern and southern kin as to the circumstances of our relocation and the equal distribution of our Tennessee property.

Signed by Mary Elizabeth Taylor, Age 80 years

Author's note: This is a story of fiction written with information provided by Tommy Webb, Historian of DeKalb County, Tennessee

Why I Shot Turner

Louvera J Webb
Letter transcribed by Larry Webb

Dear Major Clift:

According to promise, I now attempt to give you a statement for the reason why I killed Turner and a brief history of the affair. Dr Saddler had for two years previous to his death, seemed equally as near to me as a brother, and for several months nearer than any person, my parents excepted; if he had not, I never would have done what I did - promise to be his.

The men who killed him had threatened his life often because he was a union man; they said he should not live; and after taking the Oath they arrested him, but Lieutenant Oakley released him at Pa's gate. He stayed at Pa's till bedtime and I warned him of the danger he was in. I told him I heard his life was threatened that day and that I felt confident he would be killed if he did not leave and stay off until these men became reconciled. He promised to leave that night or by early morning as he had some business in Carthage to tend to. But for some reason he did not leave.

About 3 o'clock next day news come to me that Dr Sadler was killed. Poteet, Gardenhire and Turner had gone to the house where he was at; and strange to me after his warning, he permitted them to come in. They met him perfectly friendly as they had come for some brandy from Mr. Yelton, which was obtained and after drinking they all three drew their pistols and commenced firing at Sadler. He drew his, but it was snatched away from him. He then drew his knife, which was taken from him. He then ran round the house and up a stairway escaping out of their sight. They followed and searched until they found him and brought him down and laid him on a bed mortally wounded. He requested some of his people to send for Dr. Dillon to dress his wounds. It is strange to say that all of Dr. Saddler's friends had left the room when Turner put his pistol against his temple and shot through the head.

They all rejoiced like Demons, and stood by till he had made his last struggle. They then pulled his eyes open and asked him in a loud voice if he was dead. They took his horse and saddle and pistol and robbed him of his money and otherwise insulted and abused his remains.

Now, for this, I resolved to have revenge. Poteet and Gardenhire being dead, I determined to kill Turner, and to seek an early opportunity to do it. But I kept that resolution to myself, knowing that I would be prevented.

On the Thursday before I killed him, I learned he was preparing to leave for Louisiana; and I determined he should not escape if I could prevent it. I arose that morning and fixed my pistols so that they would be sure to fire and determined to hunt him all that day. Then sitting down, I wrote a few lines so that if I fell, my friends might know where to look for my remains. I took my knitting as if I were going to spend the day with a neighbor living on the road to Turner's. It rained severely, making the roads muddy so that I became fatigued and concluded to go back and ride the next day or Saturday. But Ma rode my horse on Saturday and left me to keep house. We had company Sunday a.m., so that I could not leave, but the company left about noon and I started again in search of Turner. I went to his house about two and one half miles from Pa's. I found no one at home, and therefore, sat down to await his return. After waiting, perhaps one and a half hours, a man came to see Turner, and not finding him, he said he supposed he and his wife had gone to Mrs. Christian's sister-in-law, who lived about one half mile distant. I concluded to go there and see, fearing the man would tell him that I was waiting for him and give him a chance to escape me.

Photograph courtesy of Larry Webb

I found him there and a number of other persons, including his wife and her father and mother. Most of them left when I entered the house. I asked Mrs. Christian if Turner was gone. She pointed to him at the gate, just leaving. I looked at the clock and it was 4:30 p.m. I then walked out into the yard and as Turner was starting, called to him to stop. He turned and saw I was preparing to shoot him; he started to run. I fired at his distance of about 12 paces and missed. I fired again as quick as possible and hit him in the back of the head and he fell on his face and knees. I fired again and hit him in the back and he fell on his right side. I fired twice more, only one of those shots taking effect. By this time I was within five steps of him and stood and watched him till he was dead. I turned around and walked toward the house and met Mrs. Christian and her sister, his wife, coming out. They asked what I did that for. My response was, "You know what that man did the 13th of December last — murdered a dear friend of mine. I have been determined to do this deed ever since and I shall never regret it."

They said no more to me, but commenced hollering and blowing a horn. I got my horse out and started home where I shall stay or leave when I choose, going where I please, saying what I please.

Editor's Note: This letter is a family document of Larry Webb of Williamson County who writes,' Verna was the daughter of Daniel c. Webb who resided in the Spring Creek area of Overton county which is where she is buried. The original letter which she wrote to Major Cliff was also printed in the *Nashville Times* on June 28, 1864.

Cries of Terror From the Civil War

Mary Lou McKillip

Bold fear raced through
my veins,
as I looked out my
open window.

Swift horses' hooves
clambered up the
road to our cabin.

"Josh get the rifle.
Come quick Josh,
Union soldiers are
almost here."

They dismounted and
smashed open the door.
"How many Rebels
do you hide?"

His pistol drawn before
he got the reply,
my Josh lay dead,
one single shot to his head.

I screamed in rage,
"You blue bellied devils you,
have you no pity for a
helpless couple as we?"

The soldier grinned through
his yellow stained teeth
"We are trained no mercy,
by the war we're led."

Josh's gun lay in view
I picked it up, "You son of
a dog you."

I cocked the hammer
as he turned to leave,
I aimed high and brought
him low, dead low.

Photograph by Truman McKillip

Runaway Slave

Luther Harris

Toward the first of the war, there was a man down near Muddy Pond in Overton County who had to go up to take his hogs to mast (take them to summer in the forest for the acorns). Most men during the war were pretty busy with fighting, so there wasn't anything for his wife Susan to do but get her sister Sara to come stay with her during that time. The man told Susan to get the chores all done before dark every evening and get inside and pull the latch string in and not to open the door for anybody.

Well, Susan and Sara did just like he said the very first evening. They got everything done and finished before sundown and went inside and latched the door good. Then Susan went to brushing her hair in front of a mirror, and in it she could see that across the room there was a black man crouched up under the bed. The candles were flickering a good deal, but she could see that he was ragged and rough and that he was way up in the corner looking out at her real sharp like. She said she wanted to sling that brush up under there and holler at him, but she didn't.

She just turned around quick and said, "Oh, Sara, we forgot to feed the geese."

Sara looked at her funny because they didn't have geese, so real quick Susan said, "Hurry, before it gets dark." and grabbed Sara by the wrist so she'd know to be quiet and come on.

Once outside, they ran to a neighbor's, and the men came back and caught that feller. He had a knife with him and said that if he had known those two women were going for help, they never would have gotten out the door.

Dred Fish

S.R. Lee

Dred Fish, Dred Fish
Pretty girl, don't make no wish.
He ain't coming courting or kissing
But stealing, looting, burning. and killing

Narrator: DeKalb County Historian:

We choose our own fights
no matter how somebody
down in the state capital votes.
We drink our corn before we eat it,
free-range our hogs,
'casionally have a fight.
Maybe lasts a-while,
three or four generations if
the dead man's children grow up.
Can't tell--fire of anger might die down,
might smolder,
might flare up most any time.

Came along a real war,
States couldn't get along,
That's nothing--
counties couldn't get along,
neighbors couldn't get along,
perfect time to fight.
Formed little gangs,
rode though the farms,
took what they wanted.

Warning:
Bushwhackers coming, hide, hide, hide,
Run through the woods, hide behind a wall,
Ain't nothing safe, stay out of the brawl.
Just as soon kill you, don't care what they burn,
if they miss your old mule, they're gonna return
Bushwhackers coming

Dred Fish, Dred Fish
Mother and kids, don't make no wish
He'll take the mule and your last chicken
Says "Damned Rebs deserve a lickin."

Narrator: 1863, Walk Hayes, ten years old

Dred comes over here 'bout noontime
looking for my Daddy
who warn't here right then.
Dred has his pistol
all ready to shoot some Reb,
in other words, my Daddy.

Ma says she don't know where he is.
Dred yells and cusses.
Ma just keeps quiet.
Dred hits her hard across the face.
Ma keeps quiet.

Dred looks round,
don't want the law to get him,
got to hurt us bad
without no blood to show.

Ma's loom setting there.
wool thread woven tight,
a big swatch of cloth cause
Ma's weaving me a shirt.

Dred's got a boy the size of me.
Takes his knife,
cuts the warp at the top,
quick but careful,
cuts the warp at the bottom,
quick but careful,
folds up the swatch,
tucks it under his arm,
smiles at me.
"Make my boy a shirt" he says.
"I'll damned kill you," I say.
He laughs, walks out.

Ma's pale as ice, silent,
covers my cussing mouth.
I feel her anger.
I'll for sure kill Dred,
just don't know when.

Warning:
Bushwhackers going, watch, watch, watch
Bushwhackers take all the muskets and balls
if their backs is safe, they take no falls
But the watchers got memories plenty long
and a scrawny boy might grow up strong.
Bushwhackers going

Dred Fish, Dred Fish
Folks in the county, don't make no wish.
He'll taunt you so you can't forget.
He plundered your place and he ain't dead yet.

Narrator: 1872, Judge Wilson Andrews

Last year of the war,
Dred joined the Union army.
Five more years and
his commanding officer
is high sheriff of DeKalb County.
Dred don't have no problems at all,
sold his farm; deputy sheriffing
is more to his liking than hoeing a corn row.
Rides in and out of town as suits him.
Scorns those loiterers
on the courthouse steps.

Walk Hayes has grown into a man,
young, but a man.
Loads his pistol and waits
quiet by the courthouse.
When Dred's foot touches the first step,
Walk puts three bullets in his back.
Shots spin old Dred round.
Walk puts three more in his chest.
Dred's bleeding bad all over them steps,
but he looks up,
"Well, you said you would kill me—
I didn't believe you but you done it."

Walk is arrested
but gets out on bond.
He's gone quick.
His lawyer takes that bond.
Ain't nobody seen it since,
and the story is
that lawyer chewed up and
swallowed every scrap.

Walk Hayes' family moved
to Harrison, Arkansas.
Letters come back
that Walk married and had five kids.

It ain't Dred's folks
writing the county history.

Dred Fish, Dred Fish
You thought you done got your wish
Acted like you owned the county
Till Walk Hayes took all your bounty.

Warning:
Bushwhackers, bushwhackers, war's over now
Folks get along or at least they try;
but if you was too mean, you're like to die.
Good years to come might ease up the past,
Settle in farming so your fam'ly can last.
Bushwhackers, war's over.

Manse

A Far Distant Kin

Nancy Fletcher-Blume

1948. Manse Sherrill Jolly had kept true to his promise.

The well diggers dug deeper and lowered buckets into the darkness that cold, dreary afternoon, in Upcountry, South Carolina. Skeletons covered in muck and filthy water began to surface. As the windlass was turned and ropes were lowered, Yankee belt buckles—all engraved with U.S— filled the buckets, time and time again.

Having been born and raised in Upcountry, South Carolina, I was always surrounded by my dozens of aunts, uncles, and many cousins. My grandmother saw that we made the rounds of visiting all of them now and then. It was especially an exciting time for me when she would say to my mother, "It's time we go a'callin' out at the Old Jolly Place."

The older folks sat on the front porch and we small children played in the red dirt and Chinaberry trees. There was a wooden rail hitching post in front of the house. We were young and innocent and never once wondered who may have tied their horses to that hitching post

Twenty five year old, Manson Sherrill Jolly, was one of the first from Anderson (S.C) County to join the Confederate Army, along with his six brothers. All of them enlisted at Charleston, South Carolina, where Manse was assigned to Company F, First S.C. Cavalry, later on rising to the rank of First Sergeant. To his advantage, Manse knew every inch of dirt, back swamps and mountain caves, of the Upcountry.

Photograph courtesy of Nancy Fletcher-Blume

He was a Company F scout, riding for weeks at a time from Low Country, South Carolina to Virginia. Manse on many nights searched for any campfire where he could sleep. He might on some of those nights, disappear from camp and appear again at sunrise, carrying guns, swords and many times, parts of Yankee uniforms.

It was late October in the Low Country, but still muggy hot and Manse was anxious to ride toward his Upcountry and cooler weather. He was not happy as was slowed down on this scouting trip when his commander ordered him to take one of the Alabama's 55th wounded soldiers and his slave Ben, and try to find some of their men. The slave had been found hiding behind the swamp knots in the Combahee, trying to care for his master.

"All right you—hold him upright on the back of my horse until he gets his balance," Manse yelled at the slave.

"Yassa, I done did. Massa's Marsh Tacky horse done gone," he mumbled trying best as he could to keep up with Manse and his horse, Dixie.

After several hours of this slow cautious walking, Manse finally got on The Old Sheldon Church Road close in to war torn Yemassee. He knew of a huge grove of towering live oaks with moss hanging to the ground which would hide them and felt they would be fairly safe to camp there for the night.

Manse ordered Ben to make a pile of underbrush and hide it under the trees to lay the shaking man. He tried to give the soldier a few drops of water, covered him with his blanket, and told Ben to stay close beside him to give his body warmth.

"Yassa," said Ben, as he sat.

Giving a quick glance down at the slave's blistered feet, he said to him, "You're safe here 'till I return. I'll be back directly."

Manse quickly covered a few miles as he headed toward the Confederate camps at Pocotaligo when he heard voices. He dismounted and crept closer. Two Union soldiers stood against the trees, watching their campfire and talking. Their horses were tied to the low branches.

Manse slipped up behind the trees. Moving swiftly, he slashed one across the head, stabbed the other in the chest, and then turned the knife back on the injured. Once sure they were dead, he took their shoes and guns, and then untied the horses.

Arriving back at the hidden camp with the horses in tow, he found Ben sitting up, rocking back and forth and moaning softly. "The Massa's done gone and died." Quickly tying the horses to low hanging branches, he turned toward the slave. "Get up, we have to dig," Manse ordered, jerking him up.

"I'll say a few words," Manse said, as the last shovel of dirt was patted down and brush pulled over the narrow mound. Standing back a respectful distance, the slave listened as Manse said a prayer and placed a makeshift cross in the soft dirt.

Throwing a pair of the soldier's brogans toward Ben, he said, "Now sleep...we go before daybreak."

Just before dawn they arrived at Pocotaligo, where the Alabama 55th had camped. A few soldiers were taking down tents and cooking over the morning fire.

"Mornin' there boys," Manse called out.

"Mornin' to you," said one of the soldiers, as he stood there poking at the fire. "Come on 'round and share some vittles."

"Where'd you find Ben," one soldier yelled. "Where's Private Bull?"

"Buried him back there aways. Here's his packet and watch," Manse said, as he handed the soldier a small bundle. "Be kindly if you talk with his mother; tell her that he stood brave in battle and that he went to sleep peaceful like."

The young soldier nodded and said, "We'll make certain sure that we get Ben back to his owners."

Glad to be relieved of that duty, Manse gave a half salute and said, "Thank you for the offer of food but I have need to be heading on now."

Several days of riding brought Manse to a Confederate camp about forty miles from Anderson. In a quickly built shed, three Union soldiers were held until someone could take them to Anderson, where they could be jailed.

The Confederate commander called Manse inside his tent. Spreading a large map out on the table, he pointed to the Walhalla mountain area. "I'll need you to scout on that and find the count of Union soldiers and how much artillery you can spot." Manse immediately knew that it would not be difficult. He knew the hiding caves up there.

"There's something else I have need for you to do," the commander said as he offered Manse a seat. "Those three prisoners out there...well, I need for you to take them on into the jail at Anderson before you head up to the hills."

Manse knew not to contradict the orders, but also knew that he was in no way going to let them go into the safety of jail. *'Good as dead if I take'um. Not going to be bothered with some dirty Yanks.'* "Yes sir, we'll leave as soon as my horse has rested and fed."

"All right soldier, that's the plan. We'll be looking for you back in a few days, with information on the Walhalla Union camps, and then we'll move accordingly."

It was a very disgruntled Manse that afternoon, as he helped secure the three prisoners on horses. They rode single file with Manse every so often trotting up alongside one of them; taunting that surely they did not think he was going to let them be locked up.

"Ya'll boys are good as dead." Then waving his pistol, he would drop in behind them laughing.

Upon hearing a rough knock at the back door, Mr. Mitchell grabbed his shotgun, where it was propped against the stone hearth. "Who goes there?" hollering as he walked.

"It's me, Manse Jolly, your neighbor!"

Recognizing the voice, Mitchell said, "Hold up there son, it'll take a minute or so to get this double lock unhooked." After fumbling and pulling on the heavy chain, he finally got it open to let Manse inside.

A cold gust of early November wind caught the door. It almost knocked the three men down who were standing there, with Manse behind, holding his pistol on them. Before giving any explanation to Mr. Mitchell, he waved his gun at the men, pointed at the floor, for them to sit, and then watched until the last one dropped down and sat.

"My deepest apologies to you, Miz Mitchell." Manse, had just noticed her seated quietly in a rocker by the open fire. "I felt it best not to go further on home with these men, as Ma is feeling poorly, and this would just be worrisome to her."

"No problem with that son," Mr. Mitchell said, leaning back in his chair by the fire. He held his rifle, giving it an occasional pat.

Mrs. Mitchell got up, grabbed her apron off the wall hook, and headed to the pantry. "You look awful hungry son, and we've just finished supper, but I'll be mighty glad to feed you." She stopped and stared at the empty chairs for a minute then said, "It'll be right good to have a young boy sitting at the table again."

"Yes'um. I would be mighty obliged to you, M'am, and if you could spare more for the men, 'cause it appears it will be their last supper."

Mrs. Mitchell nodded, and went to putting out spoons, plates, and a jug of buttermilk, cold biscuits and a jar of black strap molasses on the table. As she was finishing, she caught one of the prisoners looking at her.

She looked back—only for a moment at the boyish face and long lashes, and then turned away, repeating over and over to herself, '*They killed my son, they killed my son.*' She went back to her rocker by the fireside.

Waving his pistol at the men, Manse, told them to get up and find a place. He took an end seat at the long trestle table, laid his two pistols beside his plate, and began to eat hungrily.

The room was quiet except an occasional word or two between Manse and Mr. Mitchell, about family or crops and the constant sound of unhinged wood down by the well when the wind would catch it.

"You boys 'bout done," Manse asked, noticing that none of the men had eaten a bite. "If so, get up— it's time we take our leave."

Mr. Mitchell stood up with his rifle, as Manse started herding the men toward the door and said, "If you need, our table is open to you anytime."

Manse nodded, then looked at Mrs. Mitchell and said, "M'am, thank you for your good hospitality. I know that Ma will be feeling cordial about this."

"Please do tell her that I asked about her health."

"Yes M'am, I will kindly do so."

Frigid wind blasted as the door opened and Manse shoved the men outside.

Mrs. Mitchell began cleaning the table, staring at the prisoners' untouched plates, but then paused only for a moment when she heard three gunshots. She shuddered, then finished her chores and went back to her rocker by the fire.

After and sitting for a short spell, Mr. Mitchell got up with his gun in hand, and said, "Lyde Ella, I think I'll go down and see about the animals—and that old well lid was really a bother with tonight's wind. I may put a jam on it just to hold until I can seal it."

"Yes Mr. Mitchell, that'll be good, but don't put any more wood on the fire. I think I'll finish darning this sock, and then go on up to bed."

A cold mist was hanging heavy from the river that early April night; so heavy that the small group of Yankee soldiers' camping above the shoals, was hunkered down close to their campfire. Occasionally the chilling scream of a catamount, somewhere off in the distance, would bring them in even closer.

Word had reached Confederate Commander, Boyd Crawford late afternoon, about that camp not quite a quarter of mile from Cry Baby Bridge. Manse sat listening to the Commander as he laid out his plans and called for a few volunteers to clear a path, through to the bridge, where they could follow with supplies.

Manse stood up and said, "Begging pardon Sir, but this is my home and I know every inch of it. Let me go. Let me go, and I'll be back with nairy a problem, before midnight."

Commander Crawford, stared for a minute, then said, "Word's out that it's heavily guarded. It's just too dangerous to go alone... take two soldiers with you."

"Then Sir, I'll take James and Todd yonder; we'll be leaving directly." Manse felt his leather sheath, making sure the long Bowie knife was secure, nodded at the two men, and all headed for their horses. "You boys stay close behind me, always steering to the right and left."

In a short while, Manse held up his hand to stop, got off Dixie, and tied her to a small tree. The night air brought the smell of coffee from the Yankee's campfire. Real coffee—not the ground okra seeds that Manse and his men had to use.

"Stay!" Manse ordered the two men. Keep watch while I go 'round the side of the bridge."

"But—" one of the men whispered; Manse had disappeared into the fog.

He dropped to the ground, crawling stealthily, following the sound of low talk. The fog was so dense that he could see nothing— suddenly out of nowhere, he could make out one of the men. He waited a few minutes, until they quit talking and walked away, to check their posts at the bridge.

Slowly standing upright, Manse gripped his knife, and crept closer and closer to the back of one of the sentries—so close, that he could hear him breathing. With one move, he clapped his hand over the sentry's mouth, with the other thrust his knife deep into the man's throat. He went down without a sound. Manse jerked out the knife and moved through the fog again. Twice more, his knife found the sentries' throats.

Arriving back to the men waiting, he untied his horse, and said, "Let's go back to the camp boys. I'll be needing some coffee 'bout now."

As they turned their horses toward camp, sudden shots sounded in the distance, echoing off the high rocks flanking their trail. "Hold steady boys," Manse ordered, as he tried to get his bearings on the sound. Another volley rang out; the shots were coming from the Yankee camp above the shoals. "Easy boys, get off the trail—follow me."

Riding slowly, twisting their way through the thick undergrowth and dense fog, they found themselves on a small hill, overlooking the backside of the camp. Manse held his hand up for a stop. "Stay." He dismounted, got on his belly and crawled slowly toward the edge.

"Well boys, guess that'll about be it for tonight." The booming voice was that of Confederate Commander Crawford. He and a handful of soldiers were standing by several bodies sprawled out on the ground.

Manse stood and hollered out to the Commander, "It's Manse and my boys, Sir. We're coming down."

As Manse approached the site, the Commander half laughing said, "We caught one of them no'count rat scallions, trying to sneak up— spying on us back at camp.

We reckoned it be best to take advantage of this fog and catch 'em unawares. Sure did pan out! How'd it go with the bridge guard?"

"All's quite well, Sir," Manse said. "There'll be nothing to bother with there."

Beckoning for his soldiers to come sit, the Commander reached for the pot of coffee that was brewing on the glowing embers of the camp fire.

April, 1865.

Manse ignored surrender. He continued killing; but upon hearing of the capture of Jefferson Davis in Georgia in May of 1865 and all of the troops disbanded, he finally packed his saddle bag, along with his many badges for bravery, got on his horse and headed toward his Upcountry home. He had not a single scratch on his body.

While Manse worked his land for the next few months, he was brooding and planning. When word came to Manse and his mother that his last surviving brother, Larry, had been caught by some carpet baggers only a few miles from home and killed, Manse raged for weeks. He vowed to his mother that he would kill five more Yankees for every brother he had lost.

He would not allow his six brothers, who died defending their Southern homeland and ways, to die in vain.

His hatred of the Yankees grew, along with grief over the loss of his brothers. He added Freedmen to his killing list. These Freedmen were leading the Union soldiers to the silver, gold, and horses that the South had hidden. The Union authorities were using them as informers; but as word passed around, many of the Freedmen deserted those duties, chancing Union punishment over the wrath of the now widespread horror tales of this man, Manse Jolly.

Soon, Manse was becoming more and more involved, forming a group of men who had been too young to fight in the war, but ready now. He called them *The Jones*

Company. He also became partners with another Confederate soldier, Texas Brown. This man had been given the 'Klan franchise' from Nathan Bedford Forrest for the Anderson area.

Manse sat at breakfast one rainy morning at the empty McFall house, a favorite hiding place for many of the Confederate soldiers. A few *Jones Company* boys were hanging around, jesting about last weeks leaflets, handed out by Union soldiers. Three of the men were in serious talk of leaving today and heading for the safety of Texas.

"Your head's worth eight thousand dollars," one of the boys said, as he handed the paper to Manse.

He frowned slightly and looked up when the boy continued, "That's a hunk'ah bounty. Some folk'ed turn in their own kin."

Manse half laughed at the remark, got up from the table and said, "Boys', I'm going to have me some funning. I'll be back late afternoon." Grabbing his hat and guns, he headed out the door.

"Dixie, old girl," Manse said, patting his horse, "I'm thinking it's time to put this South Carolina dirt behind and head us on out."

Hat pulled low, with his red hair tucked under, he turned Dixie slowly toward Benson Street. He stopped at the Benson House Hotel and tied Dixie to the hitching post.

As he entered the dining room and began looking over the crowd of men eating and smoking cigars, he recognized a Union General sitting alone. Walking over to him, he said, "Excuse me, Sir, but my understanding is that there is an awful big price in the giving on this Manse Jolly's head. Is that 'bout right, Sir?"

The General immediately stood, looking up at the very tall man who towered over him and said, "Yes, of course, eight thousand dollars. You have him around? Money's yours, dead or alive."

In that instant, the General saw the red hair and icy blue eyes. Before he could make a move, Manse jerked out his pistols, shot twice in the ceiling and twice in the floor. Putting his pistols back in their holsters, he said, "That would be me, Sir," and with a low laugh and half salute said, "Now I'll take my leave."

The General collapsed into his chair. When he looked up, Manse had already disappeared.

Manse came home late that night to find his mother rocking and crying on the front porch. She reached out to him, "Sit Manse, sit and talk with me."

"Ma, what are you doing up; whatever is so troubling to you tonight? I'm home and not a hurt anywhere."

As he sat down, she put her arms around his shoulders. "Son, there was an awful fright here this afternoon. Your sisters were lying down up in their bedrooms, and I had just joined them, when four men beat on the side door. Not waiting for us to find their business, they broke in, and came up the stairs into our bedroom. They waved their guns and threatened us as to your where'bouts.

Manse could feel his face becoming hot and his head starting to pound as he reached to comfort his mother. "Oh Ma, did they damage you in any way?"

"No son, but your sisters have cried all afternoon."

Manse stood up, took his mother's hand and said, "Ma, you go on inside and keep your pistol by the bed. I'll be back by morning."

"No—no—Manson, no!" Grabbing his arm, she pulled him back and said, "Let's come to reason. I'm knowing that I borned eleven children and I'm knowing that I've lost six of my sons. I will not lose another one. I will not!"

"Ma, I have to go and do this."

His mother held firm.

"They'll only be back son, more of them. It's time for you to go away someplace where it's safe. You need to leave this be. We already have some distant kin from up 'round Tugalo and Oconee who're living in Texas. It's a far piece from here and you'd be safe. They'd be much obliged to take you in."

Manse knew that his mother was right. The men would be back. He had heard just that morning, some of his Jones Company group had been found beaten and shot, their women folk damaged, and their homes ransacked. Going inside that night with his mother, he knew that he would not sleep.

After hearing it all quiet upstairs, Manse slipped out and sat on the porch, holding his pistol and planning. He went inside when he heard the first rooster's crow.

Mrs. Jolly also had not slept. Upon hearing the rooster, she got up and put on her shift, then came downstairs. Manse was sitting in her rocker by the fireplace, holding his Bible. "Ma, I'll be going on. It'll be daylight before long, and I'm going by to get the boys that'll ride with me. I've heard hard talk from them this week already for going to Texas."

She came to him, and held him in her arms for a minute, knowing that she would always keep his scent with her. "You go now son, and may God be with you."

"Ma, I'll write." Manse picked up his guns and Bible and, not looking back, walked out the kitchen door.

Mrs. Jolly went back to her rocker by the fireside.

The weather was unusually warm in Anderson. People were out, enjoying the fine day. All were steering clear of the Union soldiers who were camped off Fant Street and Main where the dirt streets were still muddy from rains the day before.

A Union soldier noticed a man far in distance wearing a tattered Confederate uniform, riding toward the courthouse.

Suddenly, a screaming, blood curdling, Rebel Yell, filled the air over and over. The man, with two guns blazing and the white horse bolting, came at full gallop towards the soldiers. The gates of hell had loosed one of its own.

After the last shot was fired, five lay dead on Fant Street and Main in front of the Anderson County courthouse. The man and white horse had vanished as quickly as they had arrived.

Manse Jolly had come to say good-bye.

Late August, 1866, letters to his mother slowly began arriving. Manse and his traveling companions had been riding many weeks, down through Georgia, Alabama, and Louisiana, until they finally reached Maysville, Texas, where they had South Carolina kin and acquaintances waiting to greet them.

Later letters to his mother and sisters, told of him and the men settling down on a wide range of land, and Manse told of being contented as he worked at the crops. Several months later, another letter informed his mother that he had married. Continuing letters showed him to be happy; and finally, they were expecting their first child.

Rev. Matthew McGuffin had served as pastor of the Mulkey Baptist Church for many years. He had baptized both Mr. and Mrs. Jolly and several of their eleven children and had suffered right along with the family, when one by one of the Jolly boys had been killed by the Yankees.

He stopped by the Anderson Post Office around noon as he did each day while he was out making his sick rounds. He was surprised to find a letter waiting for him with a return address of Benjamin Jolly in Texas. He knew that this was not good, so he went outside and found a seat in the shade.

When he unsealed his letter, another smaller one fell out. It was addressed to Mrs. Jolly. '*I need to pray first, before I read this.*' Tears blurred and stung his eyes.

"Some awful' bad news there, Preacher?"

Mr. Mitchell sat down beside him on the bench. "It's Manse," Rev. McGuffin said, as he dabbed at his eyes with a handkerchief.

Taking off his hat and bowing his head, Mr. Mitchell said, "Oh Lord 'a mercy, I allow that boy done gone and got hisself killed."

The men sat in silence for a while, and finally Rev. McGuffin said that he would head on out to the Jolly Place. Mr. Mitchell stood, put his hat back on, and said, "I'll go on back home and tell the woman, and we'll go out there to call, directly."

Mrs. Jolly was out tending her garden that hot summer's day, when she saw the rider, his horse slowly walking toward the side porch. She stood straight and propped on her hoe. She knew. *'There is nothing left for me— nothing left to feel— nothing left.'*

The rider got off and, removing his hat, walked toward her. "M'am—Sister Jolly, I have this letter for you." He fumbled with it for a second, bowing his head, then handed it to her.

She nodded and said, "Brother McGuffin, I thank you kindly and now, if you'd like— it being hot and all—please use the dipper for a cool drink before you head back."

Rev. McGuffin took the dipper off the nail of the well side, carefully watching as she silently turned away. He quietly hung it back on its nail. "I'll be going now, and Sister Jolly, the wife and all will be a'callin on you in the afternoon."

She watched him ride away, then propping her hoe at the well, she walked back into the house. *'Our Father who art in heaven,'* but she could not finish.

July 16, 1868
Maysville, Texas

My dearest Aunt,

It has fallen my honored duty and with deepest sorrow and regret, that I need write to you. Your beloved son, Manse is dead. He died on July 8th and was buried Saturday, last. He was trying to cross the Little River to get home before dark set in and the current took him away. The river which was normally low had become swollen and in some places had risen to fourteen feet, due to the heavy rains. It took me twelve hours to ride to the place, where the men found him and his horse, Dixie. They had already taken him away, but I felt that I had great need to do this.

Our family, his many friends and neighbors did him a proper laying out and burial at the Little River Cemetery and there, I carefully cut a small lock of his hair for your keeping. I will attend to any matters that need, and let you know of their importance.

My sincerest sympathy and condolences are with you. Please tell my dear cousins; those sisters who Manse loved so much and our kin back in South Carolina, I am respectfully at their call.

Your faithful and loving nephew,
Benjamin

She read the letter again and again, but finally put it back into her pocket. Neighbors and kin came and went all that afternoon on into late evening, bringing food and whispering words of comfort.

Mrs. Jolly heard none of this, nor ate. She sat for hours, rocking by the cold fireplace; clutching the curly lock of red hair.

Manse Jolly fireplace
Photograph courtesy of Nancy Fletcher-Blume

AUTHOR'S HISTORICAL NOTE:

Four months after the death of Manse, Mrs. Jolly received the news that a baby girl had been born. It stated that the mother and baby and several relatives were leaving Texas for good and moving away to California.

There lies a simple slab stone in Little River Cemetery, Maysfield, Texas, under a weathered tree marked; Sacred to the Memory of Manson S. Jolly, age 29 years. The only other marking is a Masonic symbol.

This story is historical fiction based on information known about Manson Sherrill Jolly, a Confederate soldier and a far, distant kin, from Upcountry, South Carolina.

The Old Jolly Place, which held such terrible secrets, has been beautifully restored and is now a tourist attraction, along with Civil War reenactments held there each year.

A sprawling subdivision sits on Jolly Road and Boy Scouts camp down there and proudly salute the raising of the American Flag each morning, and the lowering of it each evening.

PRIMARY SOURCES:

Manson S. Jolly: letters to his mother and sister, 24 February, 1867
Letters written by Manson Sherrill Jolly 1867-1868

SECONDARY SOURCES:
Anderson Daily Mail
Greenville News
Dallas Morning News
"The Legend of Manse Jolly" *Anderson Independent Mail*, 12 April 1981 p.
    1 A and 6 A

Authors Personal Note:

Probably the spirits of many a Yankee soldier would be pleased to know that a Texas creek did, what the Civil War and its aftermath couldn't.

Some had said that Manse Jolly was an avenging Robin Hood and some said that he was a brutal killer, but in South Carolina, he will always be regarded, as a classic symbol of the unreconstructed Rebel, who never surrendered.

2012- Remembering those long ago visits when I was a very small child, visits where I played and climbed on that hitching post at the Old Jolly Place, leaves me to wonder why my grandmother, mother and I never visited again, nor was it spoken of.

Maybe it had something to do with the old well having been cleaned.

Kernels for the Colonels

Arch Boyd Brown

'Tis often said of the Civil War, " 'Twas brother against
    brother."
It divided families and angered kin unlike any other.
My great grandpa John took the Union side;
But his brother, Jesse, for the South would ride

With the 13th. Kentucky Cavalry
Against John Boyd Brown and the 5th. Tennessee.
But in that same family there's another story,
No guts, no guns, no bull, no glory.

Uncle Tom McCallie, when the troops began to march,
Did not agree politically with his Union brother, Arch.
If you supported the North, your corn crop could be sold;
But all Southern sympathizers were left out in the cold.

These two Scots-Irish farmers put kin and family first.
They came up with a little scheme because they were well-
    versed
In the art of penny-pinching and were said to be quite frugal.
It sounded like money to their ears whenever they heard a
    bugle.

So brother Arch sold both of their crops as soon as he was
    able,
Keeping money in their pockets and food upon their table.
Some die-hard rebels would look at Tom like he'd
    committed treason;
But he only knew that he wouldn't starve, at least not until
    next season!

Author's Note: Based on oral history related to Boyd Brown by his mother

5 AFTERMATH

Photograph by Randy Foster

Defeat

Randy Foster

I'm just so very, very tired
and only want to go home,
if, in fact, I've any home remaining.
I don't remember any more
what it was that I was ever fighting for
beyond my own doubtful survival, and
I would be ever so happy, sir,
to lay down my arms and leave
if you'd only just let me go.

In the early days, it was all a game,
with marching bands and speeches and
pretty girls exhorting us to fulfill
the obligation of our nobility,
calling us to serve our people
and our glorious heritage.
No doubt, General Washington,
our model Cincinnatus,
would have been proud of us
as we volunteered to defend
hearths, homes, and our sacred
and most peculiar institution.

Early on, cold or hot, ready or not
we seemed blessed by the Almighty
to find victory on the battlefield
more often, I think, due not
to any impressive military prowess,
but to the commanding stupidity
and hauteur of our enemy's
parade ground generals who,
at the final opportunity and push,
couldn't stand the sight of blood.

The romance of a summer's war
soon lost its luster as years passed
and the awful casualties mounted,
the dead in their graves and
the maimed by the roadsides to
remind me that I was hale and hearty
and still had a life that I could
lay down for my infant country.

My hope, often sickly and forlorn,
began to die in the Wilderness,
when the boys in blue began to stand
and fight and trade their lives for ours,
gaining victory in the horrible exchange,
as we lurched for a handful of months
from skirmish to battle, to siege,
and to inevitable defeat.

Aftermath

Once broken to rise no more,
hope's tattered and insubstantial ghost
passed like a fading dream
as the General, bowing his old gray head
notwithstanding the Yankees'
temporary magnanimity,
signed his famous name to our
unconditional surrender while
the ashes of Richmond smoldered.

So, there'll be no victory parade,
no boisterous cavalcade
when I arrive back home.
If God grants to me the grace,
I'll daily stare into the
south-bound end
of a sullen north-bound mule
to get some little crop into the ground
just in time for a late harvest,
just before the killing frosts.

With ghosts of gray and blue
to keep me company,
I'll toil to scratch out of
my meager little homestead
a hardscrabble living
little different from
what I'd earned before,
but now bereft of honor,
worthy of a defeated man.

Soldiers Fallen Here

Thelma Battle

Why is the Battle of Franklin celebrated and revered
when it happened so long ago?

And how many trips to bury two thousand men.
all killed in a day or so?

Some folks said their blood
ran like rivers.

Folks said their blood
ran like streams.

Their bodies hauled away
by a dozen wagon teams.

Two sides did bleed in this here soil
as their lives ebbed away.

These were the men in Union Blue.
These were the men in Confederate Grey.

Said they was stacked upon each other,
someone's son, father, or brother.

They were all soldiers...
soldiers from everywhere.

What makes this town so special?
Soldiers fallen here!

McGavock Confederate Cemetery after reinterment in June 1866

Photograph courtesy of Rick Warwick

Three Voices

Louise Colln

The Southern Soldier

I found my mother crying in the kitchen,
Empty now of all the things she loved,
Things crated out for the auction.
Neighbors
saying mebbe they might follow them
Sometime.
Meanwhile bidding, fifty cents
For this, a nickel for that.
She begged me to come with them.
Little brother Bill clung to me and cried.
I had just started taking him with me to hunt
Though he was far too young to shoot a gun.
But I was a man grown, courting Ellene,
Buying land I loved,
Land I still love, land I'm fighting for.

We kept in touch,
A letter every year or so.
The last one said,
"Your little brother, Bill,
Just joined the Union Army.
Watch for him."
Great God, Mother, he's my enemy.
Now when I rush across a grassy field
To fight,
Every man in blue I face
Looks like my brother.

Aftermath

The Northern Soldier

I recognize this land we're fighting over.
Somewhere in my mind is a memory
Of playing under southern sun
Before Father took us to Iowa.

No one talks about why
Even now that father is dead,
Brought down beneath a tree he felled,
Only a whisper of a race horse
And a falling out between partners,
Then a sudden journey north.

They tell me that I cried when we left.
My oldest brother, John, stayed in Tennessee,
starting his own family.

I always thought
That someday I would come back
To see John.
Say, "I'm your brother, Bill,
All grown up now. I want to know you."
God, don't let me see him now
At the end of my rifle barrel.

The Soldiers' Mother

Good friends were with me when they brought the news.
My neighbors came to mourn with me,
The same kind neighbors who sat with my husband's body,
Bringing food, that womanly belief
That feeding the body feeds the soul.

Those old Tennesseans, Virginians, Carolinians,
Strayed to Iowa,
Leaving graves beneath the blowing prairie grass,
Laid careful head to east
For the Day of Resurrection.

The pastor took my hand,
Folding it gently in his own.
"Bill won't come home," he said,
"Killed in Tennessee."

The war just over, I received a letter,
"Son John still lives,
Lives close enough
To carry flowers to his brother's grave."
I try to thank God.

Pony Rider

Alan Rhody

My mouth is cracked and dry,
Ain't seen trouble since late last night.
The saddle bags are tight and full,
My horse pulling like a big ol' bull.
Ration your water, ration your water,
Ten miles to the next station, hang on.

I'm a pony rider, ain't nobody going to stop me.
I'm a pony rider, Lord knows how I got here.

Heard there's a letter in here from Mr. Lincoln,
Heard there's a letter in here from Mr. Lincoln.
Fort Sumter's under fire;
Sure as shell there's going to be a war.
Ration your water, ration your water,
Six miles to the next station, hang on.

I'm a pony rider, ain't nobody going to stop me.
I'm a pony rider, Lord knows how I got here.

Then I awake in a cold sweat,
I awake from the same nightmare:
I's barely sixteen, twenty-five bucks a week.
Those days are gone, but I'm still having bad dreams.
And it was ration your water, ration your water,
Ration your water and hang on.

I was a pony rider, rode under the southern flag after that.
I was a pony rider and all I can say is thank God for the
    telegraph.

And it was ration your water, ration your water,
Ration your water and hang on.

A Breath of Fresh Air

Judith Walter

The aging chestnut gelding slowed to a walk as he approached the curve. The horse sensed home and safety, just as Theophilus did. Even ten years after the war ended, the young black man felt uneasy riding alone in the Tennessee countryside. Around a bend in the road, the two story white house with columns and porches came into view. Red brick chimneys stood at equal intervals along the north and south walls. Theo wondered if the red glass that formed a decorative pattern surrounding the side entrance was still intact. When rider and horse entered the wagon road, he saw the separate brick kitchen where his mother once cooked for the plantation owner's family. Even after years of freedom, the house had special meaning to Theophilus, as well as the community. For him, it was the place he had spent his earliest years; within the community, he knew its placement on a hill indicated wealth and influence.

Dismounting at the back door, he saw Vester coming to greet him and take his horse to the barn. The stooped black man waved as he approached. "Mawnin', Theo. Nice to see ya' agin. Miss Mamie be glad to see yo' face pop 'round the door. You always was her favorite." The old man's face crinkled into a smile.

"Good mornin', Vester. I've missed you." Theo removed his hat, brushed the dust off his riding clothes, and wiped sweat from his face. He stretched his lean brown body to its full height and reached down to pat Vester's shoulder. "How're you and your family?"

"Oh, we's just fine, Theo. Just fine. Say hello to yo' Mama for me. And tell her you's still the best talking young man I knows."

"I'll do that, Vester. And thanks for taking care of Freedom while I visit Miss Mamie. Maybe we can sit and talk when I finish my visit."

As was still the custom in this area, Theo strode toward the back door. Before going inside, he turned to watch Vester walking down the path to the barn. The slow pace was not just to cool the horse but also to enable the weary servant to keep up. His years sat heavily on his shoulders.

Stepping inside the back door was like entering the remnants of another world. The open twelve foot windows, with lace curtains that fluttered in the breeze from time to time, didn't change the cloistered, secretive feel of the house that was once so filled with activity. The smell of lemon oil told Theophilus that Nanny still polished the few remaining pieces of cherry furniture. The scent of apples and spices let him know she was busy with cooking duties today.

Walking through the once elegant dining room and across the side hallway, where sunlight filtered through the red glass, he tapped on the door and entered the sitting room. There he saw Miss Mamie in her chair by the window, looking through a box of letters.

"Hello, Miss Mamie." Theophilus kept his voice low so he would not startle her.

The elderly woman looked toward the voice. Her face came alive with a smile. "Oh, Theophilus. How happy I am to see you. Come—sit by me and let's talk."

Obediently, Theolphilus pulled a small chair nearer to the older woman and sat on the threadbare velvet seat. "How are you, Miss Mamie?"

"Old and tired, my dear. Old and tired."

"I know life's hard for you now. I'm glad you have Nanny and Vester here to help you."

"They're like family, Theophilus. Like family."

I wonder if that's how they feel. "They're good to you, I know."

"Mr. Parsons and I made sure all our people had everything they ever needed."

Except their freedom. "I know they appreciated that."

"They loved us and we loved them. "

Fear often mistaken for love. "My mother's family lived here a long time."

"Yes. We always treated our people well."

Except for owning them.

"Better than a lot of people did. They couldn't have managed without us."

Not while they were kept ignorant and defenseless. "Maybe not."

The tinkling of wind chimes interrupted the moment and the curtains blew about, sweeping long hidden cobwebs out of their pathway. Theophilus walked to the window and held the curtains aside. The wind chimes hung on a limb he remembered sitting under as a young child with his mother. The long branches of the oak tree had provided much needed shade on those hot summer days when his mother took a break from her kitchen duties. Sometimes she sang old spirituals meant to soothe him into an afternoon nap.

On the way back to his chair, he glimpsed a letter that had dropped from the box on Miss Mamie's lap. He recognized his mother's handwriting. His mother had learned to read and write in spite of the laws against it. He remembered her telling him of her fear of being discovered reading a book; but, once they were freed by Mr. Parsons, she made sure he learned to read, write, and speak correctly. Those efforts on her part had helped him succeed during the past year at the teachers college in Baton Rouge.

As he paused to retrieve the letter and hand it to Miss Mamie, the chimes sounded again and a strong gust of wind blew the curtains straight out into the room. It felt as if his mother's spirit surrounded him along with the wind. Her sweetness and grace combined with her strength, even after the horror of her youth, were a breath of fresh air in this

convoluted and cruel world. He made a decision. The time
had come to end the charade.

"Miss Mamie, I know the things you say are heartfelt.
But how do you know how colored folks really feel?"

Miss Mamie drew her slumped body up to its full height,
straightened her once elegant dress, and looked Theophilus
straight in the eye. "I know."

Without looking down, she closed the box of letters, as if
to hide them.

Her tone took on a defensive edge. "It was a different
time."

"But people have always wanted to be free, Miss Mamie."
Theo kept his voice even and kind.

Her matriarchal demeanor became more marked when
she raised her chin.

"What would you know about that? You've been free
most of your life."

Fresh air flowed through the open window once more,
feeling like a cosmic imprimatur for his decision.

He faced Miss Mamie. Towering over her frail frame, he
needed to bend forward to look her in the eye as he spoke.

"I know your son was my father." His voice was quiet but
firm. "I guess I should call you Grandmother."

Miss Mamie gasped. Her trembling hand flew to cover
her mouth.

Theo paused, before continuing in a slow and measured
voice. "I know why my mother and I lived as free people
long before others of our color did."

His gaze never left Miss Mamie's eyes.

The curtains stood still. The chimes quieted.

Theo began to walk toward the door.

Before opening it, he turned. Miss Mamie sat slumped
in her chair, tears trickling down her parched cheeks. He
knew she had kept the box of letters because she loved his
mother and him. He did not wish to hurt her more than she
had already been hurt. But it was time for the truth and a

breath of fresh air. With the scene frozen in his mind, he uttered his final words to his grandmother. "I will always be grateful that Mr. Parsons gave my mother and me our freedom."

Miss Mamie wiped her cheeks and looked up expectantly.

Theo continued. "But I will never forget that a violent act began my life."

He left the room and quietly closed the door.

The Death of a Confederate Captain

By George Spain

They said Captain Robert Taggert hanged himself in Lady's stall, on June 27, 1874, because she had been his son, Bob's, favorite saddle horse. Bob had died on that exact same day, ten years before. Years later, old Dock, the Taggert's cook, told me that the rope broke after the Captain was dead and that his body fell into the straw but the mare never stepped on him. Though he didn't leave a note, I knew why the "Captain", for that's what everybody called him, did what he did.

My mother had tried to heal the Captain, but it didn't help. In fact, something she did may have played a part in his death. That's what Mrs. Taggert and her sons and her brother, John Gaunt, the high sheriff of Franklin County, believed. After the Captain died, they said Mama was a witch. His death made a sadness in me because he was a good man and for a while I had imagined him as my father. But before it was all over, the greatest sadness of my life came to me.

Mama was a red-headed Irish immigrant born with the veil over her face and the gift of healing. Her eyes were gray and shaped like a deer's. I thought she was beautiful. Practically everything that is good in me came from her, for I never knew my father, Joseph. I was a baby when he was killed charging with the colored troops up Peach Orchard Hill at the Battle of Nashville. She told me that he was born a slave in Georgia and that he killed his master with a sickle. Then he fled north into the mountains near Sewanee.

In a valley called Lost Cove he was bitten by a rattlesnake and my mother, who lived in the valley, found him and saved his life. I have no memory of his face, or of his voice, or of his smell. All I know of him is what my mother told me. She said that he had a daughter who was a slave and that he wanted to free her. When he was healed from the snake bite, he and Mama walked for four days to Nashville where he joined the Federal Army so he could fight the slave owners.

After the battle, Mama said she looked for him for three days. She talked to the officers and men in his regiment who had survived; she walked back and forth over the battlefield, and went to the hospitals. She went everywhere, but she never found him. Some of the gravediggers told her that he was probably in the big grave where they put a lot of the colored soldiers. She went there, but all she found was a private's muddy hat.

She never got over losing him. And, though I know she loved me, there were times I could see that her eyes were sad when she looked at me. I could see that she was far away; and, though she never cried when this happened, I knew she was thinking about him. As I grew older, she began to tell me about how she still missed my father and how, at times, when my face was turned a certain way and I was smiling, I looked like him.

Now, I am an old man with an old brain. When I was young, it seemed I could remember every detail of everything that I heard or saw. But now, there are times when I cannot remember what happened yesterday and sometimes not even this morning. Yet, and this is a wonder, I still remember people's faces and voices from long ago; I can still bring them up before me, just as they were when they were alive—smiling, laughing, and crying, so real that sometimes I begin to smile or get tears in my eyes and I call them to me and hug them and kiss them.

As I write—sixty years later—about Mama and the Captain, I see her freckled face and Irish-red hair as clearly as I see my hand as I write, and I see the Captain and Lady, the Taggerts, Dock and Katey, our cabin on Elk River, and the distant mountains; they are all here with me now. I hear their voices and Katey's barking, the sudden, loud splash of a fish, the calling of quail from the field beside the house, the strong smell of hickory wood burning, of rain, of newly turned earth and the sweet scent of honeysuckle. I feel the heat waves rising above the fields in mid-summer, the cool water of the river flowing slowly over me, and the touch of Mama's lips on my cheek at night after I've said my prayers.

Three months before the Captain died, there was a full moon that was so large and bright it looked as though you could reach up and pull it from the sky. It was the last day of March, and the moon marked the time for us to plant our garden. The next morning Mama went to the shed behind the house and started getting the vegetable seeds ready, and the other seeds, the ones she called her 'soul food' for her flowers. I was on the porch whet-stoning the hoes when Katey, our red feist, jumped from beside me and ran out into the yard, barking loudly. I stood and looked up the road.

Even at a distance, I could see the Captain coming down the road on Lady. His head and shoulders slumped forward like an old, sick man; his clothes hung on him like a scarecrow. As he came closer, I could see his long beard and hair scraggling down from under a wide-brimmed straw hat. He rode slowly up to the edge of the yard and stopped. Now that he was close enough for Katey to smell him, she quit barking and came back to me, pressing her shoulder against my legs.

The mare climbed the bank from the road into the yard and walked up to the porch .The Captain looked more like a dead man than anyone I had ever seen who was still alive. His skin was yellowish gray, his eyes sunk deep into their dark sockets. Hollowed cheekbones and protruding jawbones were almost covered by a white-streaked beard; long uncombed hair hung below his shoulders. His lips, colorless and thinned back tightly into a grimace; his hands large bones and sinews and long dirty fingers, with their broken nails, barely touched the reins that lay loosely curled across the pommel of the saddle. I could smell him.

Before the war, he had been a wealthy man. He had owned more than fifty slaves. Some had worked his fields, some he leased out. He had believed God favored slavery as a way to lift them out of darkness. He had had great pride in his thousand-acre plantation and in what he had achieved with his years of hard work. He had loved his family, Tennessee, and the South and had never doubted that their beliefs in honor, courage, and freedom would lead the South to victory. He had believed that God answered his prayers and would protect him and his sons in battle.

Now all of that was gone—all of it—but most of all, his precious son was gone; and he could not bear the pain that was inside him every day. He was alive and his son was dead. Even the love of his wife and the pleading of his two remaining sons and his friends and, even with all the hugs and kisses of his six grandchildren, nothing that anyone did was enough. He turned more and more into himself and away from everyone else. As the years went by, his family gave up trying, and left him alone in his library with his books and his bourbon.

Three months after the war was over, he gave his bird dogs to Big Kinna who had served him faithfully for twenty years as the driver of his field hands and now lived alone in a cabin on the backside of the plantation. That Christmas he quit going to church and began to eat alone. He seldom left the house. When night came, he fell asleep in the library, with his books and empty bottles scattered around him on the floor.

But now and then, on a Sunday evening, when there was no rain or heavy fog, he would hold back on his drinking, just enough so he could walk without falling. An hour before sunset, he would put on his boots and tattered gray coat. Without a word to anyone, he would go out the back door, past the smokehouse, through the all-but-empty slave quarter, and down the slope to the pasture gate where he would whistle one time, high and clear. In an instant Lady would be there waiting for him as he unlatched and opened the gate, not closing it—for there were no other horses in the field—and walked through and on to the barn beyond with the mare so close behind him she was almost touching his shoulder with her head. At the barn, he led her into her stall and fed her a little grain while he groomed her coat and mane and tail until she stood glistening before him. Then he would talk to her about Bob. He would tell her what a beautiful little boy his son had been, how he tickled him at night before he went to sleep, how brave he was when he fell off his first pony and broke his arm and didn't cry, how handsome he was in his new uniform that last day at home, how he had shown no fear in all the fighting they had done, and how, when he died, he had not made the slightest sound as they fell together among the dead and wounded. When he finished talking, he would bridle and saddle Lady, mount her, and ride off down the lane to the road where he would turn right and, a mile on, cross the river over Bethpage Bridge and then, for another mile, to a place where the road climbed to the top of Lynch Hill. There he would stop and stare at the mountains until the last light began to fade away; then he reined the horse around and rode back home in the dark. He told Mama all these things and I heard every word.

When Sunday evening came and the weather was good, I would sit on the bank by the side of the road and wait for him to come by. Twice I hid in the woods beside the road and followed him all the way to Lynch Hill where I watched him from the shadows of the trees.

Even though he was dirty and skeletal and had once owned slaves, he was like a knight to me, a knight who had gone off to war to protect our land. I began to dream about him; and then, one night as I lay in bed, I began to pretend that he was my father and that he would teach me how to be like him, how to sit high up on a powerful war horse and how to fight; and, when I was ready, he would take me with him into battle where I would be wounded and would ride home beside him with my empty sleeve pinned up just like his.

Yes, he had owned slaves and, yes, my father had been a slave, but it made no matter for I was certain that the Captain loved me as he always nodded to me with a smile on his face and would say, "Good evening, Jeremiah," when he rode by on his way to Lynch Hill. And one evening, he lifted me up with his one arm onto the saddle in front of him and rode me to the bridge and back. I don't remember his saying a word until he brought me back and lifted me down, when he said, "Son, give my regards to your mother." That was the night I began to pretend he was my father. Now I know it was just his way of talking.

Long years later, I went to Sewanee to talk with Dock about Mama and the Captain and the Taggerts. I can still see her in my mind's eye: she was in her eighties and blind when I visited her in her daughter's home. She was the color of dark chocolate and was smoking a little clay pipe as she told me about being the Taggerts' slave before the War and then staying on as their cook after it was over. She talked for an hour about Mama and the Captain and Miss Lucy, and every now and then she would smile at a memory—but mostly her face was sad.

"Before the war, the Massah, he work hard, sometime he work in the field right along side of da hands. He hardly ever use tha whip on us, mostly he jus talk fuss talk when someone slackin. He sho luv Mistah Bob, he luv'd all his boys but Mistah Bob his favorite. After them dark days, fore he change so, da Massah was a fun luvin man; but when he come home, he not da same man, all his smiles done lef him when dat boy died. I's think some of him done die right der with Mistah Bob. Lawd, he done quit talkin, even to Miss Lucy, an he quit goin to da fields; he jus stay in dat room with dem ole books an all he did was drink dat bad stuff an eva now an den ride dat horse of Mistah Bob's out to da Lawd knows where. He jus let his hair grow an be greasy an let hisself get all smelly an not eat til he done shrink all away inside his skin. Lawd, Mistah Jeremiah, if it had'n been for Miss Lucy makin herself into a man, we'd all died out der for sure. She get up fore da ole rooster dun crow an ring da bell an begin yellin for da boys an da hands to get demselves up an out of bed an to da fields. She dun start cidin evathing; she say how much cotton, how much corn, how much wheat dey goin ta plant; an when to plant an when to pick. She make da sales an writ it all down in dem black books she keep in her room; she pick which mare to breed an which bull to buy; an many a day I seed her out there in da fields sweatin with da hands an gettin all burn up by da sun til she turn black as me, an her flesh gettin so scratched by da stickers she looked like she been whipped like a runaway. An she keep all dis up til she start gettin hard an her face start lookin like a stone. An Mistah Jeremiah, she get where she nevah show any hurt, but I know'd she be hurtin bout Mistah Bob dyin an den Mistah Robert same as dyin. But Miss Lucy she nevah show it. She done set her mind on holdin on to dat land an feedin her chullin an granchullin; but Mistah Jeremiah, there were times when that chile was so bone tired she could'nt even go to sleep. And Mistah Jeremiah, der was sumpin else I seed, she didn't know I seed it but I did, sum nights when I heps her carry Mistah Robert to bed, I seed it in her eyes, how she be lookin at him, like she lookin at her own baby chile dat's dyin an ain't nothing she can do to stop it no matter how much she pray to da Lawd to not let him die he jus keep dyin. I seed her under all dat hardness, that po woman was still luvin Mistah Robert. It's da Lawd's truth Mistah Jeremiah, I done seed it all long ago, how dat da Lawd he put some good an some bad in all of us so's none of us be all good an none of us be all bad, an since we all his chullin he'll try to hep us all, even da bad ones get over da river to da other side to be with him.

Ever since I know'd dat, I's done lef most of the worryin to the Lawd when I's go to sleep at night."

Dock was right, Lucy Taggert never stopped loving her husband. I know because I heard the Captain tell Mama about the nights his wife cried and cried and tried to love on him and, how he wouldn't let her, and how she begged him to do something to come alive again so he could love her and their family. I heard all of this, and I heard him say that it was Mrs. Taggert who got him to come ask my mother for help.

The sun was shining, but there was a nip in the air on that March morning, when the Captain rode up to our house and looked down on me from Lady's back.

"Jeremiah, is your mother home?"

"Yes sir."

"Would you please go and tell her that I would like to talk to her."

"Yes sir."

I stepped off the porch and went around the side of the house to the backyard, stuck my head in the shed, and told Mama that Captain Taggert wanted to talk to her. She said, "Tell him to have a seat on the porch and I'll be there in a minute. Did he say what he wants?"

"No'm," I answered.

When I came back to the front, the Captain had gotten down off of Lady and was standing by her with his hand on the pommel. He nodded but didn't move when I told him to come sit on the porch, that Mama was coming. I could see he didn't want to be there. He kept glancing over his shoulder, looking toward the road, as though he might see someone he knew passing by.

It seemed a long while until the front door opened and Mama stepped out onto the porch. "Good day to you, Captain Taggert." He took his hat off and nodded. "Can I help you?" she asked.

He began turning the hat around and around by the brim. At first he didn't look at Mama: he looked at the ground, then he looked again, over his shoulder, at the road and, seeing no one, turned back and looked at her. "Yes um...uh, scuse me...could we talk private?"

Mama pointed to a post. "Tie your horse up and come inside," and walked back in the house leaving the door open. He moved slowly as he tied the reins to the post and climbed the steps and followed her inside and closed the door.

I ran back behind the house to the corncrib, pulled an ear of corn out, shucked some kernels into my hand, then ran back to Lady and began to feed her. Her eyes were large and beautiful; I could see myself reflected in them. For a moment, I felt almost as if I were being drawn into them. Then, from behind me, I heard the first low murmur of the Captain's voice inside the house, but I could not hear what he was saying.

My mother never knew that when people came to talk to her, I hid under the window and listened to them telling her their secrets, telling sad things and, best of all, the bad things that they had done. It was exciting, though there were times when I heard something said that I wished I had not heard. Yet it never stopped me from listening.

I once asked Mama why people came to talk to her. We were sitting on the river bank fishing. There was such a long moment before she answered that I thought she hadn't heard me, and then she said, "Well, Jeremiah, there's some people who keep all their bad feelings locked up inside until it builds up and begins to poison them and, after a while, they're never happy and they start turning away from everybody, even the ones who loved them. Some get to drinking all the time, some stay angry all the time and think everybody's against them, some end up killing someone, some kill themselves; you know it's sorta like when you get risens coming up under your skin and I have to prick them with a hot needle to get the poison out. Well that's what telling someone about the things hidden inside you can do; for some folks, it lets out some of the angry things and the sad things, so, maybe, they can be a little happier."

When people came to talk to her, she told me to stay outside, away from the house, and not to make any noise. Of course her not wanting me to hear what was being said made me want to hear every word and every sound. So I was quiet as a mouse when I crawled on my belly down the side of the cabin until I was right under the window where I could hear every word and every whimper.

Lying there on my back, I heard people say some terrible things. To this day, I remember every word that was said by one of them—it has never left my ear: it was a man's voice that sounded almost like an animal, grunting and panting and talking all at the same time, it came from deep inside his throat as he told about burning alive a houseful of Negroes, "Unh, Unh, Unh...Oh God damn... I swear I didn't know those niggers had any children in there... Unh, Unh, Oh my dear God, I still hear them screaming, and I can still smell them...Oh God what did I do?" and then, from deeper down, there came a long, guttural, groan, like a dying beast might make.

And I heard a woman say that she was dead, and I believed her, her voice was so empty and lifeless she did not sound human. She scared me. I thought that she was a ghost or a spirit, her voice in a faint whisper saying, "I died that first night. I was no longer alive. And after that I felt nothing, I heard nothing, I did not smell them as they put themselves in me, over and over, two white ones, two black ones and...white and black and white and black, over and over, and you know, all the time their faces were changing above me, sweating, biting their lips, touching fire to me, I saw the corn cob, I saw the light come and go into darkness and then the light and the dark returned...and there was something else...but it didn't matter for I was already dead the first night...nothing mattered...for I was dead."

I heard all kinds of things: sad, strange, scary, funny things, cruel things that people did to little children and old people and to prisoners and idiots, to each other and to animals. After awhile, I wondered where was God, why did he let these awful things happen, why didn't he just kill all the evil people. And then I began to worry that he would punish me for disobeying my mother. I was betraying her. But now, as I look back on it after all these years, I realize that, if I had obeyed her, I wouldn't have learned how evil people can be, and how those who have been hurt badly or have done terrible things still keep on living, and how most of those who do awful things really want to be better than they are and that sometimes they do become better. How strange it is that I learned this from disobeying my mother. I know this, though: if I had not hidden under that window, I wouldn't have heard the Captain tell Mama about Bob.

And so it was, on the first day the Captain came to our house and closed the door behind himself and began talking to Mama, that I threw the corn down that I was feeding Lady and crawled under the window just in time to hear the chair creak as he sat down; and, in that same instant, I heard him begin telling Mama what had happened to Bob on June 4, 1864. The words poured out of his mouth without stopping, without emphasis, without life, and, it was only after awhile, when there was almost no more breath to say another word, that I heard his voice break.

"Sherman was Hell he'd killed us all at Kennesaw if he'd had half a chance an that mornin he was goin to try again, he set on us hard with his cannons an when they stopped the air was so full of smoke an dust you could hardly breathe, you could taste the gunpowder, an for a bit you could hardly see through all the smoke, the sun hanging like a drop of blood in the sky; the heat was terrible it was over a hundred an there was no shade for we'd cut most of the trees down an what was left had been blown apart, as soon as the cannon stopped we began cleanin the dirt from our muskets an gettin ready for them, we knew they were comin it was quiet now an everyone was whisperin so they wouldn't hear us behind that big wall of logs an dirt. Strange what you remember, way off there was a mule brayin over an over; the strangest thing, after all that noise an explosions, I heard a woodpecker hammerin away on a piece of wood just on the other side of the breastworks, isn't that strange that I'd remember it, my son was sittin by my side in the trench, he was leanin back against the mound with his eyes closed, his skin an beard were white with dust, his lips were so dry an cracked he looked old an worn an I wanted to touch him but I didn't, I let him sleep, up an down the line I could hear the clinkin of ramrods an the clickin of hammers bein cocked an uncocked, it was still quiet but then from across the valley came the first sounds of their bugles, I shook Bob until he opened his eyes an sat up an he said somethin to me but I couldn't hear an he touched my hand, I leaned close to him an spoke in his ear, 'Stay by me Bob, stay by me today;' I stood an looked over the top so I could see them an there they came seven long dark blue lines comin down the hill, the smoke had cleared an I could see their barrels an bayonets glistenin; I could see their battle flags an thousands of Yankees comin straight at us an everybody began to stand up to see them, we weren't afraid we knew how to kill, we were good at it, an then tough old Colonel Yeats shouted, 'Down boys down' an we knelt down without a sound an listened, we could hear the sound of their footsteps as they came closer an closer, until they were so near we could hear their officers shoutin commands to their men who cheered louder an louder, the ground began to shake an then above it all I heard that old Irishman's last call to us, 'Now, my precious boys, now, up an give em Hell,' an all of us rose up screamin an levelin our muskets at that mass of men who rushed towards us so near now we could see their faces, there was a great roar as we all fired together, I felt the heat like an oven on my face from the sheet of flame that burst outward from all along our breastworks sweepin away their first line, we fired an loaded, fired an loaded, slaughterin them in rows and heaps, killin them as fast as we could load an fire an still they came on stumblin an tramplin on their wounded an dead; our cannons opened on them with canister the air rushed an quivered; heads an arms were torn away, I saw half a body spinnin upward; they ran into our fire bent forward veerin away then back into the gaps firin as they came on an on right up to us; the air was filled with smoke an' blood an' the zippin an buzz of Minie balls an their thuddin into flesh; explosions an concussion were shakin the earth apart as we screamed an killed each other I heard myself screamin 'Kill em all kill em all' an tasted sulfur an smelled shit and vomit an then it happened... there came a soun beside my head an with it a swash of wetness across my face an neck an in that instant I was flung back an down hard on somethin an I saw before my eyes closed...I saw him...what had been my sweet boy...Oh Lord Oh Lord... goddamn God to Hell to burn with me forever for what he did that day to my dear boy who I did not save."

When he finished, there was a long silence. Then I heard my mother, but she was talking so soft and low that I couldn't hear what she was saying. He stayed in the room with her for a good while, long enough that Lady and I both became restless; when I heard her begin pawing the ground I crawled away from the window and went to her. Just as I was beginning to stroke her neck, the door opened and the Captain walked out, mounted, and without a word, rode away.

From that week on, on that same day, at the same hour, he returned. The third time he came, they made love; and, every time thereafter, for the next three months, they made love. I know they did. I heard it all, and I saw them six times through a hole that I made in the chinking between the logs. The last time he came, on June 27, 1874, he begged Mama to run away with him. When he said that, it scared me so I held my breath. There was a long silence, and then, in a firm voice she said, "No. I'll not run away with you...I'm sorry, Robert, but I'll not do it, I don't love you...and I think it's best you stop coming here. I don't want to hurt you, but I don't think you should ever come back. It's best you go on home now." He left.

And that night he hanged himself.

A few nights later the Taggerts came on horses. They were carrying torches. They hanged my mother high up in the big oak that grew beside the road in front of our cabin. They tried to find me but they couldn't; I was hiding deep in the cane on the bank of the river. The next morning when I got Mama's body down from the tree, I made my vow to kill them. And one winter day I did.

Even though I was a boy when all of this happened, and even though I loved my mother dearly, there was a long time when I believed that what she had done was wrong, and that she was part to blame for the Captain's death—it hurt me. But as I grew older and committed my own sins, I began to think, who am I to stand in judgment of my mother who loved me so, who cared for me without anyone helping her, and who am I to judge anyone, even the Taggerts, for I have done terrible things in my life: I have been a drunkard, and I have cursed God, I have been lascivious, and I have killed three people, so who am I to judge anyone?

Photograph courtesy of George Spain
The Lynch brothers from Winchester Tennessee:
Lafayette - Francis, Killed at Kennesaw Mountain - William

An Unlikely Promethean

Nancy Allen

La Rue Hughes, a woman who might never have been, stood before the audience at the quilt fair holding a quilt made in 1862 by her great- aunt, Suzie Haley. The quilt had a story:

Photograph courtesy of Nancy Allen

La Rue Hughes' great-grandfather, Sam Haley, left his home and family at seventeen in an emotional rush to join the Confederate Army. As an act of faith that he would return, his sister Suzie pulled a batch of material from a wooden chest and began work on a quilt, promising to have it finished when he came home.

"It will be your wedding present," she said.

At the beginning of April, 1862, in southwestern Tennessee, the Union Army, under the leadership of Major

General Ulysses S. Grant, moved to Pittsburg Landing on the Tennessee River. The Confederate Army, under the direction of General Albert S. Johnston, launched a surprise attack on Grant's forces, hoping to drive them away from the river into the swamps of Owl Creek. On the first day the Confederates gained some ground, but soon the Union Army regained their footing. General Johnston was killed; and because of heavy losses, General Pierre G. T. Beauregard, General Johnston's replacement, decided to wait until morning to attack the Union soldiers. Reinforcements for the Union Army arrived and forced the Confederate Army to retreat. It was one of the bloodiest battles of the Civil War.

Sam Haley was wounded twice. A severed artery in his arm allowed his life's blood to pour out in a steady stream. He took his shirt off and tied the sleeve tight around his arm, but blood continued to flow. Sam wanted to move in the direction of the retreat. He dragged his feet, his head swooned, his legs felt too heavy to lift. Giving over to pain and the loss of blood, he dropped to the ground unnoticed, unconscious, and unafraid. Blood soaked the earth beneath him. Vultures circled as darkness closed around him.

Two Union soldiers, making their way back to their unit, walked past. They might never have spotted Sam except for the birds swooping down near him.

"Is that a man over there?"

Taking a better look, the older man said, "He's a Confederate. I think he's still alive."

The younger man raised his rifle, "Let's finish him off."

"No, he's just a kid, not much older than my boy. He's going to die anyway. Let's put him against a log and cover him with brush so the vultures can't get to him."

So the Union men left Sam there to die, but youth and regeneration aroused him in the morning mist. He moved his left foot. Struggling to open his eyes, feeling the heavy tree limbs pressing on his chest, Sam realized he was alive.

Pushing with his good arm, he managed to begin releasing his entombed body. The morning was silent. The billowed fog hugged the ground and bathed Sam with its soft damp foam. At first Sam could not stand. He crawled to a tree. Shivering, he sat his back against the rough bark. His shirt was red with blood. He pulled the makeshift tourniquet tighter.

Looking north he noticed a flicker of light and began crawling in its direction. Once he stood and staggered forward only to fall. But he would not give up. He would find help. He would live. After two hours, as the morning light began to lift the fog, Sam reached a slave cabin where an old woman bandaged his arm, fed him some rabbit stew, and allowed him to sleep for three days. He found that he was then strong enough to rejoin his unit.

Sam Haley made it home from the war but never regained the use of his arm. He married his childhood sweetheart. His sister, Suzie, finished her quilt and gave it to the couple as a wedding present. The quilt remains today as a tribute to Suzie's faith and assurance that her brother would survive the war.

Years after the war, efforts were made to solidify the union by bringing Confederate and Union soldiers together. Sam decided to attend the reunion. As he was walking past a group of Union men, he overheard one of them say, "We found this Confederate guy who was bleeding and almost dead. We decided to let him die on his own, so we put him under a brush pile and left him."

"You should go back there and see if you can identify his remains. His family could give him a proper burial," said another man.

Sam turned pale. He looked at the men.

"Excuse me," he said, "Did you say you left a fellow under a brush pile down by the river?"

"Yeah, he was going to die, so we decided to let nature take its course."

"But I didn't die. That was me you left there."

The men stared at Sam, paralyzed in time, until tears began to flow. They fell into each other's arms, embarrassed, laughing. Sam would never forget the joy he saw in the Union soldiers' eyes. As the men sat together, a friendship formed that would last a lifetime.

Death was banished from Sam Haley on that cold April night in 1862. Life won that battle the next day to bring about a future for generations to come.

Author's note: based on a true story.

The Rampant Floods

Veera Rajaratnam

We had the sixth sense
We knew right from wrong
We laid the rules
We laid the boundaries
We hoped to bring civility
Where everyone finds happiness—
Where all civilization walks in
Worthy path of peace—but
We now shed tears of sorrow
Be warned of rampant floods...!

The Loss: A Mother's Cry!

Veera Rajaratnam

The person you did not become
And the life taken away – for YOU
I cry, from the depths of my soul
And will weep from within my grave...

6 SPANNING THE DECADES

Photograph by Emily Nance

Anger in the Aftermath

Louise Strang

That wild reckless feeling comes again.
The turbulence internal stirred by pain
Aligns us with all dark and angry eyes.
Our hatred aimed at patronizing smiles.

Who Has Ceased the Wind

Robert Coné

Among the many shades of Arlington
Lie the haunting acres of hallowed ground
And borne on carriages from Washington
Quick, young men on the move are also found.

The cannon balls so beautiful in flight
And yet were so destructive in their fall
Are quieted now when the fields are white
As entertainment of combat has palled.

'Tis said audacity carries the day,
But the soldiers look with cavernous eyes
Upon ignoble causes which hold sway
And languish in the wilderness and cry

For greater control of their destiny.
They rush madly into greater evils.
But marble men look and see misery
As in the cotton there are boll weevils.

They toil over malevolent matters
Whose sovereignty is a pillar of strength.
The American flag is in tatters
And thus humbles their noble selves by length

As if struck by a mule that bucks and kicks,
As by the Minié ball their ranks are thinned.
So they are tragically wounded (or sick)
But through their sacrifice they cease the wind.

Photograph by Emily Nance

It's Around Us

Kathleen Jack

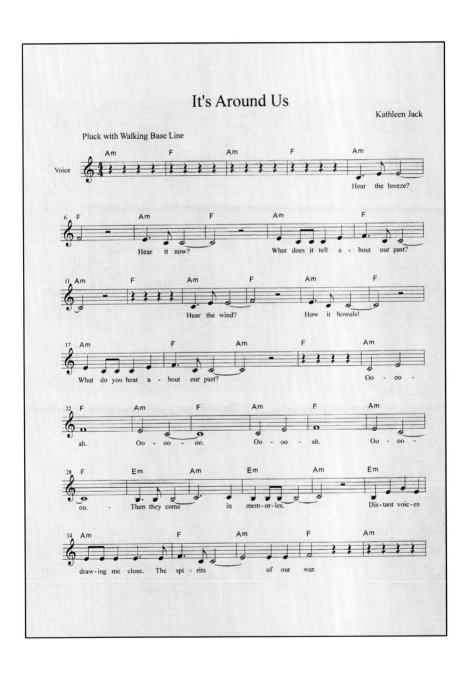

The Darker Brother

James C. Floyd, Jr.

I am the Darker Brother:

I have been kidnapped accused hunted down beaten
toyed with experimented on and sold.
I have been lied to lied on laughed at
disenfranchised drugged labeled and lynched.

My home has been burned
my churches bombed woman raped
children murdered
and I have been called uncivilized.

I have labored from sun-up to sun-down in other peoples'
    fields
and they have cashed my sweat for money.
I have discovered invented created;
they have cashed my brains for money.
I have styled designed written;
they have cashed my talents for money.
I have fought and died in their Civil War,
and they have cashed my blood for victory and glory.

Who else could have survived, thrived, kept the dream alive,
and still, even now be reaching for the sky... I.... am...the
    Darker Brother.

Author's note: This poem gets its title from the first line of the poem, "I too sing
America," by Langston Hughes.

The Scars Seen and Unseen
(Slavery to Here)

Thelma Battle

The body feels the injuries that others inflict,
And the mind does the same.

Centuries of humiliation and degradation leave
mind boggling scars.

Scabs form on sorid lashes made by whips
And fall to another day.

The same way within the mind
Scabs form on inner thoughts.

They fight a duel with the souls of those
Who have been inflicted.

Sometimes they stay forever and never go away,
These unseen scars and yet so visible.

When a man who's always been a man
But made to believe otherwise

Dies and leaves this place called earth,
Will his seeds possess those same scars?

Have they been washed away in a healing bath
Called forgiveness?

Were they taught the real history of their forgotten
scabbed formed ancestors and allowed time to heal their
wounds,

Or have they developed a full-blown disease
From scars seen and unseen?

Fire in the Cold

Lori C. Byington

An oak fire flows upward among stone cold graves
                              that house the dead.
Lost long ago in a war between brothers,
                              they are now only dust.

As autumn reaches its crescendo,
                    colors of crimson, saffron, burgundy and green
Decorate the graves of buried sons who have names,
                              but the names are unknown.

A raven rests a moment on a frigid, grey stone
                              that does bear the name
Of a youngster who heard the call to defend his home.

Do the bird's claws feel the passion that the boy did?
Are the ghosts of those children who fought
                              now watching their ebony sentry?

When the air grows cold, do the boys march again at night
                    to sneak upon those who joined the wrong side?
Do their yells and halloos break the quiet as they plunge,
              weapon-ready,
                              headlong to face a familiar visage?

The mist holds the truth as the harvest moon rises
                    and the blue-black bird leaves his post.
In the chill, golden leaves fall again
                    to blanket the boys' final cradles.

'Tis a quiet reminder that all of God's creatures
                    return to dust, where heaven awaits,
And... sometimes...a fire leads the way.

Photograph courtesy of Lori C. Byington

Author's Note: "Fire in the Cold," began while I was driving home from church one fall. I always pass the Confederate graves in historic East Hill Cemetery, and on one of the gravestones stood a raven. The leaves had turned their brilliant shades of red, yellow and orange, and they had begun to fall and pile up around the trees and graves. Simple as that, the poem erupted.

Claricy's Babies

George Spain

In 1845 my wife's ancestor, Elizabeth Darwin, the Mistress of Buzzard Roost, saved the life of one of her husband's slaves. The next year, she did not.

1844

The day started much like any other. As was her nature Elizabeth woke first. She dressed in the dark and shook her husband William awake, then went out on the back porch and rang the iron bell as she did every morning of the week, except the Lord's Day, to wake their sons and Negroes to eat so they would be at work in the fields by first light

The air was gray-white in the mist that rose from the creek beside the field. From the back of his bay gelding, William Darwin watched the dark figures of his sons and slaves moving silently in line, up and down the narrow rows, bending forward with their long-handled hoes, chopping the roots of the weeds away from the young cotton plants. Tiny brownish-red field sparrows gathered, as they did every morning, scratching and pecking in the fresh turned earth, flitting forward searching for seeds and worms almost under the feet of the workers.

Claricy, who was not yet the full age of a woman, worked in the middle of the line with her head down, swinging the hoe with a steady rhythm that never halted or showed the slightest hesitation. She was a small Negress, shiny-black with a wide nose and thick lips. Seven lines of dotted scarification crossed her forehead. She was strong and learned quickly. She never shirked or caused trouble. Claricy was the best field hand William owned. And she was pregnant.

194

She was the only slave in the county born in Africa. Her strange ways and her strange manner of speaking and the scars that lined her face frightened most of the Negroes at Buzzard Roost. They avoided her eyes and her cabin door when it was open, not that she ever did anything or said anything to them that was threatening. But there was something 'not right' about her. It was in her face and the set of her mouth; her eyes were empty, not of intelligence or of life, but of feeling. No one ever saw her smile or say "God" or "Jesus". She never looked up or spoke unless she had to when her owners or any white person talked to her. When they finished, she would nod, turn her back to them, and walk away.

No one, not even William or Elizabeth, knew who the father of Claricy's baby was. Even though Elizabeth, who was midwife and nurse to all her family and slaves, had begun to check on her every evening to see if it was time for it to come, Claricy continued, as always, to deny that she had been with a man. If any of the Negroes knew, they kept silent. Some whispered in their cabins that the Devil came to her in the night.

The other slaves were not like her. They had all been born into slavery in the South. Some were mixtures of races: mulattos, mestizos, quadroons, their blood mingled with whites and Indians. Only one or two were as black as Claricy. None had had their flesh cut into a design.

On Sundays when the sun was bright, she would sit alone on the top step to her cabin door with her face to the sky and her eyes closed, absorbing the heat into her expressionless face. After a long while, she would open her eyes and reach inside the doorway to bring out pieces of wood and a flint knife or spear point that she had found in the field near the bend of the creek. One at a time she would take the pieces of wood and run her hands over them, stroking each one with her fingers, until she selected one. Then she would take the sharp flint and begin to carve. One by one, out of the wood came strange animals and beings that no one had ever seen. If asked what they were, she would not answer. When she was finished, she gathered the carvings up and took them inside and stood them beside others that were spread across the stone hearth of the fireplace.

At night, after the night bell rang, when the last candlelights were blown out in the quarters, the others would sometimes hear her singing—in a language they had never heard—the songs of her people and of their bravery in killing lions and men, and of the great herds of elephants and zebra and buffalo, and of the rich, sharp smells rising from the hot red earth of her homeland, and of the coming of the rains.

William and Elizabeth believed Claricy loved them, as they believed all of "their people" loved them. But the truth was that she hated them, as she hated her father who sold her into slavery, as she hated the African and Arab slave traders, and the first white man who had owned her, and the next one, and the next one. She hated them all and would have killed them, every one of them, if she had had a chance.

Now, as she was bent forward hoeing, the pain came in the small of her back. She had not slept the night before for the kicking and pushing of the baby. She wanted to stop and rest and rub her back, but she did not. She stayed in line with the others all day, falling behind only once, for an instant, when she knelt quickly to untangle a small flint blade from the roots of a milkweed. She dropped it in the pocket of her frayed homespun dress and began to chop faster so that in a few strides she was back in line.

It was a dry, hot day. At noon, when they stopped to eat, a streak of dark clouds appeared in the southwest sky. The only sounds were the chirring of insects and the cawing of crows. Two red hounds ran silently across the far end of the field, stirring up clouds of dust before they jumped the rail fence and disappeared into the woods.

When she returned to work, Claricy's pains were less for a while; but as the afternoon wore on, they increased and by evening were so severe she bit her lip through rather than cry out. She licked the salty blood away so no one would see it. At the end of every row, she pressed the side of her hand against the pocket to feel the sharp edge of the flint; and, as she did, the strange and angry thoughts that had begun weeks ago came into her head again. She listened to them rather than to the thing in her stomach that caused her pain. *It will not be his*, she thought.

Finally, night came. William blew the horn. Before the long high note ended, the workers stopped. Leaning on their hoes, they stood like statues with only their eyes moving, watching the lightning flashing above the mountains—the Devil rolling his stones.

Across the field, where the woods began, a whippoorwill called. Far away a cow bellowed and was answered by another. Then it was quiet. The workers raised the hoes and laid them on their shoulders, the blades in the air. The long day was over. Night had come; and for a little while, they would eat and sleep before they returned again at the first light of day with their hoes on their shoulders.

They all left the field together, walking slowly one behind the other down the sunken lane that led back to the quarters where the Negroes turned off in twos and threes into their cabins, while the Darwins went across the yard and up the steps into the big house.

Only Claricy was alone. She entered her windowless, rough-hewn log cabin and closed the door. The room smelled of wood smoke and grease and of sumac, hemlock, jessamine, and milkweed.

Now the pain came in waves. She began to groan and suddenly was so weak she could barely stand. Holding to the wall, she knelt down by the mud and stick fireplace. She took a handful of twigs from beside the hearth, put them on the banked coals and ashes, fanned them with a slab of bark until smoke and flames wisped upward; then she put the kindling on and then four hickory logs. Slowly the flames rose, filling the room with light and shadows. The shadows of the small wooden animals leapt outward, touching her. From dozens of small pegs stuck into the wall chinking hung rags and rusty horseshoes. One wall was covered with dried herbs and roots. Above the fireplace was something shaped like an animal made from sticks and twists of yellow sedge. It had four legs, but no head. Two long sticks, like horns, came from its neck.

Claricy reached behind her back to the rope-bed, pulled a thin wool blanket off, and spread it on the rough plank floor in front of the fireplace. She sat on the blanket with her legs stretched out in front, braced herself with her hands behind her on the floor, then eased down onto her back, all the while sucking air fast and hard through her clenched teeth. Her water broke. It ran down between her hips, soaking through the blanket to the planks beneath. She raised her knees and strained with all her might, pushing against the floor with her splayed feet, squeezing the blanket in her fists, making a long high screech like an owl, over and over. Finally with one great push a piercing shriek rose from between her tightly clenched teeth, "Eeeeeeeee,!" and a bsby's head came out, and then the body, onto the blanket. It was slick and shiny and small, its tiny arms and legs squirming. It cried louder than an animal.

Claricy lay on her back, panting like a dog, letting her strength return. Within moments she sat up and looked down at the tiny girl who was wet with blood and birth fluid, and worth $200 to William Darwin the instant she drew her first breath.

Claricy stared and stared at the cord. She reached down and touched it with the forefinger of her right hand. She looked at her hand. It was rough as dried leather. With her thumb and forefinger she gently pulled the membrane off the baby's head and body, wadded it up in the palm of her hand, and pitched it into the fire where it hissed and burned.

She worked a thread loose from her dress, tied it around the cord next to the baby's stomach. Then, with her right hand she lifted the cord a few inches and with her left took the flint blade from the pocket, held its edge to the cord, and cut it.

And freed herself from what was not hers. Was his.

Now, for a long moment, she stared at the baby, watching it squirm, listening to it cry. Then, with both hands, she reached down and gently lifted it toward her face and blew into its eyes. For an instant it ceased to cry, and then its face wrinkled and it shook and began to cry louder. She put her face closer to the baby, almost touching it, and stared into its watery eyes, as though she might see something in the eyes, or even through them, something that would tell her what she was to do with it...but then it screamed a high piercing scream that did not stop. As the scream rose higher and higher, Claricy's eyes expanded and her face tightened until the bones in her jaws sharpened, Suddenly, she looked up at the being above the fireplace; and as she looked, her mouth moved as though she was speaking. Then she nodded to it four times without looking down; her arms and hands stretched out before her and she laid the baby into the fire.

Behind her, there was a sound. The air moved. She was thrown backward onto the floor. A shadow filled the room. "My God, you're burnin' your chile!" Elizabeth Darwin shouted. She stepped over Claricy, reached into the flames, burning her hands and forearms, and pulled the still-wet baby from the fire.

Elizabeth never forgot the horror that night. Every detail of it fixed in her mind. Even the smell. Long years later, when she was old, a baby's cry or flames from logs burning in the fireplace or the odor of ham or bacon frying could bring it back to her. When this happened, she would hear the baby's piercing scream that did not end. She would again feel the heat of the fire on her hands and face as she fell forward on her knees and, with her face almost in the fire, she would reach into the flames and grab an arm and pull it out; she would feel it thrashing and screaming in her arms; she would smell the blood from the birth and the burned flesh and hear her own voice screaming, "Oh God...Oh God...Oh God," as she ran down the dark lane past the slave cabins, across the backyard, up the steps onto the porch, and through the door into her house.

They named the baby Dock. She was the color of dark chocolate. As she grew older, the places on her skin where she had been burned, were as rough as the bark of an elm. In the second year of the war, William died and left Dock to his son Francis and his wife Nancy, who loved her.

Two years following Dock's birth, Claricy had a second baby girl; this one she killed.

1846

Trial transcript from the 1984 *Franklin County Historical Review.*

"State of Tennessee vs. Claricy,
A Slave For Life,
The Property of William Darwin

THE PRELIMINARY HEARING
At a March 3, 1846, hearing before Thomas Finch, a justice of the peace of Franklin County, the warrant was read, and the accused, Claricy, stated she was not guilty of the murder of her newborn child.

Elizabeth Darwin, wife of William Darwin, aged 53 or 54, a witness for the state testified:

She believes Clarisa to be the mother of the child that was killed as described in the warrant but she did not see it killed—and that the girl had found out where the child was hid in the field, the witness told her to go and get her child where she had hid it in the field which she did and brought it to the house, and washed it and cleaned the dirt off of it—and when the witness spoke to her about killing the child, she never shed a tear. . . . . that when she first saw the child in the field before it was removed that she herself turned it over and that there was some appearance of marks of violence having been used on the right side of the head and face of said child, which layed next to the ground the body of it only being partially covered with dirt.

Caty, a witness for the state, a Negro woman aged about 52 or 53, the property of William Darwin, testified:

On Sunday night 22nd February 1846 about common bedtime that Clarisa, a negro woman on trial lived in the same house with her, left the house and was gone some half hour or perhaps not so long, and before she left the house she had every appearance of being in a family way and when she returned she had every appearance of having delivered a child. The witness then accused her of having killed or destroyed her child, and she denied having had the child at that time. The witness then made known on the next morning early being the 23rd of February 1846 to her mistress, Mrs. Darwin, what had taken place the over night, and her suspicions that Clarisy having had a child and destroyed or killed it the over night—after search was made, and the child found in the field, she Clarisy went and got her child in the field when it was found and brought it to the house and acknowledged that it was her child, but denied killing it, and when she was questioned by witness how she could do an act of that kind, the defendant Clarisy replied and said that it was none of witness loss, that it was the loss of the white folks.

A son of Mr. Darwin, Thomas J. Darwin, aged about 19 years, a witness for the state, testified:

On Monday morning the 23rd February 1846 that witness was out in the cotton field with Clarisa and the balance of his Fathers hands picking out cotton, and Witnesses mother sent out for him to bring Clarisa to the house; before witness sent Clarisa to the house, he had heard that she had a child and had hid it in the fields, and witness asked her if she had killed another child of hers, to which she replied that she had had a child but said she did not kill it-witness further states that it was a female child.

James M. Darwin testified that evidence given by his brother, Thomas J. Darwin, was in substance what he knew.

Richard Sharp Jr., aged about 27 years, a witness for the state, testified that he was one of the jury of inquest held by William Reeves, J.P., on the 23rd of February, 1846, and that

. . . . in company with the Jury went to the negro cabin where Clarisa was on Wm. Darwin premises where she now lives, witness then asked Clarisy why she murdered her child, to that she gave no positive reply; witness then asked her if she struck the child's head against that rock, which lay near where the child was found, she said that she did not; witness then asked her if she tramped on the child, she said she did not, witness then heard T. N. Holt, one of the Jury asked Clarisy if the child cried after she had it, to that she said that it did, but that it could not have been heard further than to a certain bed in the house, which was not more than 10 to 12 feet off. Witness then asked her how she came to murder her child, to which she gave no direct answer, but said clasping her hands together I did so to its head.

After the preliminary hearing, Elizabeth Darwin, Thomas J. Darwin, James M. Darwin and Richard Sharp Jr., and William Darwin "for his negro woman" made bonds for their personal appearances at the next term of the Circuit Court for Franklin County on "Thursday the 4th day of the Term" to give evidence in behalf of the State of Tennessee in a suit for murder pending against Claricy.

THE GRAND JURY HEARING—MAY 4, 1846

This day the Grand Jury returned into court an indictment against Claricy a negro slave the property of William Darwin for murder, in the words and figures as follows to-wit:

The Grand Jurors for the State of Tennessee elected empanelled sworn and charged to enquire for the body of the County of Franklin and State aforesaid, upon their oath aforesaid present that Claricy a negro woman a slave for life the property of William Darwin, of said county, not having the fear of God before her eyes but being moved and seduced by the instigation of the Devil on the twenty-third day of February in the year of our Lord eighteen hundred and forty-six with force and arms in the county and State aforesaid in and upon a certain female infant child (it being the infant of her the said Claricy) of color a slave the property of said William Darwin of said County in the peace of God and of the State of Tennessee then and there being feloniously, willfully, deliberately, premeditatedly and of her malice aforethought did make an assault and that the said Claricy a certain stone of no value which she the said Claricy in both her hands then and there held in and upon the right side of the head and face of her the said infant child as aforesaid then and there feloniously, willfully deliberately and premeditatedly and of her malice aforethought did hit and strike and that the said Claricy did then and there give unto her the said female infant child by such striking at her and the stone aforesaid one mortal bruise. She the said female infant child then and there instantly died. And so the jurors aforesaid upon their oaths aforesaid do say that the said Claricy her the said female infant child in the manner and by the means aforesaid feloniously willfully deliberately premeditatedly and of her malice aforethought did kill and murder in the first degree against the form of the statue in such case made and provided and against the peace and dignity of the State.

The grand jury further indicted Claricy for murder of the infant female child by striking and bruising said child with her right hand, kicking, beating, and throwing her to the ground, assaulting her with both hands, and with beating and squeezing her, and giving the child one mortal bruise on the head and temple, two inches long and two inches wide, from all of which the infant child instantly died...

THE FIRST DAY OF THE TRIAL—MAY 7, 1846

This day came Joseph W. Carter, Esqr. the Attorney General who prosecutes for the State in this behalf and the said Claricy a slave for life the property of William Darwin is brought to the bar of the court in custody of the Sheriff, who being arraigned upon the Indictment aforesaid pleads Not Guilty...

THE TRIAL, SECOND DAY—MAY 8, 1846

This day again came Joseph W. Carter, Esqr., the Attorney General who prosecutes for the State in this behalf and the said Claricy is brought to the bar of the court in custody of the Sheriff of Franklin County and thereupon again came the same jury... who after hearing all the evidence, argument of the counsel and receiving a charge from the Court, upon their oath do say that the said Claricy a slave for life the property of William Darwin is Guilty of the Murder in the first degree, of the said female infant child in manner and form as charged in said bill of indictment. Ordered that the said Claricy be remanded to Jail.

THE SENTENCING—MAY 13, 1846

...It is therefore considered by the Court that the said Claricy be taken hence to the jail of Franklin County, from whence she came, and be there securely kept until Friday, the 12th day of June next and that on that day she be taken thence to the common gallows of said County which gallows is to be within one-half mile of the town of Winchester, and there, between the hours of Eleven o'clock in the forenoon, and Three o'clock in the afternoon, of the same day, be hanged by the neck, until she be dead; and that the Sheriff of Franklin County do execution of this sentence.

On September 12, 1846, James W. Williamson, jailer of Franklin County, came into court and presented an account for boarding "one negro woman named Clarisy from the 12th day of June, 1846, until the 3rd day of August, 1846, or 52 days at 37 1/2 cents, and two turnkeys, making a total of $20.50."

What happened to Claricy? As of August 3, 1846, she apparently was still alive. *The Review*'s editors conclude that:

...It is indeed doubtful that she was ever executed. The owner was no doubt a man of influence in the county. He probably did not condone one slave's destroying another, no matter how young, nor presumably would he have condoned murder and violence on his own property (and by his own property). On the other hand, he certainly would not have relished the idea of hanging a prime field hand whose value was certainly in the several hundreds of dollars.

Still, she may have finally been executed. But, if not, surely William didn't bring her back to Buzzard Roost. His solution (one the court might have agreed to, pending the county being paid for all its costs) was likely the tried-and-true one for problem slaves. She was probably sold to a buyer who, if they knew nothing about her killing her baby, would have paid over a $1,000.00 for a strong worker and breeder. Dead, she was worth nothing. Alive, she was a valuable piece of property.

1918

The waters in Wagner Creek still flow through the land that once was Buzzard Roost into Elk River, a small river that curves slowly across Franklin County toward the Cumberland Plateau at the southern end of the Great Basin of Middle Tennessee; there it turns west, then south into Alabama where the waters enter the Tennessee River.

Almost from the first my wife's people lived here – many remain in this beautiful country. Three generations of them can be seen in a photograph made in the summer of 1918.

In the picture are ten descendants of William and Elizabeth Darwin. They have come together on a Sunday afternoon at Nancy Darwin Pearson's: three generations of Darwins, Pearsons and Lynches, all kin by blood, marriage, or slavery. The photograph was most likely made on Sunday. All are dressed in their "Sunday-go-to-Meeting" clothes; they've come to Grandma Pearson's straight from the Winchester Church of Christ services. They've finished dinner and visited awhile on the front porch. Now they're having their picture made before they start home. Jessie, who is the oldest Lynch girl and extremely bright and funny, is not among them. I think she is the photographer.

The sun has started going down, its light is almost directly in their faces, the rays are slanted under the porch roof and are rising up the wall, moving the roof's shadow upward. The day is coming to an end.

In the photograph, sitting with the children is a small, neat, black woman: Dock Darwin. She is seventy-three. A smile hints on her face and her eyes squint against the bright sun. She will be totally blind the last year of her life. Her hands, the right one over the left, are clasped exactly like the hands of Nancy Pearson who stands behind her. Dock is six years older, though she looks sixteen years younger. These two old women were raised together, they live together and will take care of one another the last years of their lives. The year before Dock dies in 1933, they will live in the home of Frank and Leah Lynch - Nancy's daughter. Leah stands in the middle beside her mother; Frank, who will serve as Franklin County's judge for many years, is almost hidden in the back left corner.

Photograph courtesy of George Spain
Dock Darwin sitting on the front with the children,
the little girl is Katrine ("Trini") Leah, Lynck, Burton,.
Behind her is her mother Leah Pearson Lynch—
to her left is her mother Nancy Darwin Pearson

The three Lynch children, sitting in front, grow up to be good people, each one a success. Pat, the little boy shielding his eyes from the sun, follows in his father's footsteps, as do his three sons. The firm's name becomes Lynch, Lynch, and Lynch, a word suggesting a bad outcome for the guilty. Pat becomes a highly regarded state senator and will be considered for governor, but contracts multiple sclerosis in his fifties.

The pretty girl is Leah Katrine -- "Trinie" -- my wife's mother. When she is grown, many consider her to be the most beautiful and kindest woman in Tennessee. When she is 79, and near death, she asks a grandson and grandson-in-law to come to her. As they kneel beside her bed, she whispers to them. After she dies they are both baptized.

Jack is the boy in the white collar sitting beside Dock. He graduates from West Point, serves in the army, and then becomes an aide to Tennessee's congressional Senator Albert Gore, Sr. In his eighties, he writes LYNCH-PEARSON, a brief history of his family in which he tells some of his memories of Dock, though he misspells her name as "Doc":

"When emancipation came to Middle Tennessee, Doc had no place to go. She was a member of the Darwin family and stayed on, occupying the same status that many widowed aunts and old-maid cousins held in those days – something of an unpaid servant. At some point, Doc moved in with Grandma Pearson, probably when Grandma married [1873]. Doc helped take care of my mother when she was young and regarded me and my siblings as her own. And in a letter to me in 2007 Jack wrote, "She always knew her position—a little below that of a widowed aunt who might be taken in but expected to do more than just casually help out with household chores...My first memories of Doc go back to the winter of 1919-20. (She would have been 74.) She seemed to do all the work—cooking, scrubbing floors, chopping wood...Doc received good treatment by all the family, but one of our black cooks resented her. She put salt in the sugar bowl Doc was using and had to be fired."

I have long pondered Dock's unusual and, in some ways, wonderful life. It began with her mother: trying to kill her, throwing her into a fire, thus scarring her forever. She was born a slave. She lived through the Civil War and the long hardships that followed. She lived through the terrors of the Klan. She never married, never had a child. For her whole, long life, everything she had was given by her white family. They had owned her, and named her; and when she was free, they kept her with them, as Jack said, "as an unpaid servant (who) always knew her position."

But surely they loved her. She made their lives easier and helped raise several generations of their babies. Many in the photograph, both the grim adults and the happy children, she rocked and fed. Her hands bathed them and changed their diapers. Did she think of them as her family? Did she tell them she loved them? Did they tell her?

Trinie was the last of the five generations in her family who knew Dock. She told us, "I saw the scars on her from the fire. She probably would have been burned worse, or died, if she hadn't been wet from just being born... Her feet were so little she could only wear children's high-top button shoes." If Dock's feet could be seen in the picture, they would probably be bare. You cannot see any scars on her face and hands.

Jack writes that nine years after this day, "Grandma and Doc came to live with my parents for about a year. By this time Doc was rather feeble and blind. She and Grandma spent most of the time sitting in front of the fireplace dipping snuff and talking about old times."

The Lynch home is gone now. I was in it many times while "Mother" Lynch was alive. I saw the fireplace that Nancy and Dock sat in front of, "talking about old times." As I imagine them sitting there, question after question comes to my mind: Did they ever talk about Claricy? Elizabeth? Slavery and the war? Did Dock try to cover her scars, did she look at them, touch them, or wonder why her mother tried to kill her? Did she forgive her? Did she want to have a baby, to suckle, to name? Did she ever ask God why?

In the photo, Nancy and Dock are so close they can touch one another. Their children and grandchildren are all around them. Two old, southern women who lived when black people were property, were bought and sold, and owned like cattle by white people who believed in God and Jesus. They lived through a Civil War that killed 600,000 people and freed 6,000,000 slaves. They lived through years of fear and hardship and survived together. Now in their old age, they take care of one another. An old white woman and an old black woman, with their hands clasped together exactly alike. It is 1918, the last year of WWI. They live on into the Great Depression. Dock is the first to die.

BURIED BY SIDE OF
HER OLD MISTRESS
Decherd, Tenn. Oct. 24--(Special)

"Dock" Darwin, a Negress of the ante-bellum days, died Thursday night after only a few days illness of pneumonia at the home of Judge and Mrs. Frank Lynch at Winchester. "Dock", as she was affectionately called, belonged to Mr. and Mrs. F. M. Darwin during slavery days and never left them until they died. Then she went to live with Mrs., Darwin's only daughter, Mrs. J. P. Pearson. When Mrs. Pearson's health failed about one year ago she and "Dock" both went to live with Mrs. Frank Lynch, a daughter of Mrs. Pearson. "Dock" was always of sunny disposition; and though she lost her sight about one year, she never complained. She was buried at the Darwin cemetery Friday, afternoon beside the grave of her old Mistress."

– *The Winchester Chronicle*, 1933

2011

Since Dock gave the Darwins and their descendants her life and love, it was fitting that they bury her with them. There is no stone in the Darwin Cemetery with the name Dock Darwin, but I am sure that she is there. In August,

1935, Nancy died. Five months later her great-granddaughter, Jacquelyn Katrine Burton, my wife, was born. 138 years after Elizabeth Darwin, the saver (or savior) of Dock Darwin, died, her great-great-great-great-great granddaughter, Leah Katrine Flynn, types this manuscript.

From left: Jacqulyn Katrine Burton Spain, Leah Person Lynch,
Katrine Leah Lynch Burton (holding the baby) and
Elizabeth Katrine Spain Flynn— Her daughter Leah Flynn
typed the manuscript for "Clarisy's babies".
Photograph courtesy of George Spain

Aftermath

Allen Rhody

Oh hearts' blood purged forevermore
In the name of industry and opposing beliefs,
Oh hearts' blood drained from the tens of thousands,
hundreds of thousands of young lives and life's promises,
What sacrifice can be worth so much as that
so many are gone from this earth forever?

death and freedom, death and freedom, death and freedom

We live our 'normal' lives now in the after years.
Some have been raised to do battle in other ways
Of the mind and the spirit in the hopes of
No more hatred and others the perpetuation of it.
Are we not able to move on?
Are we not able to co-exist in respect to one another as
    humans?

Humans, death and freedom, humans, death and freedom

Defending America?

Bobby Calabrese

They traveled the Pikes
North and then South
Columbia, Franklin, and Granny White.
The Blue you know
      they fought for the Union
The Grey for the precedence
of their valued States Rights.
Some roads were of dirt;
Others anchored by nails.
Strategic position,
Wagons, men, and supplies,
They deployed along these roads,
Awaiting their own terrible mournful cries.
Plaster footprints of blood
      left in the icy mud
By the shoeless Army of Tennessee.
Oh Lord Your north-wind blows
      a rainy winter freeze
And men bend heavy tracks of iron
      round Your rooted trees.
Cross and re-cross so many swollen creeks,
And the importance of the rivers
Had always been foreseen:
The Duck, Harpeth, and Cumberland
And that larger Tennessee,
      Barriers
Respites of sanctuary.
Hood and Davis fight to recapture
The stoic hills of their Confederacy.
The stench of so much suffering
      will permeate Middle Tennessee.

Keep Johnny Reb
from the "Gateway to the West"
Pushing flanking marching men
All brothers
All American.
Maneuver to Columbia,
An ominous battle within Spring Hill,
But the Grey and Butternut, Brown and Cheatham
Too long did they stay still
The cautious Federal Schofield
escapes through darkened hills
To Franklin's breastworks
Where Hood's boys did come and pay
old ugly Satan's bill.
A frontal move in Grey
Divisions and brigades
Thousands maimed
Thousands dead
The open ground slickened red
Hand to hand
Rifle butts and bayonets
Trench burials dug
For the slaughtered Grey regiments
Twisted carnage
The foulness of step-laddered bodies.
Six Southern generals breath their last
With their valiant CSA thousands

Battle on you Grey of Franklin
To Nashville to meet Thomas
Your memories remain here
In so many weathered old-stone monuments
Though others died believing
Their colors flew high and true.
The little town of Franklin pays no homage
To the Americans who wore the Blue.
March again the rutted pikes
For Nashville and a final fight
With Forrest's cavalrymen away
Thomas's flanking moves carry the day.
Cold cold December skies
A routed army had been surprised.
Close your eyes
Dream no more of the glorious "Cause"
Pass south again to Alabama
Without the bands
Or the grateful applause.
Forrest returns to check your safety,
The weather a bitter cold blessing.
Open your eyes
The righteousness of Providence declares it to be so
That on this 12th day of December
In Middle Tennessee snow
Hood's remnants will vacate Nashville
And move south on those icy roads.
No more will there be glory
For the wrecked Army of Tennessee
Those Americans who fought
For an old Southern Liberty.

Now Glory Halleluiah
Mine eyes can truly see
That once again we will be Union
The brothers we were meant to be
Together
From the shores of the Great Lake Erie
To the not forgotten cotton land
That place we know as Dixie.

Don't leave Tennessee that way.

What about Tennessee today?

The Yankees have come again
Ohio, Illinois, Indiana, and Michigan
Dead brothers who had fought hand to hand
Now live and fight
Hand in hand
In Iraq and in Afghanistan.
Praise God we are that Union
Patriots
Brothers
Descendants
Of the Great American Revolution.

Author's Note: My poem is dedicated to Mr. Wiley Sword and his all-encompassing work on the decisive battles of our Civil War that took place in Middle Tennessee 1864., entitled *The Confederacy's Last Hurrah: Spring Hill, Franklin, and Nashville.*

Excavations

B.C. Nance

The gentle scrape of the archaeologist's trowel in the soil,
Peeling back the layers of time,
Weaving together the tapestry of history,
The stories woven with warp and weft
Of bullets, buttons, and fragments of bone.

Photograph by Ben Nance

Remember

Arch Boyd Brown

If you hear Lexington and Concord
And only think of places,
Of Gettysburg and Chancellorsville,
And you don't see the faces

Of those who paid the dearest price
To keep our country free,
Then you look into this soldier's eyes
And you do not see me.

If you hear Anzio and Normandy
And don't appreciate the cost,
Then you'll never know what might have been:
A world to tyranny lost.

If you think Midway or Inchon are only a name,
Then you cannot value the burning flame
Of freedom's passion in this land
Where liberty's sons have made their stand.

If you hear Khe Sanh or "Hamburger Hill"
And your soul doesn't get a chill,
Then history's lessons may not be learned
And you may lose the freedoms that others have earned.

So honor those patriots who've stood in the breach,
And vigilance to your children teach
To cherish their freedom and what has been endured
For history remembered is freedom secured!

Author's note: written for Memorial Day 2010

The Tract

Randy Foster

What bodies lie beneath the growing weeds?
What sabers rust in soil unturned by plow?
The tree knows naught of old heroic deeds
But only grows in its eternal now.
The earth turns in its slow, diurnal course,
Uncaring of the battle here once fought.
It hides remains of soldier and of horse,
Forgetting them without a single thought.
So, should this plot remain always unmarred,
Unchanged, untouched by any human hand?
Will ghosts of long-dead warriors stand on guard
And hover in dour vigil o'er this land?
Or will the march of progress claim this tract
Before the caring ever deign to act?

Photograph by Randy Foster

"The Tract" was inspired by Robert McCurley's photograph, "Civil War Battlefield"

7 SPIRITS

Photograph by Randy Foster

Spirited

Louise Strang

Sometimes I hear them call my name.
The unexpected interruption halts
The mild purpose of that moment.

From a distance and clearly
From the past
Reaching forward
Obscure images
With heads tilted back
Their lifeless breath
Carries a consonant and
The vowels of my name
Ride on air.

My very breath suspends its flow
Prolonging the quiet
Longing and listening for more.

I move forward through the tears
Past the precious sting of connection
Until I am alone again.

Sometimes I hear them call
My name.

Somewhere a Rooster Crowed in the Darkness

Sandy Zeigler

It was October 1864, and we stood on our front porch and watched as bout ready to move on?" uniformed men on horseback made their way up our dirt road, Folsom Road. I was eleven years old. Stewart, my little brother, stood close beside me. I used to call him Stewpid. He doesn't like that much, now he's eight.

"Are they us or them?"

"They're them," I said.

Stewart yanked my pants. "Henry, we better go inside. Where's Zinia?"

Stewart had no sooner gotten her name out than Zinia came bustling through the door. She must have run from the garden. It was warm for a late Tennessee October, and she was trying to find greens, apples, anything else she could store up for winter.

Our pa was an engineer for the Rebel Railroad and had taken a locomotive to Virginia. There were no two ways about it, he had to go but promised he'd be back as soon as he could. He made Zinia swear on her life that she'd look after all of us while he was gone. He gave her his Colt pistol, and she hid it somewhere. She never told anybody where it was, and it was never discovered until she handed it to Pa when he came back from Virginia. "I allowed as how it wouldn't do for me to be shootin' somebody. Either way you figure it, it'd be me what wound up in the jail house or at the end of a rope."

Zinia was hot and sweat escaped her twisted white head scarf and trickled down her dark brown forehead. She studied the line of soldiers in blue. As she tried to catch her breath, she rested her hands on Stewart's shoulders.

"Maybe they'll go on by," Zinia said in a low whisper that almost sounded like a prayer. We watched. "Lordy me, if they ain't turnin' into our yard."

"We got to go in the house," Stewart said as he tried to bolt around Zinia, but she held onto his shoulders and didn't let him move.

There were nine men on horseback, plus a leader with stripes on his sleeves; and they trotted on each side of two rumbling, empty wagons. Oatmeal-colored dust boiled up behind them as they rode, brazen as could be, past the hitchin' post, right on up to our front porch. They didn't say a thing. The man in front with stripes on his sleeves got off his horse and walked up to where we stood. He did not even remove his slouch hat, and he rested his hand on his sword like he thought he might have to use it soon.

"Where are the men in this household?"

Odd, I was always taught to first remove my hat, and then say 'how-do' and 'how 're you and yours?' He'd sure be in trouble with my Mama.

"They ain't none...right today," Zinia said as she lifted her chin and looked down her nose at him.

The leader-man smiled, "Well, all the better."

He turned and yelled at his men, "Search every building, garden, and that orchard. Get whatever food you can find and load it in the wagons."

The men dismounted and spread out. Some went toward the barn while others headed toward the smokehouse, the kitchen, and behind the house. None of them looked at us.

"What's in the house to eat?" the man said.

"Jes' some food I has for the chidrens," Zinia said. "The Missus is upstairs in the bed with a new baby. Born 'bout six week ago. Missus be very sick. Ain't no need to be botherin' her."

"I'll decide that."

The men pulled the wagons up to the smokehouse and loaded the two hams and three slabs of bacon we had left.

"What they gonna do with our bacon?" Stewart looked up at Zinia's pensive face.

"They gonna take it and eat it. They hongry."

"But if they take everything, what we gonna eat?"

"Hush up now."

"But look at the barn. They're takin' all the feed, and what they leadin' Mary Moo up here for?" Stewart had named her himself. "And they're loadin' all the corn outta the crib. All of it."

Zinia straightened her back. "Hummmp! Well," she turned to the leader-man and took a deep breath, "I...I'd appreciate it, suh, if you'd jes' leave that one milk cow. She's the onliest way we got of feedin' that new baby. Without Mary's milk, that baby gonna die. She don't get nothin' from her mama."

"Madam, I am Sergeant Thomas Everett Jenssen, Ohio Cavalry, United States Army, at your service." He tipped his hat to Zinia and laughed. I wasn't sure whether he was laughing at Zinia or at himself. A few of the soldiers laughed half-heartedly. They seemed tired.

"I was ordered to take everything, everything that can be eaten from this area. I was ordered to fill those wagons. It is my duty to follow orders and I intend to do just that. Your interest in that cow is not my concern."

Zinia put her hands in her apron pockets, and I could see big fists pushing down the pockets, straining the straps over her shoulders.

It was almost dark by the time the Union soldiers had loaded up everything out of the smokehouse, every bit of corn, jams, jellies, even a plate of biscuits. Sergeant Jenssen ordered the men to bring over the horses they rode in on and let them eat corn right outta the back of the wagon. Horses aren't very neat eaters so yellow corn kernels fell on the mossy soil around their feet. They crunched and chewed until they were pretty well satisfied.

"We're gonna set up camp on your yard here. We'll leave at daybreak to make our way to Nashville. We'll capture the chickens in the morning."

Sergeant Jenssen ordered the men to build a fire and cook up something for their dinner. He directed four men to line up the loaded wagons near the smokehouse and well away from the fire.

We sat in the near-dark kitchen in stunned silence.

"What we gonna eat, Zinia?" Stewart took one of her large dark hands in his small white ones and looked up at her. She waited and listened, then with a big grin she slowly and quietly got up from her chair and exaggerated a tiptoe to the wood cook stove. She looked like a big ole cat sneaking up on a little bitty mouse. We giggled.

As she opened the squeaky oven door, she whispered, "I left these biscuits in here this mornin'. Them big ole smart boys didn't think to look inside the stove. We gonna sit right here and eat one biscuit each, then I'll take one up to yo mama and that's gonna have to do tonight. Tomorrow I'll think of somethin' else." A wicked smile crossed her face. "I jes' wanna be sure to be out in the mornin' and watch them boys try to catch them chickens. Don't wanna miss that, no siree."

"What about the baby...Sarah?" I still wasn't used to someone new in the house.

"When it's good and dark, I may sneak out there and get a little milk from Mary, and then I can always give Sarah water with honey in it." She seemed to be taking inventory of the possibilities. "They's a little jar of honey upstairs sittin' with yo mama's perfume bottles. They didn't think nothin' of that. I can soak a rag in warm honey and she can suck on that. It helps just to have somethin' in her little stomach."

"Look! What is it?" Stewart yelled from the parlor. He had been chewing the last of his biscuit and watching from the parlor window as the soldiers bedded down in our front yard. "What's on fire?" Stewart was breathless and his eyes were wide. Zinia and I hurried to the window. On the next farm, flames lit the sky and living sparks shot up and caught in bare trees, trees that looked like Spanish lace against an orange sky.

"What you reckon is burnin'?" I said.

"Looks like it's got to be the Woodley place. Maybe the barn and the house." Zinia shook her head, "Got to fight fire with fire," she whispered to herself. We watched until the glow dimmed. Stewart had fallen asleep on the parlor floor, and the soldiers were like lifeless mounds on the front yard.

"Seems like somethin' real bad gonna happen. I feel it comin'," Zinia whispered to herself, her breath making a ghostly pattern on the window pane.

When the front yard had been quiet for awhile and a late moon eased among the clouds, a hunched-over, shadowy figure could barely be seen moving in the darkness. It carried a flickering lantern, crouched around the wagons and between the horses. The ghostly form set to work untying Mary Moo and then quickly untying the horses. As the specter held Mary's rope, a horse snorted and shifted its weight, not quite realizing it was free. The shape froze. Two or three soldiers turned over in their sleep.

When the men and horses had settled down again, the phantom went back to work leading Mary Moo to the fence where it tethered her, well away from the wagons. The cow began munching on weeds and the shape returned to the wagons.

On the wagon bed, the shadow worked quickly, scraping, heaping, and scratching. Then the ghostly form stood back and tossed a flaming twig onto the dried loot on the wagons. The smell of coal oil came and went immediately. At first, there were a few tentative flames and thin spirals of smoke. The shadow blew on the embers until in an instant the first

Spirits

wagon burst into a ravenous torch. The second wagon ignited. The greasy meat, the dried corn and wheat were fodder for the greedy, lapping flames. Untied horses whinnied and bolted, galloping over bedroll lumps as they went. They ran toward Folsom Road and disappeared in the darkness. Mary Moo jerked her head up, strained against the rope and turned to watch the blaze that reflected in her startled eyes.

The men jumped up with their blankets and tried to smother the flames; but the fire had taken control, and finally they had to stand back and watch as the wagons, first one, then the other, collapsed into fiery heaps. Only the metal rims of the wooden wheels and a few metal braces and bolts survived.

The dark shadow was nowhere to be seen.

Somewhere a rooster crowed in the darkness.

Zinia watched the flaming wagons from the front porch as she pulled a man's work shirt over her nightgown. Stewart and I shivered in our nightshirts. Stewart rubbed his eyes. The dark sky was slowly givin' way to light.

"Damn you, woman, you're in a world of trouble now," the sergeant threw his blanket on the ground.

"Me? What'd I do?" Zinia's eyes surveyed the commotion in the yard.

"All because of that cussed cow, isn't it? All because of that cow."

"What you talkin' 'bout Mary for? I didn't move that cow and I didn't turn them horses loose. If I was gonna get Mary, I'da hid her somewheres; and come to that, what would I stand to gain by burnin' them wagons anyway?"

Zinia's voice was getting louder. Stewart and I moved behind Zinia; we knew better than to be in front. If the soldier didn't believe her, we did.

"Damn!" Jenssen spit on the ground, folded his arms across his chest and watched the men as they collected

229

dropped kernels of corn into their hats. Abruptly, Jenssen pounded his fist onto a porch post. "All right then, was it the two of you? You skinny, ignorant, flea-bitten little Confederate...devils." He shook his pointin' finger in our faces as we tried to sink further behind Zinia.

I felt my face getting hot. Seemed like somebody needed to say somethin', even if it was wrong. I stepped out from behind Zinia. "I didn't do it and Stewart didn't do it either." Stewart puffed out his lower lip and shook his head. I was jes' gettin' my steam, "It's for sure Zinia didn't burn them wagons. Zinia couldn'ta moved that fast."

I'da said more if I'da had my clothes on.

"All right, then..." Jenssen made his hands into hard fists. He lowered his voice and leaned over to look me straight in the eye. He hissed, "All right, who burned those wagons? Who? Who?"

A tear rolled down Stewart's cheek.

I don't know what came over me. Trembling from cold or fright or both, I whispered, "I'm thinkin' it was that Pig Face."

"What? What did you say?" Jenssen was squeezing my arm before I had time to think.

"P...Pig Face." My heart was thundering in my ears. "Pig Face Marlin. I'm jes' sayin', he probably done it."

"Who the hell is Pig Face Marlin?"

"He...he's a spook," I said. "He used to live somewhere around here a long time ago...when he was alive. He spooks 'round these parts all the time. When he got killed, he was tryin' to set fire to a neighbor's barn. Had real good horses in it too. The neighbor shot him dead. He's set fire to lots of buildings around here ever since." I got my second wind, "And...and then awhile back he set fire to that burned up cedar tree out in the pig lot." I pointed behind the house with a shivering finger. "He set fire to the kitchen one time too, and he opens stall doors all the time. The horses and the mule get out and we have to chase 'em all over the place." I hesitated to catch my breath. "He does bad, bad things and...and he's awful ugly. Why, he even scares the horses."

I could have gone on and on, but something was happening. I felt the air shifting. The sergeant's attention had moved away from me.

"Sir, the messenger jes' come up and he says our platoon is leaving for Nashville right now. It's practically daylight. We gotta meet up with them and head on up to Nashville too...uh, Sir." A young private was standing in the yard and offering Jenssen his coat. The sergeant released his grip on my arm. He stared blankly at the private for a moment and then, turning back to me, he said, "A spook you say? Do you really expect me to believe that?"

"Well, I know didn't none of us do it. Me and Stewart are just ignorant, flea-bitten Confederate devils, and...and y'all didn't do it, so Pig Face is the only one I can think of. He just likes to set things on fire. Coulda been him that set that big fire last night, ain't that so, Zinia?"

Zinia covered her face with her hands. It was hard to know if she was laughing or crying. "Oh, that's the truth if ever I heard it." Zinia's voice was muffled behind her hands.

The sergeant stepped off the porch and picked up his blanket. "Saddle up whatever horses are in the barn and try to round up as many of ours as you can. We've got to get to Nashville. We can't waste any more time on this idiotic bunch of...".

The men didn't wait for him to finish. Two soldiers gathered up their blankets, guns, canteens, knapsacks and hurried toward the barn. A young private ran from behind the house, "Sir, me and Horton and Evers been a-chasin' them hens and we ain't caught a one yet. Rooster purty nigh tore up ol' Evers. You wouldn't thank a chicken could do such as that." The private stopped to catch his breath. "You want us to keep on tryin'?"

"Forget the chickens," Jenssen glared back at us.

The smell of burned wagons and charred meat became an acrid part of every breath we took, and the sun was getting higher over our front yard. The hungry baby screamed upstairs. Horses were saddled and the men began organizing themselves into travel formation when the sergeant turned in his saddle.

"Hold up! You, Simmons, Gardner, come with me." The two men dismounted and rushed to keep up with the sergeant.

Zinia blocked the open front door. "Lordy, Lordy, there ain't nothin' left. What ya'll be awantin' now?"

"Move out of the way!"

Zinia stepped aside and the three men hurried up the stairs. Zinia, Stewart and I followed. Jenssen threw open the door to the room where Mama frantically clutched baby Sarah. They were huddled on Mama's big mahogany tester bed that was a wedding gift from her parents.

"Now, why you botherin' that pore woman?" Zinia hurried through the door behind the men.

Startled and trembling, Mama tried to sit up. Her face was as pale as the sheets she was lyin' on.

Without looking at my mother or the baby, Jenssen coldly ordered, "Pick them up in the sheet and set them on the floor." Gardner hesitated, looked at the sergeant's hellbent expression, and then carefully lifted the linens behind Mama's head while Simmons pulled up the sheets at the foot of the bed. Together they lowered her and Sarah to the floor.

"What...what are you doing?" Mama frantically squirmed as she tried to cover herself and Sarah with a quilt.

"Mama! Mama!" Stewart sobbed and threw his arms around her neck, burying his face in her shoulder. The baby jerked and wriggled her fingers in and out of tiny fists, but she didn't start cryin' again. She sucked in her lower lip and a big leftover tear slowly materialized in the corner of one eye.

Spirits

The sergeant walked around the room, looking under things and behind furniture.

"Get the mattresses and drag them downstairs," Jenssen said. The two soldiers pulled and tugged. Dust swirled and floated in and out of a shaft of sunlight.

"I'm sorry, ma'am," Gardner whispered as he dragged the straw mattress past Mama.

"Step lively," Jenssen said as he glowered at Gardner. The sergeant, Simmons, and Gardner hurried down the steps dragging the mattresses behind them. Stunned, Mama and Zinia stared after them.

"Throw 'em in the yard and tear 'em apart," Jenssen barked.

Zinia stayed in the bedroom to help Mama while I ran down the stairs behind the straw mattresses and feather bedding.

"Why? Why?" I yelled as I leapt down the steps two at a time, but Jenssen didn't answer.

"Why are you doin' this?" I wished I knew where Zinia had hidden Pa's pistol.

The men set to ripping and tearing the mattresses; and, under Jenssen's orders, they poked around in the confusion of feathers, straw, and muslin. "Set 'em afire when you finish going through that mess." So the smell of burned feathers fused with the ruinous odor of charred meat.

"They just ain't nothin' here, Sergeant. Nothin'," a private said as he leaned on a rake he had been using to prod the piles of what had rapidly become rags and trash. White goose feathers floated in the breeze and turned gold in the morning sun.

"Damned southern trash," the sergeant muttered as he mounted his horse. The squad followed him at a gallop down Folsom Road toward Franklin Pike. Ashes and bits of muslin were scattered all over our front yard. Mary Moo balked and bawled but was tied to a horse and forced to join the march.

Private Gardner rode close by me. His saddle creaked as he leaned down and confided, "He was looking for hidden treasure. Weren't none."

I coulda told him that.

"Go on out there and scratch up every one of them kernels of corn off that ground," Zinia handed me a milk bucket and Stewart a bowl. "You stop pickin' up corn and I'll be right in behind you. You'll be beggin' me to let you pick up corn."

Zinia stood for a moment and stared toward the barn. "Least we gonna have eggs," she said to herself and then started laughing, a deep, throaty laugh, until tears ran down her cheeks.

As I bent over the spilled corn, I looked up to see Zinia in the orchard with a basket, inspectin' apples that the soldiers had left behind. She carefully whittled off any rotten spots and dropped the good parts in the basket. Occasionally, she started laughing all over again.

That night Stewart and I sat at the kitchen table and chewed boiled corn and potatoes until they became mush.

"Aw, Zinia, I wanna swallow it down," Stewart said.

"No siree, don't you swallow. Got to be real soft so this baby'll take it."

The smell of cooking apples sweetened the kitchen.

A single candle illuminated the top of our round oak table. Zinia held the bowl, and we spat out our mushy offering. She dipped her little finger into the porridge, stirred and then pushed it into Sarah's tiny mouth. Sarah sucked, smacked, gurgled and finally swallowed.

"That's a good baby, Sarah."

"Sarah is indebted to Zinia for her life," Pa would say as Sarah grew up into a tow-headed girl who was all arms and legs.

Once baby Sarah seemed satisfied, Zinia began rocking back and forth in the straight-backed chair. The baby almost disappeared in her ample arms. "You got to go down to the Estes' tomorrow and see if they still got a cow. Alright now, what made you think of ol' Pig Face?" Zinia said.

"I don't know. Just wanted to get the attention off us."

Zinia looked at me and even in the candlelight I could see the mischief in her eyes.

"All right, Mr. Smarty Pants, did you burn them wagons? Was it you done that?"

"Well...it was you said, 'Fight fire with fire'."

"Mercy," Zinia said. She laughed to herself and shook her head.

"When do you reckon Pa'll come back from Virginia?"

"Don't know for sure. Sho do hope it's soon."

I sat straight against my ladder-back chair and watched the dancing candle flame.

I lie in the mahogany bed where my mother had languished with Sarah, my newborn sister, way back in October 1864. It's been seventy years and most everybody who could remember those days is gone. But I can still see the confusion and fear on my mama's face. Every time I light a fire in the fireplace, I smell burning wagons. I can still hear Zinia cackling to herself when the thought of stumbling soldiers chasing chickens crossed her mind.

My daughter, wearing an apron, hurries across the room with a bowl of broth. "Here, Daddy, try some of this." She's breathless from rushing up the stairs.

"Can't eat. Put...on the table," I whisper. I can't believe my voice is leaving too. There's not much of anything left of me.

"That's what you always say. I know you'd feel better if you'd just take a few sips."

"Don't want it."

She sets the bowl on the bedside table and dabs at her eyes with the corner of her apron.

"Sorry," I say, and slowly lift my hand to touch her arm. The contrast of my bony, wrinkled hand against her smooth younger skin is shocking to me.

She pats my hand, sniffs, and turns to leave the room. I hear her shoes as they clump down the carpeted stairs and dissolve into the anxious whispering and bustling noises coming from the kitchen.

I close my eyes...and then...quickly, open them again. I glance around the room and there he is. I thought I had seen him. In the corner of the room opposite my bed sits the hunched-over, dark shadow of an old man. The shadow doesn't move.

"You still here?" I say.

"Yep, ain't never been nowheres else," he says with a gravelly voice.

"All this time and you're still here. Have you come for me?"

"Naw," the spirit says, "I don't do no fetchin'." He coughs and clears his throat. "I just thought I'd settle that little mystery from way back durin' the war. The day them Yankees come callin'? The fire mystery?" He laughed to himself. "If you wanna set a fire, a war is as good a time as any to do it. Just sorta fits in with what's goin' on." He sighs, "They's lots of things a good fire can settle, mind you. You got a problem with somebody, a fire sorta evens things out." He chuckles again, "Now for one thing, how'd you know that was me what set fire to them wagons?"

"Couldn't say, just seemed like a good idea at the time."

"I almost fell outta that tree I was sittin' in when you said it was probably me what set fire to them wagons. I was thinkin', 'Lordy mercy, can that boy see me?'" He shifted in his chair, "But, the most fun I had during that Yankee visit was chasin' them chickens all over this farm so's them soldier boys couldn't catch 'em. None of them boys seemed to know that chickens can fly and roosters is mean when you upset 'em. Then, them boys wasn't workin' too hard at grabbin' 'em anyhow."

"Didn't know you had a hand in the chicken chasin' too."

"Oh yeah...while we're talkin' 'bout it, you told that Yankee officer that I left stall doors open all the time. Well, wasn't me what opened them doors. Remember, y'all had that mule, name of 'Kitty Cat,' thanks to Stewart. I think y'all felt kinda sorry for the ole mule so everbody jes' called him 'Cat.' Well, ole Cat figured out how to open the slide-locks on them stall doors hisself. He'd let hisself out, and then he'd let them horses out too, if he was of a mind to. Weren't none of my doin'."

I think I smiled.

There was silence while I tried to find a breath. I was painfully aware of my own rattling and gasping.

The shadow slowly stood and grunted, "You '

"Yep, I reckon so."

The Unknown Soldier

Nancy Fletcher-Blume

The March to Glory

He was standing near a grave
Sheltered by trees,
Holding an old lantern
That swayed slowly in the breeze.

I watched his bare feet
Shuffling the leaves.
His gray uniform was filthy
And his pants had holes in the knees.

He started talking, this young soldier boy,
"Come closer, come near,
I'll tell you how I died
And why I'm buried here.

"We had marched up through Georgia
From Atlanta on to Tennessee
Just full of passion and pride
And looking for a victory.

"Then just a mile or so
outside of Spring Hill,
We heard General Hood say,
'The enemy must really give us a fight
Or we'll be in Nashville before tomorrow night.'"

Spirits

The Battle of Destiny

"So there we camped down on that cold ground
Looking up at November skies,
Thoughts of home and loved ones
Bring pain and tears to our sleepless eyes.

"A silent watch was kept, all through that long night
Until...we heard the sound of men and horses
We thought it was upon us,
The battle, the fight.

"A soldier ran to wake the sleeping General
Just long enough for him to pass the order on
And then...it became quiet confusion,
Until...that damp dawn, and
We were still standing, waiting, waiting,
The enemy had stealthily by-passed us at Spring Hill
And gone.

"On into Franklin, digging in,
The enemy was before us.
The fight was about to begin.
Now I'm not saying who was right or who was wrong
And who was all to blame
But we surely were led into slaughter
To go down in history as General Hood's shame.

"As regiment after regiment
Was ordered through fields and hills
And we were told, at all cost
To take Franklin, keep the enemy from Nashville,
Kill or be killed."

The Final Hour

"The guns were making a terrible sound
And black smoke hung thick in the air
Young boys and men were falling all around
And I saw red...flowing everywhere

"The wounded and dying were screaming and crying.
We were fast losing ground.
Then...suddenly a great blackness came over me;
I had fallen too, had gone down.

"I died, that thirtieth of November day,
On a Franklin field,
Two thousand of us, young boys and men.
Some kind folk found me, brought me in.
And then

"They buried me right here in Carnton
With other soldiers in an unknown grave.
We died for a belief and cause,
And our young lives we gladly gave."

Giving a farewell salute,
The soldier turned to leave
Saying "Do not forget me, do not grieve
As I will forever sleep in peace
.Beneath these great oak trees."

Then I watched his bare feet
As he walked away,
Just a young soldier boy
Wearing a uniform of grey.

The Secret of the Keeper

Sylvia Bouvier

The drive was longer than we thought. Dusk was already falling when we saw the sign Willow Tree Plantation Lane. The narrow lane was filled with ruts, and the tree limbs brushing against our minivan seemed like alien arms reaching down to pluck us up into another world. Actually we had been plucked up from a bustling Michigan college town to the small north Kentucky community where my husband had a new teaching position.

Suddenly in a clearing our new home loomed before us, its tall weathered pillars reaching up from the overgrown ivy covered porch and thick vines hanging from the balcony. Not at all like the picture from the real estate company. What were we thinking when we signed the purchase agreement on a house we had never seen?

As the sun set, the house became shrouded in darkness. Jonathan our oldest, our twins Jerry and Jenny, and I waited while Rob took our only flashlight to locate the light switch. Rob shouted "Linda, I found it!" Nothing happened. I grabbed my cell phone to call our realtor, no signal.

After a dinner of crackers, warm cheese, chips and bottled water, the children played Uno while Rob and I rolled out the sleeping bags and set up for the night. A nonfunctioning southern farmhouse was not what we had imagined from back in our snug northern subdivision.

Although everyone else slept, exhausted from the efforts to cope with the unexpected, for me sleep did not come. I had last looked at my watch at 4 a.m. Now at 5:30 a.m. a car horn was blaring outside our windows. The moving van was three hours early, but the muddy lane was too narrow to bring it to our porch. For the next three hours we paid our neighbor to ferry our furniture in his pickup down the narrow lane, now a small stream due to the night's rain.

With our furniture safe in the house, we started into town for groceries. We were all starving and needed refueling before putting the beds together and arranging the furniture. Rob wanted to get the electricity turned on before dark. At the diner we were the talk of the town. Willow Tree Plantation had been rented several times, but no one stayed for more than a few nights because ghosts roamed the property. This was not what our children needed to hear, so we assured them the locals were just teasing the newcomers.

With our errands done, we piled in the minivan. All this rain was not going to dampen our spirits. Well, not until we reached Willow Tree Lane which now was a raging river. Against my complaints Rob drove through the rising water. Perhaps had he known we would literally be trapped in our house for two days without electricity or phone, he would have turned back to town. Instead we ended up wading through ankle deep water with our groceries.

As the kids explored the farthest reaches of the house, Rob and I assembled the beds. Suddenly the twins ran in screaming. "Something's in the attic. Jonathon said they're ghosts."

I am not one for believing in ghosts, but this house did have an eerie quality. But in the attic we realized the noises were bats. We hurried out, locked the door, and planned to have them removed as soon as we could call someone.

Magically on the second morning the waters receded, electricity came on, and the phone line was restored. We called about the bat removal, but it was going to cost a fortune. So as long as they stayed in the attic, we decided to be cohabiters.

With utilities working, over the next few days our family life began to take on a routine, and Willow Tree Plantation began to feel like home. The kids found a creek in the woods which they followed farther into the yet unseen reaches of our land.

Then one afternoon they returned with a tall tale about an old man named Mr. John. He wore an old tattered uniform and showed them some overgrown graves in the woods. Next day we all went exploring. Mr. John did not appear, but we did uncover more graves and wrote down some of the inscriptions.

That night the children said they heard noises in the kitchen. We checked. No one was there and yet I had this strange feeling someone was watching us. Next day some of our neighbors dropped by and asked if we had met Mr. John. I explained how the children had met him in the woods by some old graves, but Rob and I had not yet had the pleasure. They assured me we would and said children are always the first to encounter him. I invited them in, but they turned and waved good bye. Their visit gave me more of a weird feeling. I wondered if they had met this Mr. John they called a ghost. After dinner I mentioned it to Rob, but he just laughed it off. Was I letting the locals fuel my overactive imagination?

A few days later the kids asked to go back to the clearing. Somehow they snuck a box of cookies, three granny greening apples, two bananas, a box of crackers, and a jar of peanut butter. After some motherly interrogation techniques, they came clean that the food was for Mr. John.

If Mr. John could eat, was he really a ghost or a person? I was both relieved and frightened. Yet he seemed to have been around for a long time and none of the locals ever mentioned he was dangerous. I decided to go with the children the next time to search for our mysterious ghost/man. I looked on the internet for the names from the tombstones. There were the plantation owner, his wife, two children and a Confederate soldier. We had also uncovered some unmarked graves set apart from the others with not even a family name. After more research, we learned these were most likely the graves of slaves.

For the rest of the summer, Mr. John did not make anymore appearances. Summer vacation ended in mid August. The kids were shocked; in the North school never started until after Labor Day. Rob was teaching full time at the college, so now I had a lot more time to continue research on our new home. I learned it had once been a large thriving plantation.

Alone one afternoon as I opened the refrigerator for the chicken breasts I had cooked earlier, I noticed one was missing. Also the grape jelly was on the shelf instead of in the door, and there seemed to be less milk in the gallon jug.

Someone had been in the house while I was in the woods, but how? I checked all the doors to be sure they were locked. All the windows were painted shut except for three on the second floor. Was someone still in the house? I felt a strange mix of fear and curiosity. There was still enough chicken to make the salad and plenty of fresh fruit although the bowl did not look as full. I turned to make sure the fresh blackberry pie was still intact. One piece was missing, but the knife used to cut it was washed and lying on the counter. Had Mr. John been watching and waiting for me to leave? At dinner I mentioned the missing chicken breast, milk, fruit and piece of pie. The kids laughed about Mr. John's appetite, but Rob suggested I lock the doors when I was home alone.

On Saturday the kids wanted to go look for Mr. John. I was ready to object, but Rob said Mr. John had never hurt us. They were gone for about two hours. On their return, Jenny seemed quieter than usual. Without much prodding, she told us they found another tombstone for 'Angel Baby' but there was no date of birth or death.

"What does that mean?" she asked.

I held her in my arms and told her "Angel Baby" probably died at birth.

Jenny's eyes filled with tears and she whispered "I think it was Mr. John's baby."

"What makes you think that?" I asked.

"We saw him kneeling there, but when he saw us he left. We waited but he never came back."

I gave her a hug, told her we would pray for Mr. John in our prayers tonight, and sent her upstairs to get her favorite doll.

While I had been taking care of Jenny, Jerry had made himself a peanut butter sandwich.

"Jerry what are you eating? You'll ruin your dinner."

"But Mom, we didn't have lunch."

"What about the picnic basket I sent with you?"

"Well we sort of lost it."

Next morning the picnic basket was sitting on the kitchen counter. Once again the mystery of how Mr. John got in the house with all the doors locked loomed over us. I decided to put Jonathan in charge of keeping the twins away from the clearing and away from Mr. John. He wasn't happy about it, but he agreed to try.

In spite of locked doors, gifts started to appear on my kitchen counter: a hand carved wooden spoon, a small wooden bowl, an intricately carved trivet, and a wooden chopping board. One morning Rob found a note leading him to the back door where he found a board with hooks and one had his car keys on it. We all laughed at Mr. John knowing Rob's problem with losing his keys. Other things appeared mostly in the kitchen: pecan nuts shelled and ready to use, a bunch of wild onions, wild mushrooms, and on one occasion a sack of potatoes. I was a little more concerned when small wooden toys began to appear in the children's bedrooms. First Jenny found a rag doll dressed in filmy old lace. Jerry found a wooden race car with perfectly carved wheels that moved, and Jonathan found a wooden holder for all his baseball caps. Soon we looked forward to the surprises Mr. John left for us. Although as much as we enjoyed them, it was disconcerting to have no idea how he got into our house. He never took anything without leaving something in return.

Then one night the children were awakened by someone crying. They ran to our room, Jonathan and Jerry were trembling and Jenny sobbing. Jenny thought it sounded like Mr. John crying because he missed 'Angel Baby'.

Next morning after everyone was gone, I decided to look for a hidden door. I searched in an organized fashion, one room at a time. In Jonathan's closet, I stepped on a board and a door opened slightly behind some boxes. I could see there was only undisturbed dust. I checked all the rooms upstairs and downstairs including the halls. No secret passage! Maybe Jenny had one of her bad dreams and woke up crying which woke up the boys.

Every night our family prayed for Mr. John's safety although Rob and I hoped never to see him again. The children chose to believe their schoolmates who said the ghost had a habit of disappearing from time to time. Finally on a crisp fall day, the children decided to go to the clearing with a picnic lunch in hopes of seeing him. Jenny was sure he had come to her in a dream and told her to meet him.

Mr. John was waiting for them and beguiled them with stories about the plantation before the Civil War. That night, he began his visits once more. Little gifts appeared and at times I'd leave food on the counter for him. The children often met him in the clearing, and in a strange way he became part of our family.

One day as they waited in the warm sun for Mr. John, a cool breeze wrapped around them and they had a strange feeling. Mr. John had a way of appearing at the edge of the clearing, but this time he suddenly appeared on the blanket, eating a sandwich, and there was urgency in his speech. "I'm going trust you with a secret. Your family comes from the North. Armies from the North came to free the slaves. We spirits want to give you our secret, but you has to promise you won't tell nobody but your folks, and they has to promise to keep the secret."

The children promised.

"We need to find the survey marker on the far side of the stable. It proves all the land to the river is part of the plantation. It's overgrown with weeds and heavy underbrush, but I know it's there cause my daddy showed me when I was made Keeper of Willow Tree Plantation. "

The children were so excited when they arrived home we could hardly make much sense out of what they were saying. We agreed to help them look but mostly out of curiosity. On Saturday we went after lunch to see what tools we needed. The children thought Mr. John would be there but he was a 'no show,' and the amount of brush to be removed was overwhelming. Rob and I left feeling somewhat deflated, but the children were not discouraged. They were sure Mr. John would help us find it.

In the morning on the kitchen counter was a mason jar filled with flowers. Next to it was a note scribbled "Look for the flowers." Jenny remembered seeing them in the brush next to the stable. Off we went, in search a treasure buried under years of vegetative growth. Jenny was disappointed when the flowers she remembered were not the same kind. Then Jonathan spotted another mason jar filled with flowers like the ones on the counter. After thirty minutes of hacking at the brush, Jerry screamed "We found it. We found it." He was right; there was a stone with some barely legible writings. I brought paper and charcoal to do a rubbing. It helped us make out some of the letters and numbers on the stone, but their meaning was a mystery. The letters seemed to be initials, so with a little internet searching, we determined they matched the owners during the Civil War.

What to do with this information was another problem. Monday I checked at the county seat to see if their records matched our findings. There seemed to be no record of that particular tract of land. The County Clerk thought it very unusual and kept on searching. She seemed delighted when she found an old survey map that showed our property went all the way to the river just like Mr. John said. We didn't understand why this mattered since it was all overgrown and the stable looked like a strong wind could blow it over, but that evening we drove into town and celebrated with ice cream cones.

A few days later Mr. John left a note on the table asking the children to come to the clearing on Saturday. Armed with the picnic lunch, they left early. Mr. John was in the clearing waiting. They told him what the survey map showed, and all Mr. John said was "I knowed it. Now I can finish telling my story."

"The Willow Tree Plantation was a stop for the Underground Railroad. A tunnel leads from the house to the stable and from there the slaves got into wagons and drove to the river where boats took 'em across."

Jenny asked "Were you a slave?"

"Yes, I was."

"Why didn't you run away?"

"Cause the only family I has is right here buried in the grave yard in the clearing. When my Daddy died, I promised him I'd stay until I found someone I could trust with the secret. My family's been the Keeper of the railroad since it started. A lot of lost and unhappy spirits walk in the woods; they're all good spirits but they're afraid to leave for fear some one's going to destroy the unmarked graves. A lot of families tried to live here, but you're the only ones ever come from the North, from that good place. I'm the only spirit anyone can see, so I don't know if I'm a ghost. I just know a lot of courageous spirits roam this woods, and now they want your family to be the new Keepers of the Underground Railroad. We need someone who cares and you children care and your parents do to."

"Wow! Keepers of the Underground Railroad! I know Mom and Dad will be willing."

"Jonathan you can't tell your parents until you become the Keeper, and it has to happen after dark cause that's when the railroad worked. I'll come for you tonight in your room at ten."

The kids were in bed and we thought sound asleep by 9:30. However, the next morning Jonathan told us about their great adventure. They were in Jonathan's room before ten. The closet door opened, and Mr. John appeared. He pushed the clothes and boxes aside, stepped on a floorboard and led them into the secret room. They went through another door into a dark stairway lit only by the lantern Mr. John was carrying. It was narrow. The smell of dust clung to the damp air and filled their nostrils. When the steps ended, they were walking on a downward slope. The passageway seemed to go deeper and deeper into the earth. The walls seemed to close in on them as the passage narrowed. When it began to level off, their journey was easier. Suddenly, the passageway widened into a small room with old rough wooden benches lining the walls. Mr. John gave them apples and had them rest because from here on the passage led up hill. Jenny was tired and cold so Mr. John picked her up and pushed the next door open. A breath of fresh air gave them hope the journey was soon to end. Jerry complained his legs hurt, but Mr. John assured him the path to their destination was steep but not far.

They came above ground in the stable. Here the slaves climbed into wagons and were covered up with sacks. Then they were driven to the river's edge where boats met them and they were rowed across to freedom. Mr. John never went. He stayed to be with his family and to help the others. Now he is passing the responsibility for this heritage on to the new family of the Willow Tree Plantation. He gave them an old tattered journal containing all of the people in the unmarked graves. He asked them to get a plaque with these names and place it among the unmarked graves. The story of the Willow Tree Underground Railroad was finally free to be told. It was all in this book. He leaned down and hugged the boys, kissed Jenny on the cheek and handed Jonathan the book. A tear rolled down his cheek as he began to fade.

The next morning it all seemed like a dream. No one remembered walking back to the house, but Jonathan woke with the journal in his hand. Jonathan handed the book to Rob and me. Our family was now Keepers of The Willow Tree Plantation Underground Railroad. There is both joy and sadness in the passing of the Keeper. We will miss Mr. John, but he had kept his promise to his father.

The Willow Tree Plantation has become an historical site. We placed a plaque with the names of the slaves in the center of the unmarked graves. The County Historical Society published the Underground Railroad journal. Most important of all, the restless spirits in the woods are at peace.

Yet, sometimes in the stillness of the night while I am sitting on the porch swing, a gentle breeze weaves through the trees and wraps around me like a warm blanket and I know I am not alone.

Double Wedding Ring

Margaret Britton Vaughn
Poet Laureate of Tennessee

Each year the Beech Creek Methodist Church
had dinner on the ground.
For miles they came with home-cooked food
and quilts to be put down.
At the age of five Jason met
Cecelia blond with curl,
and Jason swore at tender age
Cecelia was his girl.
For years they both met on Sunday
and sat in the same pew.
They fell in love in their young years
and always would be true.
Ninth grade Jason went off to school;
Cecelia stayed behind.
Letters were written every day
with love in every line.
Both wrote they would exchange their vows,
friends and family to view:
Valentine's Day, to be exact,
in eighteen sixty-two.
We were at war in sixty-one
when they both picked that date.
Jason left to fight the war,
no matter what the fate.

He swore to his darling Cecelia
he'd be there without fail.
She promised she'd be there
in wedding gown and veil.
The river they call Cumberland
Fort Donaldson sat above;
Corporal Jason hugged his gun
but thought about his love.
Grant's troops surrounded the hills
and waited for gunboat
Corondolet to fire on fort;
the corporal wrote his note:
"I must be at the Beech Creek Church
my wedding to take place."
He wrote it in the sleeting rain
but had to write in haste.
Meanwhile Cecelia lay in bed,
warming from the chill.
She whispered from too pale lips,
"Be at the church on hill."
They kept the promise they had made
for their Valentine's Day;
God joined them in matrimony
and this their headstones say:
Cecelia died of scarlet fever,
Corporal Jason was killed.
Both stones February fourteenth
together on the hill.
"No matter what, my Cecelia,
I'll be there to meet you."
"No matter what, dear Jason,
know I will be there, too."

Susan

Laurie Michaud-Kay

She hurried the visitors out the door and reached for the key in the deadbolt. Her fingers paused, gripping the cold metal. Which did she fear confronting the most—the threat from within or the threat from without? She had planned this carefully, weighed all the options. The fear was there, but also the excitement. How many people had a chance to explore for ghosts in an expansive antebellum home, its walls imprinted with nearly one hundred fifty years of history? She might not get this chance again. She planned to move out of town, leaving her job as tour guide at the historic site. Her fingers snapped the lock into place.

She had more to fear from the living than from the dead. But her stalker couldn't possibly know that she had chosen this afternoon to stay late. He never showed up here anyway, but waited for her near the apartment, scolding her in letters for stopping somewhere on the way home, disappointing him in the minutes lost until he could see her again. No, she had time for her paranormal investigation. She took a deep breath, turned, and walked down the empty hallway.

He watched her latch the door and come toward him. He could feel her nervousness. Her name was Susan. It was what had first attracted him. His wife's name had been Susan. It was nice to think of Susan in the house again. It reminded him of the golden years after the war, when he could again control everything in his life. When Susan was alive. When he could kiss her, lie beside her in bed. As he drew further back into the shadows, his hungry whisper lingered in the air. "Susan . . ."

Susan stopped at the end of the hallway to retrieve the flashlight from behind a stack of brochures. The remaining daylight would fade to a soft darkness in the hour she expected to be in the house. She did not plan to use the lights and would switch on the flashlight only if she needed to. Ghosts liked the dark. It was a tenet of the paranormal.

But she wasn't up to roaming the antebellum house in total darkness. Besides, she had to be out before the local police did their nightly check of the property. Her car was still in the parking lot. As a guide, she had the right to be inside the house. She just didn't want to explain to them why she was there with no lights on.

"Okay, girl, let's go," Susan said out loud, as much to rally her courage as to spur herself on. At least she thought she had said, "girl." Her ears echoed back "Susan." She couldn't be hearing things already. Ghost-hunting distorted perceptions from your eyes and ears, teased your imagination. Oddly, though, being a stalking victim would help counteract this phenomenon. After months of vigilance, her senses were attuned to things out of the ordinary—subtle noises, abrupt shifts in atmosphere. But she had to anchor her mind in rational thought, find logical explanations for noises and sights, or the entire experiment would be invalid.

Putting it down to nerves, Susan pushed open the swinging door and entered the original portion of the two-story house. The Preservation Society had done a marvelous job in restoring the structure and interior. Most of it reflected the house as it would have been after the Civil War. Some of the furnishings were family pieces from that period. However, the Society had kept the closets, bathrooms, heating and electric lights that had been incorporated after the turn of the century, as well as the wing she had just left, which consolidated the original kitchen and smokehouse, and now housed the Society offices and a modern kitchen.

The passage from the wing had brought Susan into the dining room. She gazed at the large oval table immediately in front of her, attuning her senses to the atmosphere of the room. Confederate generals had faced their destiny over its polished walnut surface that autumn morning in 1864. The enemy had slipped through their presumed blockade of the road in front of the house. Their boys had been exhausted after chasing Union forces as they moved north from Atlanta. Now their commander was in a rage, thumped the table repeatedly, and shouted orders. Their troops would follow the Yankees to Franklin and attack in an all-out attempt to stop the bastards from getting to Nashville.

This well-known chapter in the house's history was rumored to evoke a residual haunting. Tension thickened the air, making visitors uncomfortable. People heard dishes rattling as the General's fist slammed into the table. Others swore that they actually glimpsed the heated exchange, watching and listening as the Confederates argued the strategy of a frontal assault at Franklin—shadowy figures oblivious to the passage of time, unaware of modern observers.

Susan had read that residual hauntings could be tied to a specific hour or time of year. She had chosen this late November day exactly for that reason. It was the anniversary of the historic battle. True, the breakfast had happened in the morning, and it was now twilight; but she was hopeful the spirits would react to the day, rather than the time. She waited, focusing her senses on the room.

Nothing. Susan relaxed a bit. Even the power of suggestion had failed to produce an apparition in the room. Glancing at her watch, she realized that she needed to move on if she wanted to walk through the entire house before her hour was gone.

She entered the front parlor. The portrait of the original owner hung over the fireplace. An exacting man, he had torn down the walls of the house three times before satisfied that he could safely move his wife and children into the spacious structure. They had occupied the house just five years before the Civil War started. As with most prosperous local farmers, he had been a Southern sympathizer, alarmed at the recent government actions that threatened to destroy his means of supporting this family. He organized a local infantry company and served the C. S. A. as a Major. Captured twice, he spent nearly two years as a prisoner. And if the stories were true, eternity being a ghost.

Rousing herself, she decided to cover the upstairs next. She had no trouble seeing as she entered the central hall and started up the wide staircase. The evening light fell through the row of windows on the landing above. She was aware of the quiet of the empty house, heard the ticking of the clock in the parlor. Suddenly, she heard a brief, familiar creak of door hinges. Her hand gripped the stair rail. It was the noise made by the swinging door when she pushed it open to lead her tour group into the main house. Was it the police, come earlier than usual? She hadn't heard their car, but it was hard to hear outside noises through the twenty-inch brick walls. No footsteps. Oh, God. It couldn't be him. Her stalker had taken pains to demonstrate that he was skilled in stealth. He taunted her in letters with intimate details of her home life that he had secretly observed, comparing this activity to his covert war ops. He bragged that he had only been stopped once, on an overseas mission that had been bungled. He had been captured and held as a POW. The internment had stung his pride; and after being liberated, he had trained so that he would not be captured again. No one could stop him from being with her.

Was he here?

Susan turned on the stair, aiming the flashlight, her thumb ready on the switch. Then she shook her head. The noise could not possibly have come from the swinging door. It had a stout, old-fashioned sliding bolt that she had locked in place after entering the dining room. No one could move that door when the bolt was in place. A group of teenagers had tried it after breaking into the offices one night. They had jimmied and hammered on the door, but it never budged.

Reassured by her logic, Susan turned and continued up the stairs. As she passed the landing windows, she glanced outside. Her car was the only one in the parking lot.

He could hear her moving slowly from one room to another. Occasionally, he heard her voice. She was always talking to herself, he knew. Her progress was easy to follow as the wood floors creaked overhead. He would wait for her down here, in the chair by the fireplace. Susan must finish her chores . . . take care of the house . . . before they could be in each other's company. But he would see her from the moment she descended the lower portion of the stairs. He sighed in anticipation, leaning back into the soft cushions. So different from the hard, filthy surfaces of the prison camp. Deprivation heightened your appreciation of the comforts of home, he mused. He looked around the room, noting the placement of the furniture in the shadowy edges of the room. The silken settee, a maple floor clock, the tall secretary desk placed next to the window overlooking the garden. The hall end table, the fringe on its embroidered scarf gently moving. The side door must be slightly ajar, letting in a telltale current of air. He started to get up and then realized Susan was moving toward the stairs. Lovely Susan. Deprivation certainly heightened your appreciation of that, as well. He settled back in the chair.

Susan's footsteps resonated on the bare floor as she moved toward the stairs. She had wandered through each room, poking into the closets and cupboards, lightly touching period keepsakes, listening beside beds. She had stepped onto the back balcony, envisioning a thriving plantation, where crops of wheat, corn, and cotton grew in the nearby fields and slaughtered hogs were laid out behind the smokehouse in preparation for dressing and salt-curing.

She had spent the most time in the second floor kitchen. A figure had been seen in the window of this room by other staff members, always when the house was empty. She had tried to provoke an intelligent haunting by politely introducing herself and asking its reasons for haunting the home. She went so far as to demand a sign of its presence. As if in answer, the windows had rattled slightly and a distant clanking noise could be heard. With a whoosh, the heating system announced its presence . . . but nothing else. She was proud to have maintained her objectivity in the face of the house's dark corners and night sounds, and a tad disappointed. It was time to check out the remaining rooms downstairs and leave.

The row of windows glowed softly from the floodlights now illuminating the exterior. Stepping onto the landing, Susan was startled by her long shadow stretching across the hall floor below. Uneasiness surged through her. The atmosphere grew tense, charged. Her objectivity faltered as her eyes moved to the dark entrances on either side of the hall. Her primal sense took control, whispering danger. Her heartbeat accelerated. Something was in the shadows below.

He could see her on the landing, an angel surrounded by a soft light. Susan. She was finally coming to be with him. She would sit in the delicate chair opposite him. They would talk about the future. Then they would retire for the night. He leaned forward. What was she waiting for? Why did she suddenly seem frozen, a look of fear on her face? He was puzzled and now slightly out of humor. Why was she keeping him waiting? What was this foolishness? A whisper reached him, and he realized with a jolt that his feelings were echoed by another person in the room, a person hidden behind him, waiting in the darkness. No, not echoed. These feelings were coiled, depraved, and threatening, ready to be unleashed.

Susan heard the scream just as she turned to run. It reverberated with human agony and seemed to go on during the seconds she was fleeing to the second floor kitchen. There was a fire escape off the room. She was no longer driven by logic or objectivity. Terror had taken over. Just as she reached the window, she heard the side door slam back against the wall. She saw someone stumbling through the garden. He continually turned to look back, as if terrified that he was being followed. She recognized his face in the security lights.

It was her stalker.

Suddenly he froze, his staring eyes locked on the house. He crouched down, covering his head with his arms. His second scream was cut off as a shadow seemed to move over him. Then he jumped up and tore for the woods. This time he did not look back. He disappeared into the trees, only to reappear seconds later, the headlights of his car bouncing across the uneven ground in a desperate effort to get his spinning tires to cover the distance more quickly.

"What the . . ." Susan muttered, her own uncontrolled terror broken by the sight of the man's frantic retreat. She shivered, feeling a trace of cold air behind her. She turned, her eyes trying to penetrate the shadows in the room. It was quiet again, but colder. The night air must be blowing through the open side door. She felt the need to close it, to stop the cold and her own reactionary shaking. But this was no time for taking chances. Whatever had caused the man to flee might still be downstairs. She pulled out her cell phone and called the police.

After reporting a break-in, Susan listened again. There were no footsteps, no creaking floorboards. But the cold was becoming unbearable. She started quietly for the stairs. Hoping for the advantage, she switched on the chandelier when she reached the landing. The lower hall flooded with light. Blinking in the brilliance, she paused, assessing the atmosphere. The paralyzing knowledge of a presence was gone, even though the rooms off the hall were not completely lit. She was alone again in the house.

She could hear the reassuring sound of the police siren in the distance as she hurried down the remaining steps and across to the open side door. Standing in its shadow, she stared into the garden. There had been terror on his face. Whatever happened to him, he deserved it. She shut the door and walked into the parlor to wait for the police.

The sight of him knocked the breath out of her. He stood in front of the fireplace, watching her face. He was older than in the portrait behind him, his whiskers grayer, his hair sparser, his face lined from the months spent in the Union prison camp.

Susan knew that she should be frightened, but instead a feeling of love and safety settled over her. He came to her and looked into her eyes. His voice, deep and soothing, resonated in her mind.

"He'll never bother you again, my dear. I've seen to that."

Susan was still staring at the empty spot when the police came into the room.

Close to the Grey

Joyce A.O. Lee

So close to the Grey am I
As I stand on this land
Where they met their fate
Can they not see me as I see
The fear in their eyes
As they're led into charge
Do they know that I know
They dare not decline, but resign
To the battle that night
The sights, smells, and sounds
So real all around
Oh, my feet, have you trod here before?
A gun in my left hand, a sword in my right,
And a Yell straight from Hell in my throat,
Did I die with so many, or was I the other?
Was the last thought I had of a long dead mother?
Did I see their still faces and hear their hushed cries
On the day all the Generals died?
So, come gently this way to that Elephant Day
Of many long years ago,
And I'll tell you their story with a step back to Glory
And you too may feel close to the Grey

Author's note: inspired by Thomas Cartwright, Carter House curator, retired

I Was Warned

Tom Wood

Dear Great-great-great Granddaddy Sam,
 I have a confession to make. You were right and I should
have listened to you. We'll talk again soon, I promise.

 Sorry. I had to start out writing that way. Confession is
always good for the soul, they say. Suppose I'll find out now.
If you've read the newspapers or watched the television
lately, you know who I am. But you don't know me, not
really. Just what they're saying about me. Lots of it is true, lot
of it ain't. I wasn't always the monster they've written or
talked about. Hard? Hell, yes. I come from a long line of
hard men.
 But none were as hard-headed as me. I should have
listened.
 My name is Samuel Beauregard Hopkins V and my
revered great-great-great Granddaddy rode proudly with
Confederate States of America Major General Nathan
Bedford Forrest during what our family's always called the
War of Northern Aggression. At least that's the story that's
been handed down generation to generation. It's time to set
the record straight.
 Sam wasn't proud of what he done with General Forrest,
but he was a soldier and did his duty. Just that, nothing
more. I know, straight from the ghastly source.
 I didn't listen that night, and I didn't believe. I do now.

 My story began exactly twenty years ago on May 1, 1992
at my old, two-story brick duplex in Franklin, Tennessee. I
went to bed mad and not because I had to work the early
shift at the 7/11 the next morning.

Spirits

I was still stewing after watching Bill O'Reilly on "Inside Edition" talking about the Rodney King race riots. They kept showing over and over all the fires the blacks had set and the beating of that white truck driver and, 22-year-old hot-head that I was, it really ticked me off.

Okay, so King had been beaten and tasered by those cops. Maybe he didn't deserve it; but as my grandma woulda said, two wrongs don't make a right. Burning Los Angeles wasn't the answer.

Can you believe I'm talking like this? Maybe I'm not a monster; I hope I'm not the pure evil that they say I am, that redemption is possible in the next life. Yes, I did monstrous things; and if I could take it all back, I surely would.

I stubbed out my Camel cigarette and drained the last drop of the Schlitz tallboy as I stumbled off to the bathroom. Sitting there, I took a few tokes as hatred for what was happening in L.A. again bubbled to the surface. I wished me 'n my boys coulda been there. We'd have helped take back the city. We weren't members of the Klan, though several of our ancestors had been, but I went to one meeting in Columbia before the L.A. riots. It was more like a Moose Lodge social club meeting where they got together and bragged about who would do what if this or that happened. They were all talk; I wasn't.

"None 'a you old boys could carry your daddies' jockstraps," I said, slamming the side my fist on the wooden table for emphasis. "This ain't a time for talk, it's time for action. Grab your guns and let's head West."

The packed room was deadly silent for about ten seconds before 50-ish Bubba Malone ran a hand over his bald head and finally spoke without making eye contact.

"Well, Sammy, it's not that I don't want to, but I can't commit right now. My wife's still in the hospital and—"

263

"And you think I care? I'm tellin' you, the firestorm that's about to explode in Los Angeles is gonna sweep across the country and then where will your wife be?"

He didn't answer, but Woodrow Jackson did. His hair and mustache were white, but the streak down his back was yellow.

"You don't know that. We're ready to defend our home turf, but me, I hope they go ahead and burn that whole damn Babylon to the ground."

Woodrow grinned like a possum and looked around for support. He got a few smiles, but that was about all. Nobody else spoke.

Me? My face was turning as red as my neck.

"Dammit, boys, I got to tell you, I'm disappointed. Sons of the Confederacy? You're just a bunch of dried-up old pecker-heads."

I glared around the room, looking for someone to fight, but was met with a stony wall of silence. I just left.

Two nights later was when the riots broke out and I got so riled. After I'd finished in the bathroom, I collapsed on the unmade bed, my head spinning from the beer and drugs. I was pretty wired, but thought I might get a couple of hours of sleep.

Just me and the dog were in the room, and I was laying there with my eyes closed when he started whining lowly. I probably would have ignored it, thinking he was dreaming of chasing rabbits or something, if it hadn't been for the sudden drop in temperature in the room and the noise in the hall. It sounded like chains rattling or something, and I sat bolt upright as Blue started growling.

I reached in the drawer, pulled out my Colt .45 revolver, and stumbled down the hall in my shorts looking for the intruder. Nothing. A quick recon showed all the doors were locked, so I went back to bed a little confused and uncertain what I'd heard.

I checked the thermostat and it was set on seventy-two, but as I got closer to my room, I again felt a distinct temperature change, sort of like standing in front of an open refrigerator freezer door. It didn't disappear, but the dog had. I didn't see him leave, but he must have gone out the doggy door because I found him still outside the next morning and he refused to go back in the house.

It was so cold in the room that this time I got under the covers and huddled into a ball. I rolled over on my side, facing the wall instead of toward the center of the bed, and was almost asleep when I heard the footsteps way down the hall.

Only they weren't the quiet steps of some ninja agent trying to sneak up on you to slit your throat. They weren't the normal-sounding, thudding steps of someone walking on creaky wooden floorboards.

These footsteps were like Phil Collins rhythmically pounding on his bass drum. They were loud, and getting louder.

Thoom ... Thoom ... ThooM ... ThoOM ...

And closer.

THOOM ... THOOM ... THOOM ... THOOM ...

I lay there with my eyes shut tight, telling myself I was dreaming. Only I knew I wasn't.

THOOM ... THOOM ... THOOM ... THOOM ...

It got colder in the room, but I was sweating.

THOOM ... THOOM ... THOOM ... THOOM ...

Then the footsteps turned into my bedroom.

THOOM ... THOOM ... THOOM ... THOOM ...

My pulse was beating to match the stomping feet.

THOOM ... THOOM ...

Then they stopped.

My hand darted to the open drawer for the gun and I bolted upright, springing into action like a coiled snake, gun cocked, ready for anything.

Only I wasn't ready for what confronted me.

Standing at the foot of the bed was a pallid, grisly reflection of me.

What had I been smoking?

Except for the bedraggled gray Confederate uniform wrapped in chains, the shimmering figure looked just like me. Same slight build and rounded shoulders. Same scraggly beard and mustache. Same crooked teeth. I'd seen the old tin-type photos. But I had never seen such haunted eyes.

"Wha ... who ... Grandaddy Sam?"

The figure nodded.

"I'm here to save you from yourself."

I couldn't speak.

"This family is still paying for my sins. I saved your father and his father and my son before him. Now it is your own soul that in jeopardy."

I don't know if it was shock or just the unreality of it all, but I didn't run or scream. My arm sagged and the gun fell harmlessly to the floor. I just sat there, too stunned to do or say anything.

For the next half-hour or so, Sam explained his mission, telling me about the unvarnished truth about the massacre of some two hundred black Union troops at Fort Pillow in West Tennessee, just north of Memphis. The garrison was defended by some six hundred soldiers, about half of them black. If the fort fell, they knew they would either be slaves again — or dead.

"It was April 12 of '64 and we'd been there a month when General Forrest decided enough was enough. That morning, the General's horse got shot out from underneath him and he was going to make them pay. We outnumbered the Union boys four- or five-to-one and our sharpshooters had been picking them off. General Forrest got another mount and rode up and down the ranks, calling on us to seize the fort and save the South.

" 'Kill 'em all,' came several shouts back. All of us smelled blood.

"That was about 10 o'clock, and then the cannon fire began and we stormed the fort in waves.

"It was brutal, brutal warfare, but within the rules of engagement.

"Union commanding major Lionel Booth died early, taking a bullet in the throat. About three-thirty, General Forrest brazenly demanded unconditional surrender of the fort, telling them they'd have to pay the consequences if they didn't. Twenty minutes later, Major William Bradford sent back his reply: There would be no surrender."

Granddaddy Sam paused and his choking voice lowered to just above a whisper. If a ghost could cry, he would have.

"What happened for the next two hours was so damn awful, so damn shameful. I've spent a hundred years trying to wash the blood from my hands," he said, stretching his arms toward me.

"We had 'em on the run, surrounded and cut off from escape. Some tried to flee, some tried to surrender. Didn't matter none. We butchered 'em like hogs. Them what made it to the Miss'sip drew enough fire from the bluffs that the water along the shore turned red.

"Inside the fort, some of them white boys were allowed to surrender. But the black 'uns? Uh-uh. Ev'ry which way you turned, somebody was shoutin' 'No quarter, no quarter.'

"I shot a half-dozen point-blank till I ran outta ammo, then bayonetted two or three more. The last boy couldn't a been more than seventeen. He was on his knees, praying up at me, begging to surrender."

The spirit paused and trembled.

"I smiled down at him, took the bayonet off my rifle — and stabbed him in the eyes."

It was my turn to shudder. This was my glorious ancestor, my namesake?

I bowed my head — so he wouldn't see me smiling.

Hell, yeah!

Finally, I looked up clear-eyed, hiding the wonder and awe that I felt.

I wasn't listening.

"It was war, but it was wrong. We were wrong. I was wrong. I crossed the line," Granddaddy Sam said. "There was an inquiry, but nothin' ever came of it. Many were able to go on with their lives, but I couldn't and I eventually died of my shame, a weight that I still bear. That boy's eyes haunt me to this day."

The spirit straightened and looked me square in the eye, his own orbs blazing with the fires of eternal damnation as he pointed his right forefinger at me.

"And now you, like your father and his father and his father before him, are about to reach a crossroads. Hate runs deep through our family. Hate runs deep in YOU." There was an ethereal sigh, almost a moaning. "When I spoke to them, they listened. They never spoke of it, but they were warned and they listened."

"Choose the wrong path and I'll see you in hell!"

I should have listened.

Grandaddy Sam vanished after sounding that ominous warning, and the temperature immediately returned to normal in the room.

Man, that grass must've been laced with some hallucinogenic. That didn't just happen. No way.

I lay back on the bed and passed out.

Four hours later, the alarm started its staccato buzzing and I staggered out of bed. Damn. Three a.m.

I got the coffee going, used it to wash down a handful of pills and chewed on some stale Krispy Kremes as I watched the early news. It was a recap of the L.A. riots and fires and the trucker beaten. The irrational anger was back with a renewed fury. "Damn ******s. Something's got to be done!"

It was time to go to work, so I went back to the bedroom to get my shoes and socks. I plopped on the corner of the bed, and my heel touched something cold. The .45.

I picked it up, stared at it a minute and sat it beside me as I pulled on my socks and sneakers. Then I stood and slipped the gun in my waistband, pulling my shirttail over it.

I smiled and left.

About five a.m., at a time when the store should have been packed with customers on their way to work, it was empty. I had another Camel hanging from the corner of my mouth and was on my third cup of black coffee. The Channel 4 early show was on, and all the talk was about what was going on in L.A., and what was next.

A car pulled up to the pumps and a young interracial couple — the Lincolns, I would later learn — stumbled out, laughing. She was dressed in nurse's scrubs after working the overnight shift at the hospital. Before heading off to work himself, he had picked her up and was taking her home.

They never made it.

He opened the door for her like a true Southern gentleman, with a slight bow and sweep of his arm, and she laughed as he wrapped his arms around her.

"Hey, none of that in here," I said sharply, baitingly.

My tone had the effect I expected. The baldie and the blondie were offended.

"What's your problem, man?"

"Yeah," she said. "Mind your own business, buddy."

"My name's not Buddy," I said calmly. "The store's closing early today."

"Listen, you," he said, raising his fist as he stepped toward the counter.

I took out my gun and shot him once in the chest.

His wife screamed and I put two in her.

Then I stubbed out my cigarette, drained the cup, and got outta there.

As I walked past their car, I heard a noise and quickly brought the gun to bear, ready for anything.

But I wasn't ready for this.

Strapped into his car seat was two-year-old Stephon Laurence Lincoln Junior, newly orphaned. He was tiny, but you could see both of his parents in him. He had her nose and his mouth.

And great-great-great granddaddy Sam's burning eyes!

Boring into my soul with a glimpse of the hell I would face.

I blinked and looked again.

Tears ran from the chocolate eyes and the face scrunched into a bawl as he perhaps realized he was alone in the world.

I'd been ready to shoot; now I felt like shooting myself as I fully realized the unimaginable horror of what I'd done.

But I was too cowardly to pull the trigger that day.

Or perhaps too scared.

I wasn't ready to face great-great-great Granddaddy Sam.

I ran, with little Stephon's plaintive cries echoing in my brain.

You think you know the rest of the story, that I was caught two days later in New Orleans, shipped back to Tennessee and eventually sentenced to death in the electric chair.

By the time I had listened to all the testimony and the trial reached its foregone conclusion, I was truly, truly remorseful for the senseless acts of evil I had done. Not sorry for myself, but for the oh-so-many lives I had destroyed.

What you don't know is that in the nearly twenty years that I've spent on Death Row here at Brushy Mountain, I've only had one visitor.

Great-great-great Granddaddy Sam.

It occurred the very night after I was sentenced to death.

I was processed into my new cell, small and stinking that it was, when I felt the temperature suddenly drop. I looked up into those blazing eyes, finally cringing in terror before he disappeared for good.

"I warned you. I WILL see you in hell."

That's why I've filed appeal after appeal, to stave off the inevitable.

And why I wrote all those letters of apology to the fathers, mothers, brothers and sisters of the Lincolns.

And why I began reading the Bible again and talking about life and the afterlife with the chaplain, always leaving out one small story out of our conversations.

Speaking of the chaplain, here he comes now. And the warden is with him.

I guess it's time.

Great-great-great Granddaddy Sam, I'll see you soon.

I was warned.

I should have listened.

Civil War on Carmack's Farm, East Tennessee

Lori C, Byington

Four spirits of our war make their way down the hill
   In search of the pond that's gone dry;
They've no notice of me as I watch them glide
   Midst gnarly trees enveloped in a mist.
As the boys trudge, the smoky veil accompanies them like a
   sentry
Sent by God to guide those who cannot see the light;

Where are they going?
   Where are their homes?
Are they Union or Confederate born?
Are they brothers in arms or brothers as men?
Does their momma await in the corn?

In the mist when the sun has set behind the Holstons
   If the air is still and the temperature is low,
Boys of our war, their faces smudged by powder from their
   weapons,
   Trudge their way in search of their home.
They've no notice of me as I cry for their souls
While I watch in the crisp autumn night.

Where are they going?
   Where is their home?
Were they Union or Confederate born?
They were brothers in arms and brothers in blood.
Oh! Their momma awaits in the corn.

8. BRIDGE TO CHANGE

Photograph by Randy Foster

stone memorials
graven to last forever
fade like memory

Randy Foster

The Stone

Arch Boyd Brown

A granite stone covered with moss
Cannot convey the grief or loss.
It cannot boast of deeds 'twere done
Before the death of a gallant son.

Cold and silent it marks the tomb
Of one who heard the cannon boom,
Who fought so bravely and so well;
And of his valor it cannot tell.

About war's horror it doth not speak,
As when the carnage was at its peak,
The deafening thunder of shot and shell
While soldiers blunder through its hell.

It cannot tell the soldier's saga
Of Gettysburg or Chickamauga;
Nor historian's errors now refute,
It merely stands a last salute.

So as you're standing by his grave
Remember a trooper young and brave,
The promise of a life that was lost
To purchase your freedom at so great a cost !

Colonel Benjamin

George Spain

Colonel Benjamin Stainback and Reverend Billy Highfield on their Way to the June 3, 1898 Confederate Decoration Day Celebration in Winchester, Tennessee

"Reverend, they should uv hung that son-of-a-bitch Davis an dug up Calhoun an hung im too an then lined up an shot all uv them sons-of-bitches politicians that got us in that Goddamn war with the Goddamn Yankees, an then we should have lined up half ir gen'als, with Hood smack dab in front, and shot them too...I'm tellin you, Reverend, killin six-hundred thousand people just to hold onto a bunch of niggers wus a slop jar full of shit...an as to States' Rights, that's another crock of shit!"

Confederate Colonel
Benjamin Lafayette Stainback

"Lawd have mercy, Colonel, yo sure a booguh man today, but yo tellin the Gospel now, fo the good Lawd knows all about them dark days...you want anothuh drink outuh this jug fo I put back unduh the seat way from the sun?...Yes suh, Colonel, the Lawd knows, He knows...Get on mules, we ain't got all day, times awastin!"

Reverend Billy Highfield
Minister and Former Slave

The Colonel

Seventy-two-year-old Confederate Colonel Benjamin Lafayette Stainback was a banty-sized man, only five-foot, five inches tall and getting shorter every year. But he was still tough as a railroad spike and so stern-faced and bad-mouthed that people thought he was taller. He'd been around tough-talking, bad-cursing men since he was eighteen when he went to work for the Nashville, Chattanooga, and St. Louis Railway; and then, during the four years he fought with the 1st Tennessee, the toughness and cursing got worse; and as soon as the war was over, he went back among the railroad toughs as an engineer for fifty years. By the time he retired, he could say every curse word the Devil had come up with and "Goddamn" had become another adjective like 'the' for him. But he never used any "blackguards", as Miss Lillie called them, when children or women were around. He was as thin as a fence rail. The Colonel's uniform fit him as well as when he had first put it on just three weeks before Johnson surrendered him along with the few that remained of the Army of Tennessee over in North Carolina in the Spring of '65.

"Miss Lillie" Jane Wagner, The Colonel's wife of fifty-four years, thought he still looked smart when he was all dressed up in his outfit, especially when he wore his sword that he had not surrendered to the Yankees. She liked to brag to the women at the Estill Springs Baptist Church that he was still the fittest man she had ever seen, "Why, honey, he don't have a slice of pie anywhere on him even though he sho eats like a field hand." And, of course, hearing such bragging, the Church ladies just had to whisper behind their hands to one another about the men who Miss Lillie might have been checking over for pie slices.

She and The Colonel had one child, a boy named Marcus "Mark" Aurelius Stainback. The Colonel had named him. He was so filled with pride to have a son to

carry on the Stainback name – a name of no certain origin –
that he wanted his given name to be something special. And
it was. Whenever anyone would ask, "Where in the world
did you come up that odd name," red splotches would break
out on his neck and he would stare into their eyes like they
were fools and after a moment would hiss, "Well, I'll
Goddamn tell ye where...as sure as hell my boy's goin to be
a great man, so I named him after a great man." Then if
they asked him who Marcus Aurelius was he would shake
his head and hiss almost as if he was about to strike, "I ain't
got time to educate halfwits, so go look it up on your own
damn time." Other than him, Miss Lillie, and the Reverend,
there were eleven other people in Franklin County who
knew that Marcus Aurelius was one of Rome's greatest
emperors: an old Jewish clock repairer, six professors at the
University of the South, three lawyers, and one doctor.

Eighteen years after his father named him, Mark was
killed on the beautiful morning of October 8, 1862, at the
Battle of Perryville. Long years after he died, when Miss
Lillie had lady visitors for lunch, at some point she would
pick up one of the four framed tin-type photographs of him
she had placed around the house and hold it up with his face
toward the others and say, "Our Mark would have made
such a good daddy if he'd lived; he so loved little children."

The Colonel never got over his son's death. Afterward
he never talked about him. He never let anyone see that his
heart was broken; he just became more irascible and rough-
mouthed. People avoided him when he came to town.
Some whispered that he was the one who should have been
killed at Perryville instead of his boy; but they were careful
who they said it to so it didn't get back to him, for he always
carried a derringer in his coat pocket and always seemed on
the edge of dangerous.

You only had to look at his scarred and purple-splotched
hands and muscled forearms to tell that he was old and had
worked hard with his body all his life. But his watery eyes

were not the eyes of most old people; they could still see as clearly as when he was a boy. They had a haunting, dove-gray color that exactly matched the color of his uniform and were tiny and quick as a mink's, never seeming to rest as they scanned for something far off, or the face of the person standing right in front of him, or the magnificent words of his beloved Shakespeare.

Shakespeare was his Bible. He went to him nightly for wisdom and comfort. There were nights when he was reading a play or sonnet while Miss Lillie was sitting on the other side of the coal-oil lamp reading her Bible that were like heaven. He would look up from his reading and see her looking over her glasses smiling at him, and for a moment his heart would leap and his eyes would mist from loving her so much.

Other than her, there were only a few things in life that gave him much pleasure or rested his unyielding spirit: eating milk gravy mixed with crumbled biscuits - his dessert at every meal; walking with his dog Shep through the fields and woods of his forty-seven acres beside Elk River; reading Shakespeare and memorizing his soliloquies and sonnets – he was now on number 34; and not having to be around "fools-rampant" which included everybody but Miss Lillie and the Reverend.

For thirty years The Colonel and the Reverend had worked together as engineer and fireman in a sometimes burning hot, sometimes freezing cold locomotive cab of the Nashville, Chattanooga, & St. Louis Railway. During those years they had grown to totally trust and respect one another and once or twice they had saved each other's life. They knew they were each other's friend though neither had ever said it. They also knew that they were the two most intelligent people they knew with the exception of Miss Lillie whose practical wisdom outranked them both. They were mostly self-taught and, loving books as they did, had good libraries of history, philosophy, science, literature, and theology. Their brains forgot nothing they read or heard. In the Reverend's monthly visit to the Stainbacks for supper and conversation, the two of them sprinkled every kind of quotation into their discussions which would grow louder and louder when they were debating fine points of theology or Aristotelian logic and had had too much of Reverend Billy's homemade cider which The Colonel bought three barrels of every year and fermented with molasses. But no matter how much they enjoyed their brilliance, when they were in Miss Lillie's house; her word was law, and when they became too loud and too swollen with themselves, she could settle them down with a loud clearing of her throat or with three or four firm words, "Ya'll, that's enough now!" or "Ya'll calm down!" And they would immediately get quiet and usually the Reverend would say it was about time for him to be getting back home.

Early on in her marriage to The Colonel, Miss Lillie had realized that she was going to have to keep the bit in "Mr. Stainback's" mouth or someone was going to kill him before he reached thirty – and it might be her. Lillie Jane Wagner was the only creature on earth that The Colonel was scared of.

The Reverend

Except for The Colonel and Miss Lillie, most white people called Reverend Billy Highfield, "Uncle Billy." He was born a slave on Samuel Highfield's plantation in Greene County, Alabama, in 1836. He was a big, light-colored baby and grew into a big, light-colored, big-muscled man, standing a little over six-foot-three in his broad bare feet that didn't wear shoes until they were ten years old. Because of his color and high cheekbones, some thought his daddy must have been an Indian.

But it wasn't his size or appearance that made him special to people when he came to live near Tullahoma; it was his kindness to others, poor or rich, black or white, righteous or sinner. When people needed him, no matter how bad a sinner they were, he went quickly and prayed for God's help and always left them comforted. The same prayer he prayed for the righteous. Those who knew him well, both black and white, thought he was one of the best people God had put on this earth. He was a happy man with a face that seemed to keep a slight smile as though he was thinking something good. No one could imagine that he ever had a troubled thought. And he loved to laugh, most especially at The Colonel's colorful condemnations of mankind, though he wished he could make them without saying "Goddamn" so much.

Reverend Billy Highfield was a great preacher. He was known afar for being able to quote all of the Bible and for his sermons on "The Day Christ Died" and "We are All God's Children." And though he sometimes used words that few in the congregation of the Mt. Zion African Methodist Church understood, they were never troubled since they knew he would never speak a falsehood even with a single strange word. Every Sunday his deep bass voice rolled mercy and forgiveness over them like ocean waves, bringing hope and comfort as did the waters of baptism and the Supper of the Lord.

While he was kind to everyone and was an ordained Gospel minister, Billy Highfield made some white men uneasy when they were around him, not so much because of his size, but what really bothered them was their instinctive recognition that he was far smarter than they were. Only in a whisper did any of them ever say he was an "uppity nigger", and that only when they were certain that the person they were talking to would not pass it along to The Colonel. No man or woman who knew The Colonel wanted those words passed on to him as they knew there was a good possibility of his coming after them with his gun or a knife.

In the fifteenth year of Billy Highfield's life, he had been a prime field hand worth over a thousand dollars. However, instead of putting him into the fields, Samuel made him his groom with responsibility for caring for his two fine saddle horses and four brood mares. Three years later he brought him into the big house as his body servant and that same year began to teach Billy to read and write.

Samuel Highfield owned three thousand acres, one hundred and twenty slaves and the finest library in Green County, Alabama. A year after he was married, his wife Fannie died trying to give birth to a baby boy who was dead inside her. Within one month of Fannie's death, Samuel took her maidservant, a fine-boned woman from East Africa, to his bed. Nine months later Billy was born. And though he was their master and owned them, Samuel loved Mary and Billy; he loved them up to the second he was killed by a Minie ball on the bitter-cold, rainy Friday of December 16, 1864, fighting with the 7th Alabama Cavalry as part of the rear guard of the destroyed Confederate Army as it began its long retreat southward to Mississippi.

Billy stayed with Samuel all through the war as his body servant. He did not love his father; he obeyed him. Less than ten minutes after he heard that his father had been killed, Billy filled a haversack full of food, hung a bedroll over his shoulder, put on the Major's heavy overcoat and hid in the woods near Franklin. For two days he stayed there until he was certain all of Hood's Army was gone. Then he began to walk through the mud and ice beside the railroad tracks that led to Tullahoma where his only child Hattie who, when she was three, was sold along with her mother Liza, Billy's wife, to a Tullahoma doctor to pay the large debt Samuel Highfield owed on his land. On the evening of the fourth day, covered with mud and freezing, he stepped up onto the platform of the Tullahoma Train Station. An hour later he found his wife and daughter living with an old black woman in a green shack on the east side of the railroad tracks. They had been freed in the summer of 1863 by the Federal Army as it moved south through Franklin County.

On a warm Sunday morning in August, 1867, Liza died of 'the fever.' The day after she was buried in Mt. Zion Cemetery, Billy did what she had been praying for: He confessed that Jesus Christ was his Savior and was baptized. As he would tell his congregation years later, "The day after my Liza went home to be with our Lawd, He reached down with His big hand and lifted my old sinful soul up to Him and washed it whiter than snow...Yes, suh, that's what He done for me an that's what He can do fo all sinners who wants to be made clean...Praise the Lawd!"

Three months after Liza's death, Billy began working as a fireman for the railroad. On the very first day when he climbed up into the cab of a locomotive there was The Colonel. From that day until thirty years later, they worked side by side. When they retired on the same day, The Colonel took Billy's hand in a tight grip and gave him a fine gold watch that he had just received from the President of the N.C.& St. L. Railway and said, loud enough for everyone standing near to hear, "Billy, yore one helluva man. I'm shore gonna miss yore black ass."

Soon after he retired, Billy went to live with Hattie and her husband, John, at their small place a quarter of a mile south of Tullahoma. He began preaching full time and it was not long before all black people called him Reverend Billy, and so did some whites.

The Wagon Ride

Today is a perfect day. Decoration Day, June 3, 1898, and Jefferson Davis's birthday is as near perfect as day as can be. The early morning sun is rising in a pure blue sky; the air is easy to breathe, clean and sweet and filled with the smells of earth and new growth; the road is lined with rail fences and wild rose hedges, red sumac, pink fireweed and honeysuckle; from the thickets and fields come the callings of thrushes, quail and meadowlarks; and nearby, to the left of the road where the bank of the Elk River is lined by an old grove of oaks, chestnuts, and maples, a flock of crows rises from their roost cawing to one another as they head to the fields to feed. Almost parallel to the road is the railroad track that runs all the way from St. Louis through Nashville and over the mountains to Chattanooga. In the early morning air, the dust from the stirrings of the mules' hoofs and wagon wheels hangs close to the ground; and beyond the fences, the fields stretch away in their varied shades of green of the young corn and wheat and cotton and of the pastures where cattle and sheep are grazing. It is a splendid day! Even The Colonel feels it for a moment. Then a train whistle from far behind him breaks the splendor, and he suddenly remembers how much he despises this day.

For ten years, on every third day of June, The Colonel and the Reverend have made this trip to Winchester for the Celebration, leaving Estill after breakfast at The Colonel's, in the Reverend's farm wagon, on which he always puts a fresh coat of green paint and red for the wheels. This morning the Reverend left Tullahoma in the dark. He arrived at the Stainbacks a little before daybreak just as Miss Lillie was taking the biscuits out of the oven. After stuffing themselves with ham and eggs and biscuits and gravy and buttermilk, they climbed up on the wooden wagon seat with the woven basket she had filled with fried peach pies and fried chicken and headed up the lane to the main road where they turned left to Winchester.

The wagon bed is packed with clay jugs of the Reverend's cider which he sells out of on the square every year and gives one fifth of the money to the Church. And every year The Colonel brings his own jug. It now sits between their feet under the wagon seat. They go only a quarter of a mile when he reaches down and lifts it up, pulls the cork, and takes two long swigs. When he finishes, he breathes out hard, "Damn, that'll make you strut!" and wipes his lips with his sleeve and hands the jug to the Reverend who takes one short swig and breathes out, "Lawd, Colonel, the way you've stoutin it up is mighty fine!" He shifts his bottom into a more comfortable position and undoes the top button of his shirt in preparation for one of The Colonel's soliloquies, which he knows is forthcoming and which he knows will probably last most of the trip to Winchester.

It begins with a hack and a spit, followed by a loud clearing of the throat. His voice is like a rusty saw. "I'll tell ye one damn thing, Reverend, wearin this itchy wool uniform and walkin in a parade alongside a bunch of farty, ole toothless veterans an listenin to them beat their gums about how we could uv won the Goddamn war if such an such had happened or not happened is worse than bein in the Goddamn war; an then sure as hell they'll start on what a drunk Grant was an what a lunatic Sherman was, an all that stuff is a crock of shit...hellfire an damnation! Grant an Sherman beat our ass! An I betcha one of my jugs aginst three of yours that that damn train from Nashville is gonna unload two or three of those Nancy-boy reporters and one'll come up to me an ask that same old stupid-ass question they always ask, 'Colonel, wouldcha mind telling us why you fought in the war?' That's what they's gonna ask me, why I fought in the Goddamn war!...I tell you, Reverend, if I don't shoot 'im with my derringer I'm gonna scare the shit out of 'im with my face and voice...'Well, sonny boy, I'll tell ye why I fought in the Goddamn war: 'cause the Goddamn Yankees were gonna come down here on my land, where my house is, an they were going to upset Miss Lillie, an steal my cows an hogs an whatever else they could lay their thieving hands on...an they were gonna do all that just to free all the niggers, an I'd only owned one of 'em way back, a no account high-yellar that wasn't worth piss, an when he ran off I almost fell on my knees an thanked the Lord, so I sure as hell wasn't fightin' to keep the niggers...far as I's concerned they could uv had 'em all free.'" He paused and took a deep breath. 'An one more thing in case you wanta put something in your little piss ant paper 'bout why I waste my good time dressin up in this monkey suit an comin to these Goddamn things. It's cause I'm a Goddamn hero since I personally shot an kilt eleven Yankees an there's some genteel ladies who love havin a real bonafide hero in the Goddamn parade to march 'round the square, so's I put up with all this damn tomfoolery 'cause they pay me to come an dress up an have my picture made with all the other ole farts.' Then, Reverend, I'm goin to grap 'hold of his shoulders an squeeze down hard an look straight in his eyes an say, 'Now does that answer yo stupid-ass question about why I fought in the Goddamn war?'" He stops again. This time his neck is flushed all the way around. He licks his lips, "Good Lord, my spit's all dried up I've run my mouth so much." He reaches down and gets the jug and balances it on his knee and pulls the cork out. "Now, Reverend, you take a lick at the talking for awhile while I get my spit back...Tell ye what, I wanta hear how ye come up with those milk-sop names, Kate and Beck, for them mules of yores."

The old preacher is looking straight ahead, his face is set like an amber mask with no emotion. He does not speak for a full minute, then begins, "Colonel Benjamin, you wants to know where those names come from...they comes from a long ways back. 'Member those dark days, when my peoples were owned by yo peoples...they's the names of two of em who was owned...they's the names of a little brothah an sistah, they was twins, they's had faces like sunlight, smiling an laughin...they's little bitty things but even then yo could see in their eyes they's smart as tacks. They lived right next to us with their mama, so near yo could hear 'em laughin at night an first thing the next monin they's start all over agin."

He stops and wets his lips with his tongue an looks down at his hands holding the reins, he turns them palm up as though looking for something, then continues, "Then one monin The Major calls all us people togethah in the front yard an he walks out of the house onto the porch an looks at us sorta sad like an then he begins talkin an tellin us how he's 'bout to lose the land an if he don't sell some of us we all gonna be split up an sold away...an ever'body gets real quiet an he says he's done the best he can to sell as few uv us as possible an then he stops talkin an he coughs an then he says he's got to go to town tomorrow an settle up with the bank, an Mr. Haddus- he was the overseer - would let those that's been sold know in the monin an'll help 'em get on they ways with their new masters, an then all the rest of us could rest easy an know they's all be stayin with him. Then he close his eyes an holds his right hand up high an prays, 'Dear God, watch over these my people. Amen.' An then he turns an walks back in the house an there's not a sound or a movement...it seemed like we were gonna never move agin, an then Big Isaac, the driver, claps his hands loud an shouts, 'Les get on to the fields!'"

Now his voice is almost a whisper without the slightest inflection. The longer he talks the fainter it becomes, as though he is going farther and farther away, "So he sold off my Liza an my baby girl, Hattie, an some mo people...an he sold off them two little chillun from their mama...an that's where the mules' names come from, those chillun names be Kate an Beck. I still sees their faces right now while I's talkin, I sees em an hears em cryin for their mama an she be pleadin with them white men that were takin em away." He stops...then, "An, O my Lawd God, Colonel, I can still sees my Liza an Hattie cryin an lookin at me an I's beggin Mr. Haddus to take me an not take them an...an none of it kept it from happenin, an they just gone...an...an...." There comes another long silence, and then he speaks in a voice The Colonel has never heard. It is cold and hard, and every word is clear, "Even if it was to send me to burn in hell forevah, I'd kill any man - even my daddy, if he was to come back - that'd try to make me or my Hattie a slave agin."

The mules' slow, steady plodding has continued all this while, their movement gently rocking the wagon's seat and the bodies of the two silent old men. Both are looking straight ahead toward the distant bridge that will take them over the river and up the slope to the square and the courthouse where the townspeople and the country people have already begun to gather.

The Reverend turns his head and looks at The Colonel, "You know, Colonel, you nevah ask me what it was like bein a slave an I's nevah said a thing 'til now... folks look at me an they sees a kind-lookin, ole white-haired colored preacher who likes to help people, an that's pretty much true now, but I hadn't always been this way. A long time ago, before the Lawd an Liza change me, I wants to kill people...wants to kill white people fo what they done to us...I'd wanted to kill you I was so full of hate. Bein a slave is a bad thing, so bad you can't nevah know it, we wadn't mo than a bunch of two-legged animals worth lots uv money...the Major an his wife, they was church goin people who said the blessin at all their meals an always talking 'bout Jesus an how someday they's goin to heaven, an look at what they did...they's made me hate Jesus an the Lawd God. But all the while I nevah lets on, I's covered it all up, all my sadness an hate, even when they's sold my Liza an Hattie away, I's didn't show nothin 'cause I's promised her I wouldn't kill someone or do somethin awful an that one day I'd come an find em an we'd be togethah again...An thas what I did...An the Lawd was good to me an forgive my sinful heart an answered my prayers, an so Him and Liza, they's change me an they's teach me to want to be good and to help others an He move my heart to preach His word an help sinners like me to find Him...Colonel, there's many a night I thank Him for you bein my bes friend, 'cause spite the ways you talk, an Lawd have mercy how you talks, Miss Lillie wouldn't live with no bad man. All those long years we's workin in that hot cab, you was lookin out fo me goin up and down them mountains, and you saves me from dyin fo my time." He took his straw hat off and raised his tear-streaked face to the sky, "Thank you, Lawd God an Jesus, for given me Colonel Benjamin Lafayette Stainback to be my friend, an, Lawd, lay yo hand on him an Miss Lillie an give them comfort, an a place with you when they leaves this ole world. Amen!"

When he ended, both were quiet. He put his hat back on, pulled a bandanna from his inside coat pocket and blew his nose and wiped his eyes. Then he smiled and gently slapped the reins, "Get on up there, Kate an Beck, times awastin, we gots money to make."

The Colonel reaches out with his hand and gently pats his old friend's knee.

The mules lift their heads and step out faster. Now, in the warmer air, a little dust rises behind their hoofs and the wheels of the wagon, and from beyond the river comes the first sounds of horns and a drum and the high piercing whistle of the train.

Conflict Remaining, 1910

S.R. Lee

Margaret scrunched down in her chair, making her ten-year-old body as small and still as she could. Of all the guests, relatives, and strangers who sometimes ate breakfast at the rectory kitchen table, Uncle Louie was the worst. He only came for a visit twice a year, but Margaret felt she could remember every shameful moment of every visit since she started to school. The school building was right where a big battle had been fought. Soldiers had died there not even fifty years ago.

On the playground when she was in first grade, a big boy had come up to say, "Your Uncle Louie fought for the Yankees didn't he? You got damn Yankee kin."

She hadn't told at home. At school, somehow every time he came, the rumor seemed to run through the upper grades and quickly arrive at hers—now the fourth. Did the littler kids know, she thought. That would be terrible. Sometimes the thought made her stomach hurt so much she would ask to go home. The teacher always let her.

This morning was Saturday, sunny with a little breeze. The old soldiers would be collecting on the Square all day, chewing tobacco, whittling, talking to anyone who would listen, some of them propped up as best they could without legs, missing an arm, or with a sunken spot where an eye should be.

With good weather, farm folks coming into town for Saturday shopping would bring their old men, give grandfather a chance to sit in the sunlight with his old comrades in battle, talk and brag and curse maybe." No harm done," said Margaret's minister father.

Uncle Louie was feeling expansive this morning, talking already, even before he walked out for the Square.

"Wisht I'd been in that occupying army down here, all this sunshine, not much danger. Could have learned to love this place, might have stayed."

Margaret thought, "What's wrong with his home in Illinois? Up there he can talk to Yankees like himself." The word "damn" crossed her mind, but she didn't allow it to stay there, pushed it out like she pushed out other thoughts—the big grin on the eighth grade boy's face at school, the confusion of kneeling in church and saying she would forgive other people's trespasses when really she knew she would stay mad, the strange hurt she felt from her friends' pride in old houses. She'd stay home this morning, help her mother set up for tomorrow's communion. Be unnoticed.

Uncle Louie worked his bullet-crippled arm into his coat sleeve, took his walking cane, and left to walk the two blocks to the Square.

Margaret knew he would be there along with the first of the old Confederates, all talking and spitting, all bragging. He'd come home for some lunch but go back until sundown.

Sometimes Margaret wondered if they'd stab him with that old cavalry sword Garrison Davis's great uncle brought down there in good weather. He'd start to brag about how many men he'd stuck with it, and sometimes mothers would move their small children out of earshot. Uncle Louie ought to be afraid, but Margaret figured he was just too ignorant to know how Southerners thought. She knew; she'd been living in this town since the first grade.

The day snailed its way toward sunset. Margaret's mother seemed to have many chores for her. The family delayed supper until dark, when Uncle Louie would return.

He was clearly tired from his day of visiting, but still happy and wanting to talk.

"You should see that sword. Old Man Davis keeps it sharp as a razor, shiny as the sun. But he hands it around to hold. Margaret, I cut you this little stick with that good blade. Save it now for it's touched history."

Margaret laid the small stick politely beside her plate. She didn't want it in her room. It had touched history, the mean, dangerous part that everybody needed to forget.

School Yard Find, 1930's

content by Mary Lynch
verse form by S.R. Lee

1.
Behind St. Ann's school,
the fourth grade played outside
without thought of the indention in the ground.
Sometimes one might say, "Don't trip there."

Then a curious boy dug about.
found a metal ball,
larger, heavier than a Minie ball.
But no one told the fourth grade
it might have come from a cannon.

The teacher set it on her desk,
and there it stayed for a while,
silent, mysterious.

Now at ninety, one student remembers,
not sure what it might have been.
but it seemed to have come from war
even to a Catholic school ground.

2.
Its size was impressive,
to the younger children
who never touched it.

Not far under the grass
of the school yard,
it had waited three quarters
of a century, patient, still,
until found.

School children
watched the heavy ball
waiting on a teacher's desk,
unexplained but present.

Weight of war unseen,
sensed though undescribed.
remains in memory
without permission.

3,
Peace and a normal life
for the children, grandchildren,
decades of work for adults,
of school for children,
a few sudden silences,
some names ignored.

Years pass,
good harvests, drought,
business, family,
a city's growth,
prosperity or bad times.

Beneath our feet, relics wait.

Someone will dig.
Shovel strikes hard.
An arrowhead?
Let's make a collection.
A cannon ball?
Perhaps best not explained.

Battlefield, 1937

S.R. Lee

One hot summer day, a boy,
with little sister tagging behind,
climbs to a low crest where
three weathered trenches
sink in weedy waves,
long lines of buckbush
and prickly pears.
The boy brings friends.
Enthralled, they play at war.
Unprepared for cactus,
little sister in sun suit, sandals,
follows their violent charge
through real war's land.
Her sandaled feet are soon
darted with tiny spears.

Little sister weeps to home
where Mother with shiny tweezers
becomes a battle surgeon
claiming pain must follow wounds.
The child sobs
and in her baby way
learns that real danger
dwells in battlefields forever.

Blue and Grey

Margaret Britton Vaughn
Poet Laureate of Tennessee

"Tell mama and family I fought the good fight."
Then the soldier's soul turned out his light.
His flag for country flew in the wind,
His last words spoke of country and kin.
His buddies who stood by his side
Fought on in battle while the next one died.
Stars and Bars and Stars and Stripes
Flew in the wind like they were kites.
Blue and Grey fought for their cause,
Blue and Grey both wrapped in gauze.
A country divided in their beliefs,
A country united by the same griefs.
When the smoke had settled and gone,
The Blue and Grey returned to home.
Today we dig for buckles and balls,
Brass buttons to decorate our walls.
I wonder if the fallen's wildest fears
Were that someday they'd be souvenirs.

A Boy Understands

Jane Wilkerson Yount

A lad studied, walked the Shy's Hill woods,
Seeking to learn about that war,
Found trenches where the desperate fought,
Dug Minie balls that bodies tore.

He climbed the hills, rough, steep,
Fell on rocks where blood had been,
Knew cold rain, this worn out boy
Felt helpless misery of those men.

In three years, pulled to later war,
In diary penned, understanding this:
"Never has peace been appreciated enough."
So to the Battle that was his.

Author's Note: Jane is the sister of Bill Wilkerson (photo opposite page), killed at nineteen years old in World War II in the Battle of the Bulge. The Bill Wilkerson Hearing and Speech Center of Nashville was named for him.

Bill Wilkerson
Photograph courtesy of Jane Wilkerson Yount

Federal Cemetery
Nashville, Tennessee,
early 20th Century

S.R. Lee

endless rows of small white tombstones
over green grass
protected by a stone wall
driver of a passing car says
"Only land an invading army
ever keeps."

Photograph by Emily Nance

The Curio Cabinet

Lin Folk

When I was a child growing up in Los Angeles, California, the Civil War had very little meaning to me except for a few pages in history books and watching bewhiskered old men marching in Memorial Day parades. But when I married a Tennessean, Reau Folk, Jr., my appreciation for and knowledge of the War Between the States increased.

As newlyweds my husband and I arrived in Nashville in December of 1945. When we came to the family home where we would be living for the next year, I wasn't taken to see our living quarters but instead was escorted into the parlor to see the curio cabinet with its treasures. And there it was, on the top shelf of the cabinet, the little blue velvet pillow with the most meaningful of treasures resting on top of it: a pocket sized Bible with the top right-hand corner shot away.

Matthew Barrow Pilcher, my husband's grandfather, was fighting in the battle of Perryville (west of Perryville, Kentucky, October 8, 1862) when a shot came toward him, striking the little book which was over his heart and ripping out the corner of the book which deflected the bullet so that his life was saved. The pillow and the book occupy an important place in the curio cabinet today, a reminder of one life saved and the many lives which were lost.

After Matthew's injury, he was cared for by a good woman, Mrs. Rochester, who lived near Perryville. His father and mother, Nancy Barrow and Merritt Pilcher, journeyed to Perryville from Nashville to be with him. He was a prisoner while at the Rochester's.

Photograph courtesy of Lin Folk
The Bible that deflected the bullet is still preserved by the family.

Later he was exchanged and sent back to his command when he was again wounded in the battle of Franklin, and another good woman, Mrs. Carter, took him to her house. He was expected to die, and Mrs. Carter sent for his parents. It was December with snow and ice on the ground. They had been warned not to make the trip from Nashville to Franklin, but nothing could stop them. They started out with a carriage and two horses, but the ice was so thick that the horses had a hard time pulling the carriage. Merritt Pilcher got out of the carriage and walked up all the hills. After reaching Franklin, the parents saw their son, but the father was weak and suffering from pneumonia. With every house in Franklin full of the wounded, Mrs. Carter squeezed him into the same room with his son. The father, Merritt Pilcher, died there in the bed next to his son. The son, Matthew Barrow Pilcher, recovered and lived many years after the war.

During my years in Nashville, I've learned of many episodes similar to this and the hardships that the Civil War brought to so many families.

The bearded men marching in the California parades are all gone now, but my thoughts of them and what they represented remain as I think about the Civil War after living for nearly seventy years on the ground where they fought.

Boyhood of a Tennessee Educator

George Northern

In the early 1930's when I was growing up, sharecropping in Williamson County, Tennessee, was alive and well. My Daddy had found a good job with an educated family who were better than most of the white landowners in the area.. He earned a salary when he worked on the farm except when he worked for himself. We lived in a peach orchard where my Daddy was caretaker and part-time farmer.. Our family was poor; but compared to other black families, we lived pretty well.

Mama was an excellent cook who could make a meal when it looked like there was nothing in the house to eat. We always had lots of chickens, and it was the small children's job to scare the crows off to prevent them from eating the baby chicks. She gave the farm the name Ringcrow Valley as it seemed that we were always watching out for crows. The only time I saw her shoot a gun was to scare the crows away because I was too small to chase them.

Growing up in Ringcrow Valley, I never thought that I would become a principal of the most prestigious school in Williamson County, let alone the state of Tennessee. Being black, poor, and a stutterer as well as being the eleventh child in a family of twelve children, all I could hope for was to get a job like my older brothers. My Daddy believed that if you worked hard, stayed out of trouble, and learned a trade, you would be all right.

In a way I was fortunate because my older brother was three years older and my younger sister was four years younger. Mama was a natural born teacher even though she only finished the 6th grade. After that, she was expected to either work for a white family or stay at home to take care of the other children while her mother worked.

My Grandfather had married once before he married my Grandmother. Both wives died. Mama was the youngest girl in the family; and when she finished school, she went to Nashville to live with her father's sister. This aunt was well to do because she was a head housekeeper for Chancellor Kirkland of Vanderbilt University. She got Mama a job working with her for the Chancellor. That is where Mama learned to love books. We always had books in our home. Mama kept the school books until they were out. We always took the newspaper as Mama would sell eggs to pay for the subscription. We also subscribed to a magazine called the *Farmer's Home Journal.*

During the early days before we got a radio, Mama would read the paper aloud to us, especially the funnies. I also read from the newspaper plastered on the wall to keep out the cold air as well as from the labels on boxes and cans. So hearing Mama read and helping the older children with homework, I had a head start with school.

My older sister taught school in Kirkland, a rural community in Williamson County, so she was able to come home on weekends. To watch her grade papers and do other school work made me want to become a teacher. There was a boy named Charlie who had a hard time reading so he got a whipping almost every day. I felt sorry for Charlie, so instead of playing at recess, I would help him practice his reading lessons.

One morning we met on the road to school and Charlie started running. He was so happy. "George, I can read." he shouted. We sat down in the middle of the gravel road, and he read his lesson and did not miss a word. I was hooked. I must have been about fourth grade. I knew at that time I wanted to be a teacher.

Reading was my favorite subject. By the end of the fourth grade. I had read every book in our library which consisted of a homemade book shelf. Because I would stutter, I would sing my lesson. I never said speeches at church because I would stutter so badly. I would always sing a song that I learned from Mama and Daddy's singing.

Because my mother was a kind and compassionate woman, she would always put a finger over my lips and tell me to slow down. She would take time with me, read to me slowly and then ask me to read it back to her. Mama was truly my first teacher. Her patience paid off; by the time I started to school, I could read without stuttering. Miss Mattie was a very strict teacher, and I was afraid of her. I did not know at the time but I was one of her prize pupils. She took me to spend the night at her home so that I could participate in a contest. I won a blue ribbon for first place.

I guess there were advantages to a one room school. There was always noise except when we had study periods and then it would be quiet. Often the older ones would teach the younger ones. In such a school you could learn leadership skills. I was school president for two years. Each year we had an end of the year program when all the parents would attend. I cannot remember there being a discipline problem. Children played like brothers and sisters.

Somehow I always loved learning new things. I wanted to go further because I knew if I was to be a teacher I had to go to high school and then college. Daddy saw to it that my sister went to college because he did not want her to work for a white family or work on the farm. He had his reasons.

We had a Home Demonstration Agent who worked for the University of Tennessee and served also as our 4-H teacher. She asked my parents if I could go to Tennessee A&I College for a summer camp. Of course my mother said yes. Miss Epps picked me up and took me to summer camp. I had the best time of my life. This was a life changing experience. I got to live in a college dormitory, eat the cafeteria food, go swimming in the pool, see movies at night, attend college events, and hang out with college students. For the second time in my life, I was hooked. This was the only state-run black college in the state of Tennessee, so I was exposed to students from all over the United States. This was my first time to be away from home, and I loved every minute of it.

I knew that someday I would return to go to school at Tennessee A&I College and become a teacher. That fall I would start to high school.

Landowner's Meeting, 1964

S.R. Lee

The County sent each landowner
an orange postcard
validating the right
to vote on this issue.
The night was warm;
the school cafeteria packed,
people standing along the walls
down both sides.
"What was this zoning issue?"
"What changes were to come?"
Each man had an orange postcard,
often a wife by his side.

The County official raised his voice for quiet.
At that moment, the door opened,
once more admitting men,
three, stout, overalled men.
Orange postcards peeped from bib pockets.
Dark skins contrasted with pale green walls.
All standing along the sides noticed.
Among the seated, a few quickly glanced back.
The County official called the meeting to order.

It was a long, hot meeting
with many asking questions,
offering opposing points of view.
Finally a resolution was proposed
and counted by a "show of hands."
The County official read it loud and
clear to the listening crowd.
The heavy door clicked open.

The three black men walked out silently.
There were calls to "Vote!, Stay and Vote!"
But they had disappeared into the night,
toward their cars parked in the dark,
gone before the uneasy crowd
escaped the building.

Slaves and Skeletons

Von Derry

I moved to the infamous Civil War town of Franklin
   Tennessee in 1975.
It was a hotbed of secret wife swapping
   homosexual identity hiding,
      educated, eccentric characters.

All manner of interesting folks flowed in and out
      the quaint pretty little town:
rednecks sly as foxes,
   how they could be so lazy and get by,
drug dealers hiding out in the countryside
      all around town,
several sheriff's deputies hooked on sex and drugs.

Seems like every one or most were keeping skeletons
   locked in closets.

One of my dearest friends was a gay artist. who loved the
   drink.
He bought Clouston Hall
   and ran a myriad of renters through his house and life
   in the old town manse
once a Civil War hospital
      with blood and bodies
where he and his posse now painted parties
      and parlayed their insanities.

Blood stains were still visible on the original wood floors
   occupied by Miss Ninny, the Ghost.

One of the renters was a writer who,
      unbeknownst to anyone,
   liked to asphyxiate himself
     in front of his mother's wedding dress.
One day while doing this, he died.

Four days later,
   the body stunk so bad
everyone in the house
      complained of the stench.
The landlord, of course, had the skeleton key to unlock his
   doors.

Later he told me that when the ambulance guys
   picked up the bloated body
"He popped." he said,
     "He popped, dear."

More fluid on the Civil War floor
and the landlord/artist who was a slave to the Civil War
   house
     in the Civil War town
was so distraught
     he stopped drinking for two weeks.

The Absurdity of War

Nick Dantona

I saw a cache of newspapers today, from 1936.
Pages and pages of musty, frail newsprint
browned with Hitler's rampage
while Miss Irene Nesbit of Mt. Pleasant, Tennessee,
conducted a successful tea
for the United Daughters of the Confederacy.

Steak was on sale for 83 cents a pound,
while a negro broke his leg stealing a car.
How does a body do that?
Sounds like the local Constabulary
took their pound of flesh
while the nice Ladies were sipping tea.

Chitter chattering, protecting the honor of
Confederate poor boys dumb enough
to believe that war could be gallant,
even chivalrous. The enormous, profound loss
sends shivers chattering down my spine.
Don't worry, boys!
The Ladies will remember
you 150 years later while
eating Po' Boys in Naw'lins.

Oh, yes please, a Beignet and a cup
of chicory coffee. Please pass the newspaper
before they make a fresh brew of news
to fill the pages that will get musty and brown
to stack in some abandoned building
waiting for a guy like me who is filling the pages
of his own book to shatter the silence.
Everyday I write this book with abandon.

Author's Note: I've had the good fortune to walk some of the battlefields, particularly Gettysburg, with retired Special Forces General Officers. Their insights on strategy and the pain they still feel for these men have left an indelible mark on my heart. Many times during these tours we were left speechless and more than occasionally, breathless. Anything that honors their memory is precious to me.

The Herringbone Way

Randy Foster

There is no glory
on the herringbone way.
There is no grandeur
in the cold bricks
connecting Carnton to
the land of the living.
Neither does magnificence reign
on the back porch
where the generals lay
after the smoke cleared
late that November night.
Only shades remain.

When flashing sabers slashed
and angry sergeants barked
their officers' final orders to advance,
the gray-clad privates
fell in obedient rows
as fodder for shallow graves
that swallowed them into eternity.
But the generals' wraiths still hover,
And with regretful, silent steps pace
to a cadence called by their demons.

For them, there is no end to
the high carnival of death
born of hailing canister shot
and sleeting Minié balls that
tore through the air
and through the unwilling
flesh of horses and men alike

to lodge at last for all time
in the silent walls that
keep vigil to this very day.

For Franklin's gray generals,
only unceasing, hopeless,
bitter memory remains
of the death of their dear army
and of their misbegotten hopes
before the battlements of a sleepy town
now gone to seed with urban sprawl
and the unhappy fumes of modernity.

Carnton with its herringbone walkway
Photograph courtesy of Rick Warwick

Looking Back

Gale Buntin Haddock

They were gray and blue,
Ragged and starched,
Barefoot and booted.
Brother with brother,
Brother against brother,
Yet brothers all
In misery and in jubilation,
In grief and in gratitude,
With vengeance and with remorse.
Rushing, plodding, falling, crawling,
Yelling and cursing and praying in whispers
Before and after and in between,
And then, at some point, ending,
Perhaps with fury and roar, maybe quietly,
But whether in mayhem or a still corner,
Often unnoticed, or barely so, until later.
And for others, ending only after long memories
Trail into twilight at some distant edge of life.

Photograph by Emily Nance

What do we who weren't there know of this?
Nothing really, only maneuvers and strategy,
Statistics, famous names, and certain exploits.
We are left with remnants, tattered incomplete shreds
Of what took place at that time.

9 THE LONG VIEW

Photograph by Emily Nance

The Long View
content by Norman Nash
verse form by S.R. Lee

My adolescent self thought,
"Those men lost."
Huge stone monuments progressed
through the center of Richmond,
commemorating failures all

while we living, working, blacks
felt no sense of victory
though slavery was no more.

Older, I too became a soldier,
attentive to the needs of country,
an officer responsible
for military materiel
and the lives of men
in the Vietnam jungles.

Meanwhile, civilian housing practice
in the States decreed that
an affordable home for wife and child
was not for families like mine.
Infuriating! to fight for others' freedom
while racial prejudice
humiliates us in our own land.

I thought of my predecessors:
the Tuskegee Airmen of World War II
World War I black troops in French trenches,
the black Union troops of the Civil War.

Amazing courage in those days,
both military and civil:
Frederick Douglass spoke out;
field hands volunteered for combat
in a nation confused as to loyalties,
its motives unclear,
stumbling bloodily toward a new age.

How proud I am of their courage
facing the slaughtering bullet sweeps of battle,
facing the Ku Klux hangman's noose
in the decades following.

I think much of the present and the future:
where, when, and why we face obstacles?
what will the next decade bring?
the next political change effect?

I think also of the past:
with pride rejoice in those Black Union troops
fighting in the cold mud of winter,
the dry dust of summer,
black men giving their lives
for equality, trust, and respect of persons.

Out of terror and loss,
the end of that Civil War
brought a real beginning
from which we have spent 150 years,
a full fifteen decades,
working toward respect and freedom,
objectives desired and worthy
but only partially achieved.

The Coyote's Den

By Michael J. Tucker

I saw the coyote in the darkness before dawn
Running with his prey
To a den hidden among abandoned graves
Where soldiers lay

No one remembers on Memorial Day
Nor do they find their way on Veteran's Day
How did these men get forgotten
When everyone came to pick the cotton?

Have things changed in any way?
Do the old still send the young away?
Do poor men go to war so
Rich men can keep slaves, or gold, or oil?

What happened to his leg, or arm, or eye?
Was it a token sacrifice?
Mother, father, sister, brother, husband, wife,
Children wait for what will never return

What idea is gone, what child never born,
What story never told, what song never sung?
Are the tears falling from heaven
God's, or Allah's, or Buddha's, or merely rain?

These soldiers went to early graves
Believing they died for a worthy cause.
Today these soldiers rest in peace
Where a coyote rests after his feast

Officer R.E. Lee 1838

Lori C. Byington

Glancing left, the young man stares-
Afraid the artist will not do his portrait justice.
The model doesn't move
Lest his ebony curls fall onto his perfect, ivory forehead.
But the artist did well,
For the young officer's agate colored eyes pierce through the
    canvas.
His handsome nose, once broken, slopes forever downward;
It seems to point to the slight smirk that rests above a strong,
    cleft chin.
The handsome visage displays a sly hint of what he thinks he
    knows.
Dressed in the dark uniform of the US Army Corps of
    Engineers,
the youngster already sports gold buttons and feathered
    epaulettes.
His high collar displays a petit gold star ensconced in golden
    leaves
That represent a more peaceful time.
He knows this picture is the last that will portray his
    innocence,
So he waits patiently to see the finished piece.
Soon- he will be heralded in an older, hoary, bloodier light-
He will be a hero.

*Written upon seeing the picture of the painting of Lee as a young officer of the
U.S. Army Corp of Engineers in an article by Gary W. Gallagher, "Robert E.
Lee's Conflicted Loyalties" in *Civil War Times*, Oct. 2011. (opposite page)

Photograph courtesy of Lori C. Byington

Commitment

Elizabeth Roten

I guess I never really realized I was growing up in a Civil War town. There was the statue of the Confederate soldier in the Square in Franklin, and we took school field trips to the Carton Plantation and Carter House. It never really clicked for me how much history I was living in; where my neighborhood was built, there could have been soldiers camped. The road we drove on everyday was where they could have marched to battle, knowing that they might not survive. I remember asking my father which side Tennessee was on and associating the war with just slavery and not the whole load of other things it involved.

I started getting more interested after a while. We went to a park and saw where they would hide to avoid the whizzing bullets of the enemy. I went to museums. It took me weeks to get the feeling of death and fear off my shoulders after visiting a Confederate cemetery. I read up on women in the war, feminism growing in me. What made me realize where I was is an event that took almost everyone by surprise. There was a body found while digging for construction. I thought on this for weeks. What about his family? Did they just leave him behind? I was later told in a walking tour that there was no exact battlefield. I looked around at the streets and the scarred church, the house waving yellow flags indicating it was a hospital back then, and realized the magnitude of what I had taken for granted. This is where people gave their lives for something that they believed in, a freedom that they thought worth dying for. They left their wives and children and walked hundreds of miles to meet their death with a battle cry.

I've never really been committed emotionally to an idea or belief. I've always questioned the religion and political beliefs of my family, promising myself to come to conclusions on my own and not blindly accept whatever came my way. The technology is available now that we can view hundreds of articles of information on a single subject in just a few hours. One hundred fifty years ago this was not possible unless one lived close to a prominent library and knew it like the back of one's hand. Education like I possess now, being only a teenager, was the equivalent of a well educated person back then. People relied on what they heard. There was no C-SPANN or Fox News to let them know of the activities of our leaders 24/7. They relied on interpretations heavily; and off these interpretations, they made the decision to join the cause and fight.

It amazes me that the citizens of that time could give up so much for knowing, in comparison to today's endless stream of information, so little. How someone could sacrifice everything they possessed for one thing is amazing to a coward like me. I'm always afraid I would be wrong and make a fool out of myself. But they weren't. They stared death in the face, many of them seeing their friends, sons, fathers, and others go forth and never come back, and marched onward, willing to give it all for one object. Victory.

You could call it dumb or half-witted. I know plenty of people who would do just that. But I won't. I can't. My family was in this war as much as anyone else who is from the south. I don't know of a single member of my relatively close family that lives farther north than we do.

There were so many that left and never came back, leaving their families wondering what happened and what their last words were. Who put them on the ground and closed their eyes, said a prayer, and returned to the battle? Or did anyone even bother to take care of the fallen comrade and just keep going, determined to save their own skin. I doubt every family got a telegram or letter depicting how their son or father met their end. I know mine didn't.

My great-great-grandfather was an honest man. He made his living off a farm. He couldn't afford to own a slave (and didn't want or need one). He did all of the farm work himself with his sons. His wife, Betsy, only produced two boys who went throughout their lives relatively healthy. The last baby to be born was a stillborn baby girl that they buried in the woods. The family was heartbroken and no one could speak of children for months, as my great-grandfather told. When the war came to Tennessee, both of the boys were too young to do anything but hold their mother's hand as she waved her husband away. My great-grandfather says he didn't ever think his father wouldn't come back. But he didn't.

My great-great grandmother waited for him to return to her. She would do the housework before sitting outside on the front porch in his rocking chair with some mending and staring out at the horizon as long as she could, looking for a figure on horseback to gallop up When evening came, she would sigh, stand up, and go inside to bed. The boys managed the farm. There was always just enough money for food. When Sherman came through during his march to sea, they hunkered down with the valuables and prayed the cattle and horses came through unscathed. Luckily, they did. When the newspapers told of the end of the war and Lincoln's death, Betsy stayed silent for days. The whole family knew that Dad wasn't coming home. But Betsy never stopped her evening ritual on the back porch. She died there at over eighty.

I guess when you are leading an army, you don't really think about the man who falls behind and is buried in the dust, the one that made it through the first couple of encounters but couldn't take the weather on his old bones anymore. Maybe that's why no one ever wrote down what happened to the man who was found over a hundred years later. And if they did, maybe he just wasn't important enough to be bothered keeping. Someone cared though.

This unknown soldier was buried, oddly enough, in a wooden coffin.

It's a long shot, but somehow I think of that corpse as my own. DNA testing to prove it would be all but impossible, even if we had the money to foot the bill. The skeleton has been reburied anyway. I don't know who that man is or why he died there. But I guess he is the closest thing I have to closure for the demise of my great-great grandfather. My family and I went and put flowers on the new grave of that man and whispered a prayer for his soul. I will never tell them that I have mentally claimed that soldier as mine. They may come out with who he is sometime, but I hope they don't. I like to consider him part of my family. I wish I could have known my great-great grandfather. From what my great-grandfather has said, he entered the war for all the right reasons. He was determined to protect his family from any Yank that dared to traipse over us. He refused to believe that the leaders he had voted for had made a bad decision, and so he supported them in it, though not knowing the full story the way we know it now. He believed in the rights of the state he lived in and wasn't going to let anyone take them away without a fight. My great-great grandfather was one of those who martyred himself for what he believed in some way, though we don't know exactly what.

We don't really do that today much. Though there are the brave men and women of the armed forces, they do not fight in a war as involved as the War Between the States was involved in us. They are overseas, not fighting their brothers. There aren't too many of the brave men and women of the Civil War around anymore in the numbers that were apparent then. Yellow-bellies like me don't have the guts to stand up for what they believe in with everything they have and more. We take what we are given with little complaint.

But the fact is we have this desire to fight for what is right in our blood. Maybe it's that the right issue hasn't come along yet. What will tug on my heart might be something different and that might just be what I am willing to give up my life for. I'm going to do something one day. And it is going to be big.

Author's note: "This essay is actually totally fiction. I really have no idea about the professions or anything of that sort of my ancestors. I just started writing and couldn't stop."

Editor's note: Elizabeth Roten was fifteen years old and a sophomore in high school at the time she wrote this essay in autumn of 2011.

Where the Old South Died

Bill Peach

My ancestors first landed in Marblehead, Massachusetts, and eventually settled in Boston (Tennessee) eight generations before me. The Franklin Main Street community welcomed me, a naïve country boy who came to Franklin by way of Leiper's Fork in the early 1950's. They let me have a small corner at Fourth and Main and participate in whatever projects they pursued They also were tolerant in allowing me to not participate in some projects and even on occasion voice some opposition.

I came from rural Williamson County, raised on stories of benign and compassionate slave owners. I heard stories of pillage of henhouses and smokehouses by Yankee soldiers. I sat at the feet of great-grandparents born in the late 1800's. I learned of a time that needed to be remembered, documented, and critiqued. To many in my generation, particularly those of the liberal ilk, the shackles of involuntary servitude continued to be, for a long period, shackles on the mind.

I was part of a generation which struggled with our perceived conflict between the 1860's and the 1960's. In 1964, we celebrated the 100th anniversary of the Battle of Franklin. I wrote a letter to the editor in the *Review-Appeal* critical of something that I believed had the potential of perpetuating regional and racial animosity. The response was an emotionally divided barrage. Ironically, an equal number of respondents expressed a similar opposition to the event. What for many was a reverence for our military heritage, to others was the haunting image of a redneck in a pickup truck with two Confederate flags

The year was 1964. The "Old South" continuum was present then. I admire and respect our historians of the previous generations who saved the essential linkage with our past. However, that generation was too few years removed from plantation life to admit the pain of segregation and prejudice and to give attention to a delicate depiction of artifacts and symbols. A broader base of historians, civic leaders, preservationists, writers, property owners, and business people have recognized and defined our complex heritage and its contribution to the economic, cultural, and educational uniqueness of Williamson County.

My change of attitude has come incrementally over the ensuing 45 years. I now give much praise to the leaders of reenactment events who have brought peace to the battlefield with period authenticity of clothing, ordnance, and strategy. This has been and continues to be an unequaled teaching treasure.

If I had to cite the seminal moment of my truce, it came from an experience at the Carter House. Until approximately twenty years ago, I had not been in the Carter House or on the grounds of Carnton Plantation other than to chase an errant tennis ball. In the mid 1990's. my wife and daughter carried my daughter's elementary school students on a tour of the Carter House. On their return, my daughter called me and insisted that I should meet Tom Cartwright. Tom had conducted the tour. At the end, he did a closing admonition to the children graphically explaining the carnage and reality of war and the finality of death in battle. That singular speech changed forever my attitude toward the historical landmarks of our heritage.

It took me years to appreciate the valor of young men who died defending their homeland and family and property. For me, their struggle was lost in a partisan allegiance to a Confederacy that was not my homeland and was a vestigial enemy in my efforts for racial harmony and resistance to an unnecessary war a century later, equally bloody and ideologically divisive, conceived and destined to failure.

Twenty-five years later (1989), I came to know and appreciate the men who planned and participated in the 125th reenactment. While, I did not attend, my interpretation from most of the media coverage was that the event had reflected the true historical and academic portrayal of the battle and its place in history. Leadership in Franklin has accomplished much not only in making Franklin a tourist haven but also in giving us an image of maturity in this historical and academic advancement.

I struggled with the merging of the Downtown Franklin Association and the Heritage Foundation. Having been a Main Street merchant for 52 years, I often found the effort at shared events more often distractive than productive. In our efforts to preserve our architectural and academic heritage, I was in constant battle with the iconography of sacred land, military deployment, battle site markers, and ancestral tenacity. The Old South had an oppressive presence of those who "liked things like they were" with a connotation beyond architecture and academia.

I believe that the local partisan allegiance is ancestral, historical, and academic. It is not philosophical, ideological, or prejudicial. I share moments with our Yankee immigrants in the shadow of the monument or in the Confederate Cemetery and voice our reverence for both sacrificial folly and uncommon valor.

Much of the change in my reverence for the period has come from Robert Hicks, author of two novels set during the Civil War and its aftermath. His literary genius has carried the human side of the Civil War to an international readership. He has been a dynamic person in changing the demographics of Civil War tourism in Franklin.

I applaud the shared progressive efforts of battlefield preservationists, with the vision of Streetscape, Harlinsdale, Heritage Balls, the Franklin Theater, the Heritage Foundation, Franklin on Foot, and Franklin Tomorrow. One exciting part of this is the dedication of those who have just arrived and been immediately immersed into a love for a town (city) and county.

The recent reburial of an unknown soldier in Rest Haven, and the national attention it brought to Franklin, may have been an unprecedented moment in our tribute to the restoration of the Union. This reburial was monumental in that we do not know for which Army he fought. The message that it doesn't matter is a tribute to the historical leadership of Franklin. He was honored by re-enactors in Blue and Gray and by visitors including surviving sons of Union Soldiers. His identity is truly unknown. His remembrance was honored in a memorial at the Episcopal Church, and he was re-buried with ceremonial reverence and national attention. I don't know whether, or by what criterion, we are Old South or New South. We are Franklin, and that defines who we once were, who we are now, and maybe what we may become.

Living on the Battlefield

Louise Colln

There's a spot in our yard, he said,
That's greener than the rest. I see it when I garden.
I measured it just now;
It's big enough there's
Maybe several soldiers down there
Covered up that day-forgotten.
I think I'll dig.

No, she said. Leave them.
They're not your story.

My land, he said. I bought the land.

Leave them, she said.
They bought that part with their blood and their bones.
Fought for the land.

Maybe not, he said,
There's other side buried here.

Fought for the land anyway, she said,
It's all over now.

Reenact

Janice A. Farringer

Reenactments
Battles fake
Lots of smoke and sometimes snakes
Those ancient chickens
The Yankees stole them
Great Grandma starved but she told 'em,
"We don't like Yankees.
We won't forget."
We stand around the Coleman kit
Cooking bacon in honor of our dead.

BATTLE OF FRANKLIN, NOV. 30TH, 1864.
AS SHOWN IN THE "HUMAN MILL." FRANKLIN, TENN.

Photograph courtesy of Rick Warwick

Author's Note: My father, Dr. John Lee (Jack) Farringer, headed up the reenactment of the Battle of Nashville back in the 1960s.

I was dressed as a nurse on the "battlefield" at the steeplechase course in Percy Warner Park. His papers and the papers about the Battle of Nashville reenactment are in special collections at Vanderbilt University.

Spirits of Remembrance

David B. Stewart

"Brawley, we is in Heaven! Sutlers was scarce as hen's teeth, but these folk cain't watch a whupin' on a empty stomach. Well...won't you look at that...don't mind if I do..." said a voice that was lost to the breeze and buried in the murmur of the crowd surrounding me. I paused as I picked at a plate of fried sweet potatoes. A chill tickled the back of my neck as Confederate and Union uniforms moved out of view at the corner of my eye. They disappeared into the crowd.

"It is not quite right is it, William? The old gin would have been to the other side. Do you remember?"

A cool breeze combed warm grass into ragged columns that struggled across open pasture where hints of wildflowers withered long past their season. Troops in blue and grey materialized at the edge of a thought, then faded with the retreating breeze. Like ghosts amongst the living, soldiers-in-waiting rammed powder and patch down hungry gun barrels and pushed percussion caps into place.

I heard her call "Dave!" about the same time as I spotted her arm waving. The crowd was eager for action, but pleasant enough. All were there to pay homage to a little bit of history (and watch grown men play with gunpowder.) The only things missing were beer and whiskey. I would have appreciated a julep. Instead, I steadied the plate of food on top of my cup and began picking my way through the crowd of uniforms and onlookers.

"Do you see the two Yankees forward of the battery at the breastwork? It is as if Corporal Ollis Mason died right there, William. It was not long into the fight until each battery became a terrible phantasm lost in smoke and burning eyes. We were deaf to it after a time, but no one

could hide from the thunder. And we had to stop that thunder! We all could see and feel the flame sure enough, but the flash was so quickly gone. Like a gallant knight of old, Ollis ran into the mouth of a belching dragon. He disappeared in point-blank canister fire. You know, before the war, a canister was just something on my store shelf. Ollis was just a boy. He knew nothing of knights...though he would have moved the hand of God to stop the thunder.

"One of your boys saw it and got sick on himself. I opened him with my bayonet, then ran on past. Pieces of the corporal held fast to my arm. If it had not been for nostrils blackened by gun smoke, why, you could have smelled him like a split hog on butchering day. Blessings come where you least expect them, William. I do not wish to remember these things."

Sharon bobbed up and down moving from tip-toe to heel as she weaved in-between and craned to see past others in front of us. I peered over heads and shoulders seeking an opening in the ranks.

"Can you see well enough from here?" I asked. She just laughed.

Horses once roamed the acres now occupied by tents, concession stands, cars, trucks, and families—Butternut and Yankee, alike. Period costumes mixed with name brands one-hundred and fifty years past modest style. No longer rural Tennessee, the city encroached just beyond a fence row that was newer than the massive stables nearby—stables younger than today's memories, but longing for repair.

We needed to find a better view. Children rode fathers like mounted military observers positioned at a safe distance from the fight. Dozens of arms reached upward like a shouldered rifles heading into a conflict, but these were peaceful arms held high for better camera angles. We retreated and advanced cautiously through the ranks looking back now and again toward anxious field pieces on the hill and forward for gaps or shorter, hatless, or childfree spectators.

"They got it wrong. They done got it all wrong! Hah! They's on the wrong dang side o'the river. Wrong side o'the Pike, too. Hell, this is where our boys would a'been safe! Should a'been well on their way to Nashville hours before Hood could get here. Hah!"

Most of the crowd had gathered earlier in the morning. We came only for the reenactment. Flocks of early birds roosted in the best seats along the ridge closest to the pike and above the staging area. Guns of the Army of the Tennessee lined the eastern slope as if peering down from Winstead Hill.

"This ain't even Carter's farm. We was to the east of the pike where Rebs tried hackin' through a Osage Orange hedge. They couldn't do nuthin' but move slow. They was easy prey, too, but I guess nuthin's so easy in that twilight and gun smoke. I could just make their outlines, but it was e'nuff. I'd pull the trigger. The hackin' would stop. Sometimes they jes' hung there. Upright. Usually a'screamin'. Then quiet. Jes' hangin' in them damned inch-long thorns. No roses fer them boys. Just thorns, like they give the Good Lord hisself.

"Like you and that cannon feller, it was them or me. They wouldn't o'stopped to do no decidin', neither, if'n they'd a made it through."

"Yes, they got it wrong, William, but they remembered. Look at all these folk. Women. Children. Watching just like they did that day, only they are not on roof tops or hiding in root cellars."

"Or runnin' fer cover, neither."

Brawley's spirit lifted. He shook his head as he agreed, "Or running for cover, 'neither', William."

I passed my plate to Sharon and raised my camera above the heads of onlookers. The scene slipped back to an Indian summer day in November, 1864. As then, today was unseasonably warm and sunny. Our picnic with an unlikely expectation of spring flowers was overpowered by earthy, leathered scents of autumn.

A young woman strolled unaware and carelessly near William. She was dressed to be seen leaving little to the imagination.

"Lordy! Brawley...do you see...whoo-weee! Wouldn't a'been no fight left in me after gettin' a'hold o'that! My, my! Mrs. Wright's place ain't never seen such as that!"

Confederate cannon fire erupted from the ridge to my right. The Battle of Franklin had begun.

Cavalry re-enactors mounted in the shade just behind my right shoulder. Their mounts pulled forward. Hooves crunched across the macadam before padding onto to the mown field. The reflective "One Way" traffic sign at the opposite curb steered the moment toward something humorous. The joke faded as Union cannon returned a volley from the distance.

"Let's try over there," I said. We moved toward a porch, farther from the action, but on slightly higher ground. Parents, children, pets, and a mix of fresh and tattered uniforms criss-crossed beneath our new position. It wasn't long before we joined them, again, seeking a better view.

Rifle and small arms popped and crackled over the pastureland ahead of us where ragged troops joined rank and maneuvered across the field. William and Brawley gazed southward to the Harpeth and the battlefield just a mile or more beyond the river.

"You wouldn't have been here, you know that, William. It was the Devil's own work that the bridge was out. You boys were so well entrenched in such a short time. I still marvel at the works of dead men seeking not to be so. Even in retreat, you were better prepared than we!

"Oh! What I wouldn't have given for a stand of trees that afternoon! Some of our boys could have picked yours off the

line with just the slightest grove for cover. Why, I think even you should have appreciated some of their skill, William."

William laughed as he spoke, *"I 'preciated it often e'nuff. Too often for my taste! Now, we had our share o'country boys, too. Hell, listen at me! Hah! I never was such a shot, but I was better than most o'them city boys. We did seem to have more than our fair share o'city boys! But you was a crazy, fearful lot with steel flashin' in the sunlight, you was, Brawley. Several o'us boys peed ourselves. Now, that's the gospel truth."*

William tried to spit, but found neither wet nor dry in the effort.

A wan smile settled upon Brawley's face. He thought old habits die hard, if at all, as he shook his head at William's actions, then studied a broomweed flower swaying with the breeze near his boot. The field of battle was no place for flowers. Nature seemed as confused today as in the past.

Kettle corn popped downwind at one of the concession tents. Blank musket fire puffed across the hillside as field guns erupted from opposing forces. Dragon's breath swirled through the battlefield crowd. The breeze swept aromas of brimstone, cane caramel, fried cornbread, horses, and smoked pork with vinegar. I moved to get a better view of the battle scene. A thin young man in butternut and grey met me with his musket crossed between us.

"I'm sorry sir, but y'all cain't cross through here. There'll be horses in and out o'here. I gotta keep the area clear for safety," he said. We looked at the cavalry men to our right then moved back into the crowd and split up in hope of better vantage points for each. I snapped my camera randomly at arms length above my head as we parted.

"Brawley, do you smell that corn?"

Brawley's thoughts were somewhere else as he admired the young man's weapon.

"That musket is genuine enough, William. 1862 Richmond High Hump. Fifty-eight caliber. Harpers Ferry

parts. It was in the hands of boys about his age, back then, too. We were indeed young then, William."

The young sentinel seemed to turn lily-white with a chill then moved toward the sunlight. Brawley surveyed the field. Confederates were forming up to begin their advance across horse pasture into what was proffered as the Union entrenchments at Carter's Gin.

William reached out for a fried sweet potato. A cool wind buffeted my plate and I grabbed it just before it tumped over.

"Look, William, they have built over most of the battlefield. Too much loss to want to remember, I suppose. Surely there were fields to plant and starving mouths to be fed. Lives to be rebuilt."

Rifle barrels smoked beyond the creek. Their grey blossoms were harmless enough. Memories of bullets that once sang, whirred, and buzzed in great swarms seemed as deadly as if they were fired today. Brawley's spirit winced.

"Do you ever hear the hornets, William?"

Shouts of orders barked from the field as grey and brown columns moved downhill toward the creek. Cannon flashed above and behind them. Thunder rolled over the grass and blue columns fell where they stood just beyond the creek. Survivors dove, crawled, and rolled to the safety of trenches to return pistol and rifle fire. Stars and Bars fell only to be picked up and resume their course toward the Federal breastworks.

"I do, Brawley. But ain't for a long while. I heard 'em that day right up t'the time I got stung. Then, it didn't matter no more. That's a long time ago, I s'pose, but I ain't been a'skeert since. I miss my ol' place now an' ag'in, but right here's a nice place t'be, too. My ol' place was gone pretty soon, anyhow. My wido', Jaydene, married my brother, Nathanial. They raised a nice family. That woman could cook whatever I brung in; fit for a king."

William grasped hopefully for a taste of slaw from a plate that passed too closely within his reach to be ignored. An unsuspecting father tripped over his daughter *as William actually managed to tip the plate.* The child's bright bouquet of balloons sailed free just beyond reach of the young sentry and away into a clear autumn sky.

The crowd snapped photographs and captured live-action video with hundreds of cameras. Observers bounced on shoulders. Other arms wrapped tightly around parent's knees. Small hands covered beaten eardrums, and mouths of all shapes, sizes, and colors sipped on soda straws. Lines shifted and rotated as other late arrivals struggled to find a better view. *Brawley stared blank-faced toward the battlefield seeing things spectators would never wish to imagine.*

"You see all them fancy cameras there, Brawley? Folk is so fickle. Why, if'n I'd a'had me one o'them fancy moving cameras I'd a'been richer than a fella sellin' dime novels. Yessiree! I s'pose I'd a'had to live past the fight, though. Hah! Darned Devil's alwa's in the details."

William had taken position closer to a concession truck selling fried catfish. Even as the mock battle raged, he couldn't understand why the line was so small.

"Brawley, I sometimes think I must be in Hell. Who wouldn't eat a fried catfish? Must be a bad cook. I don't recollect many bad cooks on campaign. Anythin' was better n'hard tack. 'Tween dried flour paste that could break ev'ry tooth in man's head or half burnt squirrel or catfish (if'n y'could find such) why, they wasn't no choice a'tall. A burnt piece o'meat was precious as my mama's Christmas dinner!"

A thunder clap of cannon fire rattled the sides of the concession truck. A young girl with a paper flower in her hair rushed past William to the safety of her father's knees.

"But, we were home. Really, truly, back home on Tennessee soil. Given the chance, you would have walked home, too, William.

"I will never understand why I lived so long as I did. I had a fine family and a business. Folk came from as far as three counties away for our dry goods. War came and it was all 'appropriated' to troops—some strangers and some who used to be local boys. The army needed every man that was able. But that was long, lean years ago. Years before.

"At Franklin we saw a flicker of hope. Just a flicker. Then we ran toward what was surely certain death. A man can walk through anything when he believes he is taking back that which was taken from him.

"Angels must have led me through the Yankee lines. Boys falling left, right, in front, and behind me. I could not even stop to reload; just kept my bayonet pushing forward. Ball and bullet sang past, finding home in others and in other things around me. Wooden splinters bit my skin as I finally reached the outbuildings of the farm. I was not ungrateful to have made it back to Tennessee.

"Private Dell Henry Robinson made it all the way to Nashville, but he froze to his death there in December. The General was more for pomp than for provision it seems, William."

"Brawley, they ain't a Johnny Reb fought at Franklin that day I'd be 'shamed of standin' with. I couldn't a'done what they did and that's gospel. I'd a'been froze with fear and prob'ly shot dead by Forrest if'n he'd a'been near. Hell, sure as I'm here now."

Union cannon belched and distant rifles puffed toward the oncoming Confederates. Johnnies raised their voices, broke into a headlong run of flashing bayonets, then disappeared almost to the man beneath the Federal line. Yankee forces re-formed ranks and retreated in the direction of Nashville.

It was quiet for time before William spoke.

"Brawley, one thing I learnt in all this time is dying is just a part o'living. It's a callin' to some. A thing to be fought ag'inst by others. But it's alwa's a'gonna come. Glorious or

t'otherwise. Don't have t'have no purpose other than finishin' what's done been started with a life."

Re-enactors gathered themselves and their gear from the field and moved back toward the tents to re-hash broken strategy, compare costumes, trade names and numbers, and share a cool drink. Spectators folded chairs and blankets. Babies were packed away into carriers. Dogs barked. Children stroked satin-soft horse noses. Sneakers and sandals marched toward waiting cars grown warm not from the heat of battle, but of an afternoon full of autumn sunshine.

"Look at them, William. They remember there was a battle. Perhaps they are also brave enough to remember its cause: utter stupidity of officers and gentlemen."

Too many spectators were already in their cars. Others dawdled to ponder modern sutler's goods and dwindling concession snacks. I looked at a long line of traffic going nowhere, gathered my wife and headed toward the parking area.

This was remembrance of a day long wished forgotten by many. A day of remembering the battle that never had to be. A day of battle that saw no winner, yet judged an unquestionable and undeniable loser in a flawed campaign of haughty pride that drove itself to utter failure and misery.

"I'm a'thinkin' war sure 'nuff had t'happen, Brawley. Will folk learn the wrong past, or forget everythin' they should'a learnt? Mebe. Mebe they alr'dy have forgot what they need t'have learnt: That some things is worth fightin' for n'some things ain't; some things is worth dying for n'some things ain't. But theys alwa's gonna be someone a'pokin' 'em in t'the wrong direction. They jes' gotta pay better a'tention."

"William, this battle did not have to happen. Perhaps, in the greater scheme...perhaps it did...but not on that day. It could have been avoided to secure later victory. Opportunity had been lost. I am certain of this one thing: a harvest of hopeful souls was laid to waste and rot in the fields of

Franklin. The general could have been relieved of command! And...history knows that accidents have turned the tide on many a contest. An accident should have happened! Sometimes, manners be damned, a gentleman just needs to shoot a bastard when he knows that bastard needs to be shot."

William was silent.

The living retreated slowly. Franklin Pike seemed impassible as it had been before the original battle. There was no other way out. Concession lines dried up and disappeared like the dead flower stems now trampled back into the meadow. Hints of fried foods, spice, and sulfur clung to the breeze refusing to admit defeat.

"Oh, just smell that, Brawley! I do miss me some catfish! You think my mouth a'waterin' over all my tongue cain't taste is my punishment? Mebe this is Purgatory."

"I smell my father's corn liquor from time to time and my Mary's lilac water, but nothing of this day. I smell the musty odor of my old dry goods store and I do forever wonder if I am in Heaven or in Hell, William. You should think we would surely know the difference. But, today, William...today brings visions of Hell, yet I think we must surely be closer to Heaven. I sometimes smell the blood of Carter's field on my boots and wish for something more pleasant. And it comes. Mary's lilacs."

Peace, Franklin and Lviv

Sharon V. Thach

Lviv, Lwow, Lemberg, Ruthenia, Galicia...so many names,
  so many battles
A thousand years, generation after generation, all in the
  same place
Their children came to America to study
Creating a new civil society in a new state.
Watched Americans from everywhere re-enact a terrible
  battle, one from our own Civil War.
Wondered about the cooperation, the tourism, the owning
  of it by America,
Thought of creating something like that at home,
And then,
"But all our wars are still alive"

Editor's note: The names in line one all refer to the same place,

Games We Play

Susie Sims Irvin

As for me, LORD
Give me
Peace.

Build No More monuments to WAR
For me to see.
Glorify no more Dastardly Deeds
And call them heroic because
We are "at WAR."
War is killing.
Give us Peace.

Congress used to declare WAR
They don't do that anymore. Do they?
Somebody decides it's over
A treaty is or is not signed.
And the victor and the vanquished
Go Home.
We used to have Armistice Day
But there were too many wars.
Now we have Veterans Day
And we can have all the wars
    we want.

We still have surrenders. Wave a white flag
    still means Halt and Put down weapons.
How do you Put down a Nuclear bomb, Hydrogen bomb
    or unmanned missile?
We still count casualties and take territories though
    territorial lines are debatable and often not enforced.

346

One TV station carries pictures of the casualties.
I watch and say, "Thank you."
"That's the least I can do."

Then there's territory, too
Whoever takes the most territory wins.
We sang, "Over There - Over There - and we won't
    come home til it's over, over there."
Over Where? There are too many "theres" now.

Both sides go home
    to make bigger and better weapons,
    to rebuild countries they destroyed
    to find better and stronger allies
    to prepare for the next one:
        "Red Rover
        Red Rover
        Let China
        Come over."
Nobody wins at war - EVER.

Just ask the Fathers.
They must tell the Mothers.
"No, Dad, I can't come home.
    They got my buddies."
"You got the Purple Heart, Son. You've done your part."
"No, Dad. It will be over soon. Then I'll come home.
    Tell Izetta to make the biggest, best chocolate cake ever.
    Have the Grannys and Granpas too. . .
    I'll be home for my birthday.
    See if 'my Marine' brother can get a leave."

There are NO winners in war.
Just ask the Mothers.
They are busy though.
Scrubbing red stains from the fabric of war.

Colorblind. Mothers wash blue with grey, khaki with
   camouflage.
All become "no color" – color of fighter planes   G.I.
   helmets   sand
  smoke   tanks   desert and burnt wood.
"No color" - the color of war.
Mothers dye their own clothes black.
Change the blue star at the front door to gold.

Sisters keep the guest book, the food list.
Run to the mailbox for his E-mail,
   our returned letters unopened.
Sisters cope their own way.
Sisters write to their Belgium pen-pal
   "Plant your poppies thick and red
   Round the plot where our brother lies dead.
   Tell him for us far away
   His sisters miss him today."
They sing walking to the school bus
   to escape the grief
   "Oh! what a beautiful morning. . . "
Sometimes, out of sight, they put on lipstick.

Their Marine brother wired,
   "Cancelled leave. Too painful. love."

President Roosevelt said,
   "It won't be over until we bring ALL the boys home."

The mothers began to make ready. Some had headstones
   cut.
His copied a window from All Saints' Chapel in Sewanee.
   "Tell Dr. Guerry to save me a place. I'll study this time."
The boy who struggled in school had come this far
   on a smile and a very large heart.
Who knows where he might have gone
   what he might have done.

Sergeant Cecil Sims, Jr.

Mother, Grace Wilson Sims
Sisters: Grace (Susie) Sims Irvin & Betty (Bebe) Sims Hatcher
Brother: Wilson (Woody) Sims,   Cecil Sims, Jr.

From their family home on Honeywood Drive, Nashville

The seeds of His War had been planted for those to follow.
  We, the victor, would rebuild the vanquished and dig
  our economy into recession.

"He was my favorite. He kept our spirits up," wrote his
  Chaplain, "always in church when the war allowed. Said
  he came to make his mother proud."

"He was our favorite," wrote the crew in his tank.
  "We took a couple of motorcycles from the front of a
  beer joint. (The Germans weren't too anxious to get
  home anyway.) Threw them up on the deck of our
  tank. Headed back to our woods. We built a track –
  jumps and everything. We bargained with an old
  Belgium lady I knew, for a chicken. Cooked it outside.
  Had ourselves a real feast."

War is killing. War is tears. Red stains. Unfinished lives.
  Broken hearts.   Trembling lips.

There is Hope.
Some rise above
  above it all.

As for me, LORD
Give me
Peace.

"Games We Play"
is dedicated to the unfinished life of
1ˢᵗ Sgt. Cecil Sims, Jr.
Company A 746 Battalion; U.S. Army,
by his sister Grace Sims Irvin,
whom he nicknamed Susie

Unmarked

Dewees Berry

. . . [N]ewly released archaeological findings . . . offer . . . insight about the . . . skeleton that was accidentally unearthed from an unmarked grave in 2009. . . . [But] [p]reservationists and historians have said the matter of which side the man was fighting for is irrelevant today.

The Tennessean, December 23, 2011

When I enlisted that fall day,
The sergeant somehow failed to say
That in a month I'd be found dead
As both the armies moved ahead.

For me there were no candles lit,
And that is not the least of it.
They put me in an unmarked grave-
Small tribute to the life I gave.

Now, there are some who seem to care
What color did this soldier wear.
But does it matter, after all,
Whose bugle did once sound the call?

Unknown

B.C. Nance

When did they forget his name,
This long dead soldier
Beneath a simple stone.

I brush at the lichens,
Trace my fingers through the graven letters,
And read the word, "UNKNOWN."

Somewhere a family tells of the ancestor
Who marched away to war
And never came home.

Unknown soldier's Grave Franklin, Tennessee
Photograph by Emily Nance

How to Hold Your Arms When You're in Love

Stellasue Lee

Something beyond levels itself over the night sky
Fog, yes, but a denseness of emotion too.

And this morning, separation. It moves through trees.
catches at branches. No one but us notices.

It drifts sideways, hiding important knowledge,
overjoyed that a world might take in such relief

at feeling so alive. Time wants to show me
a different country. It says that North and South

can join and take away separation. So that one man
one woman can live in a place both call Home.

Home is wherever they are. Family will become
the common denominator, and time will allow this gift

in a million different ways. I have saved for this day
tucked my love away in the museums and churches of my
    heart

knowing that one day a love that can endure for all time
would step forth. This is the way I hold my arms when I'm
    in love,

outstretched, palms up, seeding all the light my body can
    manufacture
to learn both sides of our nature and become one.

Acknowledgements

Poems by Thelma Battle: "A Prayer for Stillness" "Going Home: Black and White" "Soldiers Fallen Here" "The Scars Seen and Unseen" used by permission of Atelier Publications, Inc.

"Come Home, My Love" by Louise Coiln was published in *Our Voices, 1998 Williamson County Literary Review*, Roger Waynick, Publisher, Cool Springs Press

"Two Voices" Louise Colln used by permission of the author first appeared in *Two Voices*, published in *Echoes Of Two Voices* in 2008, Design and Photography by Laurie Michaud-Kay

"The Unknown Solder" by Nancy Fletcher-Blume used by permission of the author first appeared in *Two Voices*, published in *Echoes Of Two Voices* in 2008, Design and Photography by Laurie Michaud-Kay

"Susan" by Laurie Michaud-Kaye was first published in *Gathering: Writers of Williamson County*, 2009. Copyright is held by the author.

"Runaway Slave" by Luther Harris is a passage from the book *Granny Lindy* by Margaret Killifer Harris and S.R. Lee published by the Overton County Heritage Museum. copyright held by S.R. Lee

Both "The Silent Wall" by Joyce A.O. Lee and "Dred Fish" by S.R. Lee are based on copywriter material sent by DeKalb County Historian Thomas Webb with permission to use the material in fiction in any way we chose.

Acknowledgments

"How to Hold Your Arms When You're in Love" by Stellasue Lee has been published twice: *Crossing the Double Yellow Line*, 2000, Bombshelter Press, and *Animes*, Winter 2003, Shelter Pines Press.

"Pony Rider" by Alan Rhody is used by permission of Sony, Inc.

Author Biographies

Nancy Evelyn Allen is a graduate of Tennessee Tech University and Southern Baptist Theological Seminary. She has published a book series called, "The Covenant Woman," is published in two anthologies and a few magazines. She has also published over 150 short stories and feature articles in newspapers. Nancy and her husband, Joe, have been married over 51 years and are the parents of two, grandparents of three and great grandparents of one.

Thelma Battle lives in Franklin Tennessee where she is a renowned local historian, preservationist, and author. She is a founding member of the African-American Heritage society and of the McLemore House museum. The Thelma Battle Archive of Photographs is now part of the collection in the Williamson County Main Library

Dewees Berry is a life long resident of Williamson County and has always been interested in both history and poetry. Dewees practices law in Nashville. He and his wife Kathy have three grown sons.

Arch Boyd Brown is a native of Chattanooga, Tennessee, a Vietnam Veteran, and a retired postal employee. Since 1987, he has been an active member of Hixson Presbyterian Church where he has served as a Deacon, Ruling Elder and a Shepherding Elder while being involved in various ministries for a number of years. He and his wife, Kay Hampsher Brown, currently teach English as a Second language and tutor "at risk" children after school in the church's TASK ministry. He is the author of the C.D., "Angels, Anthems and Irishmen - A Journey of Faith and a Legacy of Freedom" which contains about 100 poems.

Lori C. Byington is a Bristol, VA native but now lives on the Tennessee side of town. She teaches King College, and absolutely feels blessed to be doing so She has been writing ever since she can remember.

Author Biographies

Bobby Calabrese was born and raised in a small Italian neighborhood in Cleveland, Ohio. He moved to Franklin Tennessee, about a year and a half ago to join a daughter and grandchildren. He is a bus driver for the Franklin special school district and a part-time driver for the Franklin trolley. He has been captured by the rich civil war history and finds that the whole social and historical fabric of Franklin instill a wonderful spirit in him to write.

Christy Cole grew up in Paris, Tennessee, the great granddaughter of William Winsett who was killed in the battle of Atlanta in 1864 and without whom she would not have had her dear grandmother Annie or her beloved mother Dorothy. She was an English major at Ole Miss, received her law degree at Vanderbilt, and is now a partner on a private banking investment team at Merrill Lynch in Nashville.

Louise Draper Colln is the author of five national and internationally published books. Her poetry and short stories have won statewide awards and have been published in several anthologies, including the Williamson County Literary Anthologies She lives in Franklin Tennessee, where the natural beauty and sense of history inspire her writing.

Robert Coné is a former teacher, journalist, and editor. He is author of three books: *The Butcher and the Hag and other poems, Thirty Days hath September* (a novel), and *The Candy Bandit Strikes Again* (a children's book). He lives in Kewanee, Illinois.

Nick Dantona is an award-winning fine art photographer whose work may be found in The Tennessee State Museum, the Cumberland Heights Foundation, the Indigo Hotel and private clients. His photographs are exhibited regularly throughout the US and now, internationally. A Jacob Riis Award Finalist, his portfolio: *Like Hemingway, but smaller*, was published in 2011.

His career has included TV cameraman, photographer, producer/director, creative director and interactive media innovator. His education was a 1970's smorgasbord, assembling and consuming the best of Emerson College, Suffolk University, SUNY and NYU School of the Arts.

John Neely Davis was born and raised on a farm at Chesterfield in west Tennessee, He dropped out of college long before it became popular. Most of his adult life has been spent working as a real estate appraiser with various federal agencies across the southern United States. He and his wife, Jayne, enjoy living in Franklin near their two daughters, Cindy and Melissa. His first novel, *The Sixth William*, was recently published.

Von Derry lives in Franklin/Brentwood, Tennessee. She is a hairdresser, poet and painter. She loves to drive her 1979 red Corvette named Rose. Her poetry is awesome and recently published as *101 Poems by Von.*

Dorris Douglass is a librarian, historian, and genealogist She has written professionally for library journals and has been a historical columnist for the *Williamson Herald.* She also writes historical articles on Williamson County subjects and occasionally ventures successfully into poetry.

Lydia Esmer was born and raised in Michigan where she met and married her husband, originally from Chicago, They have spent the past thirteen years in Tennessee. They are very fond of their adopted state that has become home and where they plan to retire.
Although she did some poetry writing in Michigan, in Tennessee the inspiration was rekindled, leading to the publication of a book in 2011 titled *Potpourri of Poetry and Song.*

Janice A. Farringer's hometown is Nashville, but she has lived for many years in Chapel Hill, North Carolina where she is a full-time writer and poet. Her work is widely available on the Internet and in print anthologies. Her website is
www.amidlifebooksandpoetry.com.
Email her at jafarringer@gmail.com.

Nancy Fletcher-Blume is the recipient of the Kay Tricki Award which resulted in the publishing of a children's book, *The Cast*

Iron Dogs. Her short stores and poetry appear in all three of the Williamson County Literary Anthologies. She condensed and adapted two classics: Robert Louis Stevenson's *Treasure Island* and *Kidnapped*. which were published both nationally and internationally She lives in Franklin, Tennessee, where she writes, teaches graphology, and dabbles in music and gardening.

James Floyd, also known in Nashville as "The Jefferson Street Poet," is a poet, screen writer, and playwright. Some of his hobbies are collecting rocks, photography, acting in community theater, exploring thrift stores ,and real flea markets. He has one book of poems presently in print, *Some Gentle Moving Thing.*

Lin Folk was born in Los Angeles. She joined the US Navy in 1942, a member of the first group of enlisted WAVES in World War II. She served as Link Trainer Instructor (Instrument Flight). She married and moved to Nashville in 1946. In addition to raising a family, she was a broadcaster for Public Radio, At the Nashville Public Library, she was the Lollypop Princess who told stories to children for many years.

Randy Foster is a lawyer and a former member of the Metropolitan Council of Nashville and Davidson County, Tennessee. He is a Boy Scout leader, has a son in college, and enjoys photography in his spare time. Co-author of a chapbook of coffee and tea-oriented poems with Amy E. Hall, *Sugar and Spice and Nothing That's Nice,* Randy shares his poetry at http://randyfosternashville.wordpress.com.

Micki Fuhrman, a Louisiana native, loves a good story--whether real or imagined. She has been collecting (and fabricating) them during her years as a singer/songwriter, carpet salesman, riverboat waitress, draftsman and construction project manager. Micki lives near Nashville and enjoys road trips, cooking for friends and family, and flea markets.

Gale Buntin Haddock was born in Franklin, Tennessee and was raised there and in Nashville. She loves the beauty of Middle Tennessee, read avidly as a child and cares about how words are used and punctuated. After a career in accounting, she is now an artist and occasionally writes poetry. She holds a Bachelor of Fine Arts degree from the University of Georgia with a major in Drawing and Painting and a strong minor in English.

Amy E. Hall with a background in music journalism and business speak, currently focuses her creative writing energy composing free verse poetry and haiku. The southern-born, northern-bred Tennessean has self-published three haiku chapbooks to date. Co-authored by Randy Foster, her latest chapbook, *Sugar and Spice and Nothing That's Nice*, features bitter and sweet poems about tea and coffee. Visit Amy online at lineuponlinepoetry.blogspot.com.

Luther Harris 1900-1989 grew up as a farm boy near Livingston Tennessee. He earned a Masters Degree in Sociology and became a Rehabilitation Officer for the state with a district of seven counties on the Cumberland Plateau. His grandmother, Lindy Smith Harris had been born before the Civil War and could clearly remember the stories she had heard as a child on the mountain farm. Luther Harris himself remained a great storyteller and repository of oral history all his life.

Susie Sims Irvin: Ours, the perfect family. Two bright attorneys, two sons, then two daughters, all two years apart. I began life as Grace Sims. Brothers nicknamed me Susie ("Susanna, Don't You Cry.") The perfect town provided the perfect schools (Parmer, Hillsboro, Vanderbilt.) All I had to do was show up - with pen and brush and work - and they would label me, *Southern poet/painter.*

Kathleen Jack was born and raised in a Navy family and consequently had the opportunity to travel a lot and visit many parts of the United States. This afforded her with a rich background from which to compose her over 1,000 songs. She settled in one of the most active civil war areas, Franklin, Tennessee and has been creating songs ever since. The songs in this anthology are a snapshot of the whirl of emotions that must have been felt during the Civil War.

Charlene Jones was born and raised in Old Hickory near Nashville. She loved to write from childhood .and grew up to write fiction and song lyrics in the midst of the normal life of husband, children, and various practical jobs. For a time she was also a performing musician. She has lifetime memories and a strong love for Middle Tennessee and so enjoys depicting its people's lives in both story and song.

Laurie Michaud-Kay began a career in writing because she was curious. Writing provided an excuse for digging deeper into subjects, both human and academic. After obtaining degrees in both English and History from Adrian College, she turned this personality quirk into a seventeen-year career in public relations and internal communications, earning individual awards for writing and design, and a team Silver Anvil Award from the Public Relations Society of America. Now retired, Michaud-Kay lives in Fairfield Glade, Tennessee, where she has returned to crafting novels, essays and short stories drawn from the meandering of her curiosity.

Joyce A.O. Lee is originally from Kansas City, Missouri. She has lived in Tennessee with her family since 1973. She is a full time writer of fiction and poetry. He work can be read in *Our Voices*, a local anthology, and online at "Muscadine Lines: a Southern Journal." *The Length of a Love Song* is her first published novel, and she is currently working on a second book of fiction.

S.R. Lee lives on family land in Middle Tennessee where she has written a history of her neighborhood, *Beechville, Then, Now, and In Between*. She enjoys grandchildren. writing, poetry, history, and the out of doors.

Stellasue Lee was an entrant for both the 2000 and the 2010 Pulitzer Prize. In 2003, she received *The Poet and the Poem* Special Recognition for Excellence from the Library of Congress. She is the author of five books in print: *firecracker RED, Crossing the Double Yellow Line, 13 Los Angeles Poets, After I Fall,* and *Over To You*. Her poetry has been published in numerous anthologies and literary journals.

Now Editor Emeritus of *RATTLE*, a literary journal, she serves presently on the editorial board at Curbstone Press, She teaches privately.

Mary Lynch 1922-2011 was born in Nashville and attended St. Ann's Catholic School on Charlotte Ave. for elementary school. In her last years, she lived on Old Hillsboro Road where she enjoyed her neighbors and kept up an interest in history.

Robert McCurley is a fine art photographer based in Franklin, TN. His artistic muses are varied and sometimes eclectic, but of late he has been expanding his artistic expression to poetry. His poems in this book are in support of the photo series entitled "Civil Conundrum". To see more of his photography, visit www.robertmccurley.com.

Mary Lou McKillip is an Appalachian author and story teller, a native of North Carolina, and a retired Activity Director who devotes herself to making others around her happy. She has many God given talents and enjoys, singing ,dancing, and traveling RV style with her devoted husband Truman along with their furry friends Lady and Precious.

Ben Nance is a native of Nashville where he lives with his wife Susan and daughters Emily and Sarah. He has worked for the State as a Historical Archaeologist since 1988 and has worked with many Civil War period archaeological sites, Ben occasionally write fiction and poetry as a hobby.

Emily Nance lives in Nashville where she is a ninth grade honor student at Franklin Road Academy. At school, her main interests are science and math. In her non-academic life, she makes jewelry, does photography both as a hobby and on request for special occasions or publications, plays golf, and as a musician both plays and composes for the piano.

Norman Wallace Nash was born March 16, 1939 in Richmond Virginia. Education includes a B.S. and Master's degree in mathematics. Service careers include twenty years as a commissioned officer in the U.S Army, 18 years as Administrative Officer at Vanderbilt University, and 6 years with the Tennessee Dept of Veterans Affairs as Budget Officer and Assistant Commissioner.

George Northern is a native of the Grassland area of Williamson County where he grew up on the historic Ring farm. He attended Franklin's Natchez high school, did a stint in the military, and finished college at Tennessee A&M, now Tennessee State University. He was appointed first principal when Scales Elementary School opened on Murray Lane. the first African-American principal appointed in Williamson County after desegregation. At Scales, his innovations raised children's reading scores so much that he was invited to Washington for an educational meeting in the early 1980's Later Northern was asked by the Tennessee State Department of Education to train effective principals. He is now retired, and his family is urging him to write of his experiences.

Bill Peach is now retired from his long term work as a Franklin, Tennessee, Main Street clothier, owner of Pigg & Peach from which central position he observed life from 1956-2003. He is a former school board member, (1976-1992, 2002-2010) and the author of four books on life and thoughts in Williamson County, He has a wife, Emily, and three daughters, Becca, Lucie, and Dea.

Veera Rajaratnam, PhD., a resident of Franklin, TN, hails from Uduvil, Ceylon (now called, Sri Lanka), is married to her husband Augustine, and has three children. A graduate from Marquette University, Milwaukee, WI, she has been on the faculty at Vanderbilt University, Meharry Medical College, and Aquinas College (adjunct), Nashville, TN, and is currently consulting as a Scientific Editor and Grant writer. In the creative realm, she is a Poet and an Artist, who trusts in God, believes in peace, loves nature, enjoys world travel, and credits her mother, Jessie, for instilling a love of poetry.

Alan Rhody Born in Louisville, Ky., Allen Kohnhorst, (a.k.a. Alan Rhody), is a multi-million selling songwriter; a touring musician, independent recording artist and workshop facilitator. He started writing poetry at age eighteen, before taking up music. Prior to this book, he has had two poems published in the Louisville, Kentucky weekly, LEO. A Louisville Art Center graduate and accomplished painter, Allen lives with his wife Kathy in Nashville, TN.

Jeff Richards' fiction and essays have appeared in more than two-dozen publications such as *Gargoyle, Pinch, New South,* and *Southern Humanities Review* and four anthologies. He is presently working on a series of interrelated Civil War stories, two of which have won best story of the month in *Frontier Tales.* He lives in Takoma Park, Maryland, a mile from Fort Stevens, a Civil War battlefield.

Susie Margaret Ross writes about relationships and life (as if they could be separated!). She is not sure that she has a theory of writing, but if she does, it is that what the reader brings to a piece is equally as important as what the writer brings. She lives with her very bossy little dachshund, Talullah (nicknamed Lulu), in Franklin, TN.

Elizabeth Roten lives in Spring Hill, Tennessee where she attends Independence High School. She is involved in debate, theater, physical training, martial arts, and church activities where she maintains the position of journalist and historian on the CCYM of the United Methodist Church. Elizabeth's goal is to be a veterinarian and she regularly shadows for this occupation. She lives in a family of three other people as well as three dogs and two guinea pigs.

Charles Rush is a retired Air Force officer. While researching family genealogy, he found family letters and official documents relating to his Great-grandfather, William H. (Billy) Jones, a Confederate officer in the 8th Texas Cavalry, Terry's Texas Rangers. Thus began several years of research , resulting in the publishing of, not only his family genealogy, but also two Civil War novels and several short stories.

Author Biographies

George Spain Native middle Tennessean. Wife, Jackie Burton Spain. We have five children, thirteen grandchildren, three great grandchildren and many close friends. Retired mental health worker. Maternal, great grandfather was in the 7th Tennessee and fought with Lee. Many of his stories are based on his wife's family history.

David B. Stewart a native of Northwest Arkansas, spent most of his life in Texas and Oklahoma. His mother's family set roots in Middle and Eastern Tennessee several generations before he arrived in the area. He credits that family line for his talent in poetry, prose, and art. Once a budding broadcast journalist, he chose engineering as a profession. Writing for hobby and pleasure saves him from the monotony of technology while giving his grandchildren something to puzzle at. Stewart lives in Franklin, Tennessee.

Louise Strang earned her PhD in Psychology at George Peabody College, Vanderbilt U. In addition to writing poetry, she is recording the inner and outer experience of life of her canine companion and activist, Arthur Todd, at Misty Meadows Farm south of Franklin TN.

Sharon Thach is a professor of international marketing and supply chain at Tennessee State University. Professor and student exchanges are a regular feature of her work, She was a Fulbright Professor in Lviv, Ukraine.

Margaret (Maggi) Britton Vaughn is Poet Laureate of Tennessee. She is the author of 15 books. Her songs have been recorded by major country music stars and her plays have been produced regionally. She resides in Bell Buckle, Tennessee. She has given encouragement to many who hope to become writers.

Judith Walter combines her love of history with her love of writing. She grew up in middle Tennessee and the home described in her story was that of her great grandparents. Judith is a columnist for *Mature Lifestyles*, Nashville, and has had creative non-fiction and poetry published in *Muscadine Lines*, an on-line journal for Southern writers. "A Breath of Fresh Air" is her first published piece of fiction. Before her retirement, Judith was a counselor of adolescents and families.

Louverna Webb lived in Overton County as a young woman during the Civil War. Her family treasured her spirit and passed her letter down from generation to generation.

Tom Wood is a North Carolina native, who went to high school in East Point, Ga., and graduated from Middle Tennessee State University in 1977, recently retired from *The Tennessean* newspaper after 35 years in the sports department . As a sports journalist, he primarily covered local college athletics, boxing, the Iroquois Memorial Steeplechase, Olympic sports and general assignments. He also contributed an interview to the 1989 book *Feast of Fear: Conversations With Stephen King.* In 1996, he served as the Nashville newspaper's lead beat writer at the Atlanta Olympics Since his retirement, he has served in volunteer public relations roles with the Iroquois and Killer Nashville conference for thriller, suspense and mystery writers and appeared as an extra in 'Nashville,' which airs on ABC.

Jane Wilkerson Yount as a child, followed her older brother, Bill, on many of his explorations. Now, unable to tramp after, she writes simple poems for friends, the lonely, and the needy. She sends out over 6,000 poems every holiday throughout the year.

Sandy Zeigler has had a lifetime of passions: three children, drawing, painting, learning, designing. She has reinvented herself several times. She established a children's gift manufacturing company; then she explored graphic design and created her own event design and production company. Now she adds a new passion—writing.

Index by Author